The Buckseller

The Buckseller

F. E. Mazur

Royalty Ridge
Springfield, Kentucky

FIRST ROYALTY RIDGE EDITION MAY 2014

Address correspondence to:
ROYALTY RIDGE BOOKS
1610 Royalty Ridge
40078

ISBN-13   978-0692215746
ISBN-10   0692215743

*Dedicated to the memory of
Frederick Joseph and Helena Pauline,
my generous, hardworking parents*

I
Buck Season
1st Week

Chapter 1

"I've wrecked six automobiles in ten years. Four because of them. Two thanks to the hotshots drinking behind us. They can shoot every one of them for all I care!"

"And just who are you referring to?"

Flashlight in hand, the fat man lumbered through the field of fog.

Lungs. He was panting. He could feel the gradual elevation of the terrain underfoot as it led to the mountain. *Go on. Don't slow, you stubborn coot. Force the old bagpipes to blow out like those winter recaps you bought.*

Heeding his better judgment, he paused to suck in several deep breaths, hacking after every third or fourth. Convinced he would not be keeling over and leaving his wife downstate a widow, he then attempted to slice the light through the vapor.

Come on. Show me something. Horned or not, it doesn't matter squat this early.

From one side to the other and back he repeated the process with the light, but there was nothing.

Returning the flashlight to the front, where it remained steady but a second before darting wildly in all directions and alerting the other hunter to his presence, the fat man next shifted the heavy rifle with its variable scope from one shoulder to the other. Following this, he joined hands to raise his ponderous belly and the smallest fingers reached below and yanked upward on his trousers that had gravitated earthward. Satisfied with himself both inside and out, he resumed his push through the field, crumbling the sod, felling stubborn weeds.

Eventually, the tree line melted into view, signaling an increase in the rate of elevation as well as the fat man's need for frequent breathers. On this occasion he reached under his mackinaw into a rear pocket of his pants, from which he removed a white handkerchief. He shoved the cloth under his runny nose, wrestling the big protrusion like a chunk of rubber. A double snort sounded between gasps, a solid one-two punch.

At his age the mountain was nothing to screw around with, he warned himself. Deadfalls and widowmakers. Soil depressions. Thin saplings with thinner branches that might poke at a man's genitals or put out an eye. Tangles of laurel that could trip a person up and leave his flesh cut open against a rock, or his ass lying in bear shit. Plenty of things to hurt a man if he wasn't careful. He searched the surroundings once more with the flashlight, but the familiar woodland forms maintained their invisibility.

"How is a man supposed to kill a deer when he can't see it?" he groused aloud.

📖

When the light had shot skyward, the second hunter, upon observing its beam, thought of the rotating beacon at the regional airport, but the watery curtain all around was so thick the landing strip would have to be within a stone's throw and that just wasn't the case. *Give it more attention anyway*, the cautious psyche advised itself, and the hunter, more calculating in self-preservation than most, waited patiently with one foot thrust forward of the other, determining if the light in the sky would repeat at constant intervals. As it did not, the indulgence of an analytical game followed: Who was this first victim? Gender, the hunter assumed, but everything else—size, shape, age, habits, the make and caliber of gun—came under consideration. Of course, nothing was conclusive. It was, after all, only a means of passing time until the moment arrived.

The fat man enjoyed his own game to while away the time as he trudged up the mountain—a spontaneous tally of the deer he had slaughtered in his lifetime of hunting. Twenty-two, maybe twenty-three or four, he counted. In the end, the actual number remained elusive. But nine were buck, he could swear to that, with the biggest being a ten that had hauled around a ton of poundage on its monstrous frame. Yet it was the eight-point on display in his den that sported the longest tines and the most symmetrical rack of all the buck he'd sighted on. For a while he tried to recall this animal's girth. No use. Too many years between the good old days and now. Despite the fading memory, he remained proud of nailing that eight—one slug through the neck! Let the world's Trumbos and all the other field-and-streamers argue till the lights went out, it was a tidy way to dispatch a deer. Grunting with satisfaction, he tugged approvingly on the rifle's leather strap while at the same time the earth seemed to fissure beneath his next step, causing the left leg to disappear. The man let out a terrible groan of alarm that was picked up by the other hunter. He peered down along the tunnel of light. The lower half of his leg was buried to the knee.

"Hog hole! Damn 'hog hole this far up!" The fact amazed him.

Bracing with the rifle and giving no thought to an accident, he dislodged himself from the animal excavation and massaged the flesh around the leg's vulnerable front bone. Other feet, he could tell, were lurking nearby, yet they didn't seem alarmed. They resembled deer, but it was impossible to be certain. How many times had chipmunks and squirrels alone made a fool of him! He straightened himself, shined the light across his watch. *Half past five.*

Continuing the climb, he put himself on guard for further groundhog holes. Before he advanced a dozen steps, a taut branch triggered loose from another, lashing his forehead.

What a relief it would be to get up top, settle on some deadfall. There he could relax and catch his breath. Sip a little coffee from the thermos, too. *Nothing like hot coffee and a smoke!*

Panic seized him. The free hand flew up, slamming against his chest.

📖

"Thank god…" drifted across the slope to the other figure and the volume confirmed the pair's convergence.

The stalker stopped to ponder the phrase uttered by the target, and with cold sarcasm muttered unwittingly the reason the hunter had expressed his gratitude to a deity.

"Poor thing's probably relieved he didn't forget his cigarettes."

Upon completion of this statement the respite should have

ended, the legs have started to climb again. Instead, the deadly figure remained immobile as the one argument that could not be won re-surfaced. Only now, with the moment so close-at-hand, it was rebutted callously.

If it turned out the victim was from Sagerville, so be it! *Write it off to bad luck. Only keep your focus.*

📖

Presently, the mountain angled skyward with greater sharpness and the target began to perspire like cold porcelain on a humid day. The fat man chuckled as he compared himself for a self-demeaning instant to a sweating toilet. He flapped the ends of the hunting coat in the fashion of a large bird air-drying its wings in an effort to dissipate the wetness. The outfit was damp from both the fog and his own effusive moisture. It appeared, though, the fog was abating as he had hoped. His light now penetrated deeper in every direction than it had only minutes before.

Despite the labor it required of anyone who climbed its steep slope, the mountain with its compelling serenity and mentholated atmosphere soon stirred the hunter. Year after year he had accompanied his friends on the four-hour drive up to Bingham County, located in the center of the state's northern Tier of counties, to get away from daily life, which for him was rife with stinking concrete, the choking fumes of oil-burners, and the acrid odor of sulphur issuing from the company's uptown pickling works. It wasn't bad enough he had to work inside this last. He smelled it with his bacon, inhaled it with his beer! And he couldn't recall a single lousy day when the only sounds he listened to had developed from nature. Like simple wind, nothing else. Water over rocks. Jays squabbling at a feeder. Deer crunching old apples on the ground in the dead of winter. Nor could he point to a night back home when the illumination had come from only the moon and stars—when the fog was away, a common occurrence here in the Tier. Fuck no, in the city or anywhere near it, the clamor and lights of humanity were without let-up, never once cutting a man a break. He was hardly a wishy-washy sentimentalist, but he was hoping to move the wife and himself north to the Tier. Maybe after retirement from the mill. Hell, he might even accept the company's early offer.

A shade of pink appeared throughout the forest canopy and the tuning-up cacophony of winter's birds was quick to follow. Near the top he crossed a thinly wooded bench cut into the side of the mountain. This break in the rough ascent reminded him how his friends had chosen less rugged terrain to hunt.

Too steep for deer, my peter! A bunch of pussyfoots. Too goddamn steep for themselves!

Thinned mucus dripped out his nose onto his upper lip. He could taste the salt. This time he determined to flush himself entirely of the irritating fluid. He stopped once more and squeezed the flashlight between his pants and shirt. The pressure from his paunch against the belt pinned the light in a vertical position, causing his face to glow with fiendish tumescence. He tugged the white handkerchief from the rear pocket and whipped it in the air to loosen its wrinkles. At once he felt extremely warm, strangely cold. Like a leaf, the handkerchief floated earthward. The rifle slipped from his shoulder and fell to the ground. But for a fraction of a second the meaning of what just happened escaped him.

An explosion of light.

An eruption of sound.

His hand then wrenched on his throat of torn flesh and frayed tissue, gushing ripe, aerated blood. Like a tree free of its roots, the massive body toppled onto the annual cerement of decaying leaves, and the rushing, gurgling complaints of severed artery and windpipe rapidly diminished. Seconds later, the ruin of a rattle sounded.

📖

Maintaining a distance, the killer watched and listened. With the fat hunter's death, premeditation had turned to murder. Yet, strangely, the killer believed it was someone else who was to blame.

Chapter 2

"I was born and raised in the city and had all that la dee da."

"You haven't any regrets then about the move?"

"I love it, love our little farm and everything. My husband loves it, too."

"What of the kids? They didn't have any choice. Must be a big change for them?"

"My kids here will pick me a bouquet of dandelions. Down there they'd be swinging bats at each other."

Below in The Buckseller, not far from its solitary street lamp shrouded in fog, Seneca "Pig" Chandler emerged from one of the dilapidated dwellings and swung its wooden door behind him. The door clapped against the frame in its refusal to shut securely, a kind of summer rhythm in December. The lean six-footer had overheard the single rifle report come rumbling off the mountain and it disturbed him on a couple of scores.

For one, during the past month the Buckseller man had been keeping a vigil on a big buck displaying an impressively sweeping set of antlers. Every evening the animal foraged in an apple orchard gone wild at the back of the long field extending from the rear of his place. Usually a small harem of doe moved about too in standoffish attendance. On several occasions he had approached the orchard for a closer view, but the buck each time drifted off, disappearing like a mirage before he could steal a meager twenty yards. Maybe some flatlander hunting atop the Den had gotten lucky and spotted the animal in the fog, before sunrise, he thought, then took it down.

For the other, there had been no follow-up shot, and normally there was.

He shook his head to deny the possibility of the first and the puzzlement of the second, then bulldozed a hand through his disheveled crop of graying hair to remove it from his eyes. Swiftly but delicately, as though a dancer were arrested in his gait, he strode to a wired enclosure penning several swine, a trash bag swollen with squandered food in hand.

Listening to the animals gorge on the fodder, Chandler questioned again why he troubled with fencing. Only the sorriest of fools would argue a hog didn't exhibit a special personality. When disposed to break out, the animals would dig and likely succeed in the effort. Then, always, before he could haul the wandering porkers back to The Buckseller, he had to wait until some pesky landowner ran him down at the 'seller's Inn, whereupon he got his ear chewed about them rooting in some garden, corn crib, or buried fruit cellar. Still, when it came to this flight of his stock, he considered himself fortunate. Labor Day past marked twenty-two years his stay in The Buckseller, and this Christmas he would celebrate nineteen years since Beryl Victor, following the cat incident, had taken him aside and told him he could carry on his life rent-free for the remainder of his days. But before the evening was over and after a few more drinks, Victor, not so gray at the time, would change his mind and present Chandler a gift instead. Throughout those years, there had been only one escapee. No sir, he could see no sense to a fence, even though last August they had busted free and ravaged a light crop of corn that he was tending in the back field.

A lot of folks, hearing of this, advised him to beef up their confinement: "Now, Pig, you see for yourself it don't make no sense fussin' over a crop just so's an army of grunting hogs can assault it!"

Didn't make no sense? Some farm types half-shucked their corn and later fed it to their stock. Wasn't he saving himself a task to allow the hogs to harvest their own? So they'd gotten into the sweet ears, too! They hadn't destroyed it all, and when the summer was over, was he clamoring for a few more? No sense? The editor of the paper who drove out a few days afterwards from Sagerville, well hell, even Meredith Tome understood the stupidity of the statement.

"It was about all he understood," Chandler complained to his swine, although he couldn't really make himself believe it, because in the end he came to like the man. Sure, Tome had taken up a chunk of his time with the interview and the picture-taking, and by now he must have realized that the life of someone in The Buckseller was of no interest to those living in town. But Chandler's tale had sparked excitement in Tome and the swine-handler had recognized it as genuine. Like many, the editor believed everyone had a story worth telling. Unlike them, Chandler suspected, he believed everyone else would want to hear it.

Using his boot, Chandler nudged the slop that had fallen outside the pen under the bottom wire. Following this, he made an inspection of the entire enclosure. At each support post he gripped the top and shook it vigorously, an act of duplicity of which he was aware, for in checking the foundation of the pen he weakened it.

Finished with the last post, he turned back to the shanty and at the door picked up his lever-action rifle. A large sorrel cat arched its back on an adjacent woodpile. It burbled at him and he burbled in return.

"There's a little something for you inside, whenever you're ready," he said. He pulled gently on the animal's tail before turning his gaze skyward into the fog.

To warm himself this morning, the Buckseller man wore only a faded flannel shirt under a vest of grimy denim. Telling the animal that he had better get a move on, he started off through the brown and brittle goldenrod that covered most of the hollow's foot hill, a thin but strong man, light on his feet. Unlike many hunters, Pig Chandler carried scant equipment— the rifle, a Case knife for gutting, and a rope for dragging home the kill.

Doubling his step, he soon arrived at the trees. Overhead, the sky was losing its pallor. He froze in his track to listen carefully, deductively. Deer normally departed an hour or so before sunrise those fields exposed to roads. Frequently, they did not make a beeline to the safety of remote timber, however, so it was rather common to discover them gliding about like ghosts inside the tree line. The rash fellow who stumbled onto them might better turn a one-eighty and hunt elsewhere. They'd hightail it, more often than not, and hard-press their stalker to locate them any time soon. Fumbling in his vest, Chandler counted out five rounds, slipped them into the clip, slapped the clip into the bottom of the rifle, and chambered a shell. Then he raised his eyes and scrutinized the grand steepness before him.

The mountain loomed into the higher reaches of the fog with an awesome and statuesque stillness. On a clear day, it was difficult to imagine any creature but a bighorn sheep or mountain goat scaling it, despite the absence of both in the East. Although the small number of people in The Buckseller labeled it a hill, those in the county seat declared it a mountain—devoid of crags and a scenic precipice, lacking moraines and cascading waterfalls, but a mountain all the same. Chandler's destination this early hour was a natural shelf that cut into the face of the slope a hundred feet below the peak. It was a popular runway for resident whitetails, and he was familiar with its lay. Following the close of last season, he had ambushed a button buck at its north end. His plan this morning was to hunt the shelf for an hour and if nothing developed, continue on up and hunt the Den. He positioned his feet at a penguin's angle to each other and began the difficult climb. The blanketing fog of earlier was shrinking steadily to a patchwork quilt of varying densities. Adequate light now outlined most rocks and trees.

The long climb afforded the climber abundant time to think without human interruption and Chandler got to musing on the shot again, the only cracking disturbance of the morning so far, a singularity that continued to bother him. A one-shot kill was a rarity. Even when the hunter was lucky enough to drop his quarry on the first pull of the trigger, he often followed with a second up-close to put the thrashing animal out of its misery. What he had heard, Chandler mulled the matter, was more the bullet to the back of someone's brain, or a self-inflicted, stick-the-barrel-in-your-mouth episode. Ending one's life in the woods wasn't out of the question either, as he recalled the teenager who had walked away from his camp and family two years earlier and blew off his head with a shotgun. Emil Carter's crew searched the county for weeks, but it was a birdwatcher eight months later who discovered what was left of the boy in the upper reaches of a tall hemlock. The teen had climbed the tree, strapped himself to a limb, then done the unthinkable. But most likely, Chandler told himself, the single shot was an instant kill. Maybe even the big buck.... No matter, really. He was a hunter for the belly, not the wall. It was venison he was after.

Winded but not exhausted, he stood on the glacial bench a short time later. Selecting a deadfall intact and relatively dry in spite of the pervasive moisture, he settled down to wait, peering into a diminishing succession of broad openings among the tall hardwoods that stretched below.

The faintest notes of brush underfoot soon struck at the stillness of the mountain. The leaves and dead undergrowth, he could hear, were crunching in a lazy, almost gentle fashion, from the pressure of delicate body weight and not like something was pounding down on them in panicky flight. Even so, he was unable to make up his mind if, in fact, it was a deer approaching. Nor could he judge the direction of the sound. Fog was often a fooler. At the moment, it floated a foot above the floor of the bench and surrounding slope.

He waited and watched. The crunching ceased. He strained his eyes. They uncovered nothing. He slid a finger onto the rifle's safety to make certain it was off. Wagering with himself a deer was about to show, and with luck a buck, he stilled himself. He refused to turn his head even, instead letting his ears double as eyes.

Within a minute the cadence resumed and the volume grew. At last, he was able to pinpoint the direction. It was advancing on his front, coming around and up the slope. He studied the layer of clarity sandwiched between the fog and forest floor and searched for four long legs, brown and generously streaked with a winter's gray.

Out of the fog ahead gradually materialized the sketchy form of another hunter, thin in detail like a black-and-white negative severely under-exposed. And changing, too, like a face drawn hastily in a window's condensation. A Kool-Aid face, though not so chummy. Chandler spotted the ethereal image. Luckily too for the stupid sonovabitch, he realized, had leveled his rifle and was now scoping the slender breeder of swine.

He rose up and, throwing an arm overhead, waved it side to side to make the hunter realize he was lining his crosshairs on a man, not a whitetail. The distant form reluctantly lifted a hand in cursory acknowledgment, and Chandler let out a breath of relief.

Too many of these careless jokers, he thought irately. Yet, equally upset was he at himself for confusing the footsteps of a man with an animal's. He was a splendid hunter, a woodsman who felt subject to his own rules first. He hadn't thought he'd see the day he would ever do that.

Chapter 3

"You are outta your gourd! This is the county seat."

"Two thousand people. Guess how many stoplights are in the county."

"Only two with another on the way? That's somethin'. No wonder I've heard it said they're not qualified to make the decisions about their own property."

"I've heard it's a small miracle if you can get enough of them together for a good chat."

"And I've heard it said the men and women both will tell you to kiss their ass. And they'd be within their rights."

"Who asked you?"

In Sagerville and similar upstate communities, the first day of deer season doubled as a time for celebration. Professionals and employees with a union scheduled vacations around the whitetail months in advance. Others who fought for their dollar with only minimal relief took the day off under claims of sickness, dental appointments, and family deaths. Schools across the region locked their doors to allow students and teachers to enter the surrounding woodland and compete with the visiting horde.

That evening of the opening day of the new buck season, John Meredith Tome sat behind his desk, dictating the news budget for his weekly newspaper, the *Tier Sentinel*, to his secretary of long standing. He was a man of medium build with an age and disposition that kept himself in good shape, appeared somberly righteous at times under a full head of dark rangy hair, but he would often display an interest in the most insignificant of things. This was the case with the tablet that Mary Kiel was using to record his instructions—the Kurtz Bros. tablet, popular among educators. Tome could not recall examining its cover, a map of the state, since his enrollment in a school system northeast of Pittsburgh.

"Then you're ignoring your children's assignments," Mary Kiel scolded him.

"Who is?"

"Meredith, your kids are in elementary! They're issued these tablets four times a year."

"Yes, but with paper at the house, they don't lug anything home but books, which are taking a thrashing. Jesse is doing what I did as a kid and giving the drums a go. We've yet to come up with a percussion pad for him to practice on." Employing both index fingers, he laid down a double paradiddle on the edge of his desk, a juvenile action from which his secretary wished he would refrain, as it compromised his credibility with the community.

"As kids, we used to color in these counties. My own I'd make an azure blue. Up here I probably used an earthy brown or maybe red, although I can't begin to tell you why. I had no idea what it was like up here. When vacation time rolled around each summer, my folks were partial to the water and the beach, never the mountains."

The state map adorning the cover showed every lineal feature—road, river, boundary—printed in blue. The Northern Tier appeared to be an orderly board of box-shaped counties that were misleadingly flat, bland in the pejorative sense, and empty of promise. Only Route 6, The Grand Army of the Republic Highway, scarred the neatness of the region as it dead-squirmed across the Tier like an earthworm deracinated under a sweltering sun. Tome took hold of the map to regard it closely. In particular, Bingham and its neighboring counties which made up the heart of the Tier. Although the map's cartographer had chosen not to reveal their contours, they formed a huge mountainous span of land in reality that invited the traditional epithets, "God's Country" and "Hunter's Paradise." The commercial tone of the former inspired some isolationists to joke that the Lord drove a Ford and chainsmoked Marlboros. At the same time, in recent print orders for two-color brochures, Tome had noted a switch by some regional promoters to the less hearty phrase, "Land of God."

"Nothing's changed on this map, Mary. It's the same as when I scratched out my Peterson specimens in the second grade." He flashed her a mischievous grin, the same look she had seen when they started working together and which she had wrongly interpreted as flirtation. "You don't suppose the Kurtz Bros. have been making a statement all these years, do you? Some cryptically derogatory comment about the progressiveness of the Commonwealth?"

Handing the tablet back to her, he proceeded with the budget dictation. Mostly, this consisted of an extraordinary number of hunting-related items, many of which, if they were not granted space in the issue at hand, would be assigned some in the next. They might have finished the collaborative task within the hour, except for a commotion outside.

"Looks like it's starting in earnest," remarked a worker named Monk.

Tome got up from his desk and moved to the window offering a view to the street. Mary Kiel and two other female employees joined him.

A man and woman were bending over and retrieving debris from the sidewalk, all the while complaining loudly, the man especially. He spotted Tome behind the blinds and signaled to the woman, the wife of Emil Carter, Sagerville's fire and rescue chief, that they should go inside the print shop. Mary Kiel opened the door and Tome greeted them.

"Moonlighting, Mr. Roman? Suzanne, how are you tonight?"

"Forget the jokes and amenities, Tome! Why can't you do something about this trash? You know who's responsible for it. It doesn't qualify as no mystery."

"Now you can't blame every piece of—"

"We damn well can blame all of this on them!" The man held up several cans and bottles and thrust them at Tome's face. "You can't buy any of these around here. They came up from below, and you and I both know who brought 'em. The same's true of what she's holding."

"Which is what, Suzanne?"

"It's the soggy remains of a newspaper," said the man. "Don't worry, it isn't yours. It isn't any newspaper from around here…. You ought to know she didn't want to come in here, Tome. Grumbled it would be a waste of time because a paper can't put a stop to a thing like this."

"King-of-Prussia," Tome muttered, leaning in to inspect the copy of a readable story. "Looks like it might be from Philadelphia."

"It's wet, but it isn't old. You can see it hasn't yellowed," said the man, who relinquished his irateness and lowered the volume. "But why can't you run an occasional story on the subject is what I want to know. Nobody would come back at you through the courts on this sort of thing if that's what's worrying you, and I imagine it does in light of what you recently went through with that libel suit. Look, I don't mean to imply that every hunter who travels here does this sort of thing. I've got friends who drive up every year and they're respectful. They religiously haul their trash to the dump. But too many others just eighty-six it behind their camps or along the road. Then some, who really don't give a hoot about those of us who live here, they toss this stuff right out in the middle of town."

"My mother is also one who once believed you could pick and choose among them," Suzanne Carter said without looking at the man.

"What? Wait a second! My friends are good people. They're responsible. They don't—"

"You aren't with them every minute." Suzanne Carter waved a hand in the air as a sign the topic should be dismissed. "Forget it. It's too late in the evening for this."

"Well, I can't agree with you," argued the man. "Some of our own right around here are worse. Like Perly Bechtel and a few out of The Buckseller for starters. Ask your husband, why don't you? He's been all over the county. Emil probably knows the location of every private dump there is. Talk to Monk here. He's got more than a few of those decorations out around his way. Isn't that right, Monk?"

The worker Monk kept his face averted from the group. Tome intervened to cut off the bickering.

"All right, I'll see if I can't come up with something, Mr. Roman. In the meantime, there is something I can do immediately to help each of you." He extended a foot and slid the nearest waste can across the floor to them. Roman bent and quickly disposed of the bottles and cans filling his arms.

"Suzanne?"

"Not so quickly, Meredith."

"Oh? Somebody having the sale of the century?"

Mary Kiel nudged him at the shoulder.

"Too far to travel, I'm afraid. But there is something of a personal interest at which I do wish to take a closer peek. I'll discard it elsewhere if you don't mind."

Once the pair left the shop and were on the sidewalk again going in separate directions, Tome and Mary Kiel returned to their chairs and finished what they had started. Then, as was his habit, he broke from the evening's labor to visit the Buck 'n' Doe Restaurant and Lounge. The weekly newspaper appeared every Wednesday morning, and on each of the two preceding days he skipped the late meal with his family and settled for a sandwich and a beer at the lounge, where a discussion of some issue was often underway.

Leaving his Ford window van, Wednesday morning's delivery vehicle, parked at the rear of the print building, tonight Tome opted to walk the short distance to the lounge. This led him past the main block of stores opposite the town square and courthouse, past Popov's Pantry where pastries and pizza were specialties of the owner, past St. Mary Margaret's Roman Catholic Church, past a service station and barber shop, and finally past Graff & Aufderheide's Memorials. Concerned for his safety, he paid extra attention to the SUVs and campers running about. Occupied by downstate and out-of-state hunters with voracious appetites for revelry, and prominently displaying rifles in their rear windows, they careered up and down the coolly lit streets, cornering sometimes wide, sometimes sharp. Had he been unaware he was in Sagerville, the county seat of Bingham County and pride of the Keystone sportsmen, Tome might have guessed they were on patrol in the Australian Outback, or cutting a trail into the Amazon, or on some special excursion, in any case, because no one needed that sort of jacked-up clearance and oversized tire here in Bingham County which was rugged, yes, certainly more so than what most of them were accustomed to, he'd wager, but excepting parts shading The Buckseller, still not all that rugged or all that wild.

"WATCH IT, BOOB, OR YOU'LL GET WAFFLED!"

He waved a meaningless hand at the passing truck.

Although he was aware a hunter was missing above The Buckseller and that a search party was out, Tome did not attach any great newsworthiness to the matter, despite the possibility the man was lying dead somewhere, the victim of a heart attack, a self-inflicted wound, or another case of mistaken identity. Already he had heard of the tragedy down in Luzerne where a boy had killed his father in mistake for a deer, while in neighboring McKean County paramedics had delivered two men D.O.A. to Paul Bingham Memorial Hospital, both the victims of a cardiac arrest. All of it was par for the course.

He crossed to the lighted parking lot fronting the lounge, zigzagged among several vehicles, read "Don't Californicate Bingham County" on the bumper of one—a giveaway the controversial pharmacist Bill Lill was inside—and entered. The uproar drilled him!

"IN HEAVEN THERE IS NO DEER,

THAT'S WHY WE SHOOT THEM HERE,

AND WHEN WE'RE GONE FROM HERE,

OUR FRIENDS WILL BE KILLING ALL THE DEER!"

Men and a few women in the safety garb of hot reds and vibrant oranges flooded the normally roomy lounge. Other men, fearing an unexplained emasculation from the highly visible colors, wore personalized, savage garments. Sheathed knives hung prominent, and the talk was as loud as the beer abundant.

A nest of hunters repeated the polka parody many times over, each beginning bringing an increase in volume and the spilling of beer from plastic steins waved overhead, some emboldened with the names of their annual customers. Tome stood his ground searching for a familiar face, gaining but slight advantage from his above-average height in the erratic crowd.

The Buck 'n' Doe Restaurant and Lounge reflected plainly its visiting clientele and mountainous location. Ornamenting the long panel above the bar was a string of whitetail racks of stunning dimensions. Several antlered heads with glinting glass eyes peered down at customers in booths. Recently the proprietor had added to his collection a mounted posterior with a photographic vignette of a local buffoon embedded beneath its upraised tail.

This comical display jutted forth above the jukebox whose songs were barely audible against the stentorian din. From a high shelf in a distant corner peered out a stuffed owl and a fox, their final survival efforts a posthumous struggle with dust and the ugly film of tobacco tar and nicotine. And tonight, beyond the picture window that framed a string of motel units, whitetail carcasses, caked in blood, were hanging head-up from naked, spotlighted trees, safe from unleashed dogs.

Monday was normally an opportunity for the lounge to lock its doors two hours before the state-mandated closing time of 2 a.m., but with the season underway for the sought-after buck and in two weeks the smaller, soft-eyed doe, the dull rhythm of the bar accelerated severely. Extra waitresses, mostly young, buttressed the daily work lists while frumpy regulars, never questioning why, found timeworn schedules altered to begin after breakfast and end before dinner. Bands had been booked months ago for the biggest evenings. In anticipation of continuous spillage, tablecloths had vanished.

An arm shot up from a booth next to a window overlooking the parking lot, and Tome elbowed his way through the throng to the druggist Bill Lill, a small but heady thunderstorm of a figure whose rounded eyes, forehead, and robust promontory of a chin did resemble, in some minor way, a collection of thunderheads. Sitting opposite, impeccably dressed, was a rich and highly influential real estate broker named Harmon Drake. A strange pairing, Tome realized, knowing both.

"Sit and relax, Meredith. Pay no attention to Drake. Once again he's selling off our beautiful county."

"The *Sentinel's* B section is a product of the Realtors," Drake responded drily. "Anymore, Meredith can't afford *not* to listen."

Tome removed his parka and signaled a waitress for his usual cold beef sandwich and a draft.

"You're not about to let me forget that I lost that libel suit, are you, Harmon?"

"What does it matter to me if you put that behind you? More to the point, I don't want you to forget that you've been unable to pick up insurance against any similar allegations in the future."

"Don't be too sure." Tome slid into the seat alongside Lill. "With the proliferation of property ads, some people are calling the paper 'junk mail with a subscription.' Enough of them get to thinking that and they won't bother to read anything, your ads included."

"Weeklies like yours have always promoted a region's enterprise, Meredith."

"Never their only role, and certainly not the most important! Publishing the viewpoints on all sides of an issue, that's what counts. Do away with that process and the fairness that goes with it, and you'll find some people deciding to take matters into their own hands, no matter what the issue."

The broker, who made it a habit to sit tall among others, released a faint smile toward the ceiling. "Whatever. Just remember which of the local industries is currently providing most of your revenue."

Although it was the evening, the broker continued to wear a tailored suit of gray with the accompanying tie still knotted at the throat. Reaching a hand inside the coat, he removed a black leather billfold. Out of it he slipped a business card, larger than standard and folded in half so that he could leave it sitting upright on restaurant tables. He held it out to Tome.

"I'd like another run. But on this order, in the box on the back?... Make certain to include the county figure for last year's harvest. That, I understand, runs about nine thousand. But if one of your staff would check to see if that's accurate, I'd appreciate it. Maybe Mary could look into it."

"Times ten for the hunters!" Lill snapped as Tome withdrew a pen from somewhere and made a notation on the card.

Tome chuckled perfunctorily and surveyed the bar. "One crazy time of year, isn't it?" he said, putting the card away.

As he spoke, an explosion of laughter ripped from a corner booth. A young hunter who had emptied his beer onto the hair of a friend—the man was swinging his long crop back and forth as though he had just surfaced from a pool—was receiving a similar sudsing from one of four women sitting alongside. At least the fellow was taking it like a trouper, rasped a tracheotymized old man standing over Tome.

Lill spun his head around to stare briefly at the rectangle of cloth concealing the hole in the man's shriveled throat. "How does he think we're taking it? Every year it's the same. They arrive and abracadabra, Sagerville converts to a giant party room."

"Hardly a high price for living here," Drake remarked.

Lill motioned Tome's and Drake's attention toward the first table inside the serving room. Three blacks and a white woman occupied its surrounding chairs. "That another part of the price?"

It was the kind of statement from the druggist that silenced most voices in the community, and neither Drake nor Tome made exceptions of themselves. Seven years earlier, pretty Anna Lill had run off with a hunter according to rumors, and rumors which continued to grow later said the man was black. In the past, neither fact of hunter or color had forbidden sympathizers from taking advantage of the druggist's fate to convey to his ears their thoughts on either "gun-toting flatlanders" or "uppity niggers," the latter usually voiced by some neo-Nazi hanger-on hoping for new recruits for their weakened Aryan compound located in a northern niche of the county. But in recent years a new dimension emerged making such callous efforts no longer a breeze. For the past two hunting seasons Lill had put up at his house outside of town a trio of hunters, all of whom he said were friends from his past and all of whom were black. It was likely they were visiting Bingham County again this season and, thought Tome, just as likely to be the men at the table with the white woman. It was likely because, simply, Bill Lill was a difficult man to figure. In any one sentence he might offer an emotional concoction of personal belief, self-effacement, soft chiding of those around him and himself, and even condescension. Such a compound was hard enough to break down on reflection. In the flow of conversation it was impossible. Thus, everyone kept quiet.

The druggist went on, sweeping his head up to include everyone inside the Buck 'n' Doe. "They're repugnant, these people. They sing out like some wise old codger that those of us residing here are unaware of the paradise we inhabit, and then promptly follow with their story of how this is their only chance to get away from it all." He raised his glass to a toasting position. "Here's to the great hope for the American suburbanite, gentlemen. 'The chance to get away from it all!'"

"My God, we all get in a rut!" said Drake.

"Like the buck?… No quarrel," Lill quipped. "Only they didn't get away from anything but a foul residue of what they themselves fundamentally are. You allow them to dwell in the Tier for long and eventually they'll uproot to get away from here. Consider their camps for a moment. Festering sores on the land! Small monstrosities of squalor and ugliness! Each year they live in them for two, maybe three weeks—I'll be generous—and the remainder of the time the dumps exist for the visual delights of you, and me, and all the rest."

"Bill, you're making my head spin! Concern yourself with an eradication of the welfare tribes out in The Buckseller! Leave the sportsmen alone. At least they're spending money."

"Not all are on welfare," Tome interjected matter-of-factly while looking for his waitress' return.

Drake, striking a weary pose, shook his head, the action implying greater marvel than perplexity. "Meredith, my head spins on your account as well. Still speaking on behalf of the little guy. Am I supposed to be impressed?"

"Listen, I'm talking about the Bingham Counties throughout America. All of them, Bingham for certain," Lill said, "they're an endangered lot."

Drake continued to hold his attention on Tome for another second before turning back to Lill. "You know what I think, Willie?"

"Let's not become overly friendly all of a sudden. I'm already quite aware of what you think."

"I think you're one selfish s.o.b. All that land you own and you don't want anyone but yourself to live on it, walk on it, hunt on it. Tell us, what are people who live in and around a city supposed to do? If you had it your way, you'd keep on bunching them together where they already live and have them hunt each other."

"They already do that," Lill responded flatly. "And without a season. Remember, you're not talking to an ignorant man. You and your fellow salesmen have contributed your own share toward bunching people together. If thirty chicken coops were what you had to offer, you'd sell them within the blink of an eye. What's more, if you had twice the buyers, you wouldn't hesitate for a second, Harmon, from converting each into a duplex. I don't want people on my land because I like unspoiled land. And that's how I want to leave it for the guy and gal who get it once Bill Lill is pushing up daisies."

"Bearing that in mind, I should hope for your early demise," said Drake, unable to suppress a grin. "Maybe that guy and gal will be more flexible is what I mean."

Presently, another waitress delivered Tome his order, then squirmed away through the crowd with a bearded young hunter near the bar snaking his tongue after her in cunnilingual imitation. Tome examined the slices of meat inside the roll and added a layer of horseradish. Jersey, Philadelphia, Pittsburgh, Ohio—the regions from which most hunters traveled. Repeated time and again in the game law violations the paper used as fillers. In spite of not knowing the number of infractions, he suspected the tally to be far greater than any arch-defender of the hunting fraternity would prefer to contend with. As Lill had charged, they were here to "get away from it all," but whatever else that might imply aside, the phrase did hint strongly at leaving the wife behind, as one eye in most foreheads, he observed—and it wasn't difficult—was busily in quest of a possible night's take.

Except for hunters new to the region, who satisfied themselves with a motel room, most came to favor ownership, to band themselves together and pool their money, so that a meager plot of land became their own and they could haul in an old mobile home and sink it among the trees or beside a stream. The more industrious constructed small cabins, and still others nested like wasps in wheelless school buses, brush-painted aluminum with a stovepipe projecting through the roof. Hanging at the front of each makeshift abode was a sign. Some residents of the Tier assumed the purpose of the shingles was to provide amusement to passing motorists and first-time guests. But Tome had found too many signs, whose cut and lettering displayed more planning than the buildings in back, reflecting a crassly perverse humor. Poachers Retreat. Stag Party. Love's Hunters. Fawn's Demise. The Cubbyhole. Mons Venaticus. This last, doubtless, a self-satisfying show of contempt of the region's intellect by the owners, arising from their misguided view.

Moreover, the signs were increasing lately at an alarming rate. His weekly attested to the rise. Each issue opened up to real estate advertisements inundating its columns. The *Tier Sentinel's* exposure, however diminished because of the recent judgment against it, remained extensive, reaching out to uncounted sporting clubs and to a dozen out-of-state federations. All that he currently read relating to property merely corroborated the obvious—the buyers of upstate realty were chiefly Americans from the cities and their peripheral infections of crime, the suburbs. The protection and solitude of rural life now fostered less of a joke about hicks and more of a tremendously desirable way of life. So with demand up, prices skyrocketed, and pioneer descendants, who had no pocket change but did have land, began to sell off sections of it, encouraged at times by the horrors of inflation, while at other moments by the well-rehearsed, progressive talk of mechanical investors and unctuous real estate men, who pressed for large chunks they could subdivide, cut into squares so that it all resembled a cafeteria Jell-O salad, and resell piece by piece for greater profit.

To say the least, it was scary. It was all too easy for Tome to imagine the county as a checkerboard of camps and rotting trailers. Fortunately, he had found himself joined by others who were not indifferent to the problems facing the Tier, and this past

September the first set of regulations regarding land use had undergone adoption. Their implementation would get underway in the spring, once the small team of enforcers and its corresponding payroll were decided on. He had pushed for them by assigning the matter front-page coverage week after week, admitting to himself it was no panacea, but neither was it a placebo. The modern guidelines—first of the kind for the county—declared to prospective dwellers that instant camps and ramshackle cabins were out because they did not preserve the innate beauty of the region. New camps, according to the regulations, would resemble a moderate home, subject to loose interpretation of course, but still complete with a septic system that would have to undergo the inspection of the county commissioners' office and its men selected for the field. No magic elixir by any stretch, but nevertheless a start. One that was promising to wind up in court, as threats were being heard already from some nonresident landowners whose backhome prominence wouldn't allow them to be told what they could and could not do with their property by what they arrogantly and disparagingly termed "a bunch of xenophobic local yokels." It was likely to come to this, Tome surmised, and even likely to be countered in some instances with what Drake was now demonstrating to Lill.

The glib broker was flicking his hands at the druggist as if they were revolvers. "They'll come in spite of you. Unless, of course, you erect a wall around the perimeter and skirmish with them at the county line. On the other hand, if it's merely a point of remaining civilized...." The sleek voice sank to the dramatic level of an attorney's summation, and the barrels turned left to center on Tome's heart. "If it's that and nothing more, then I advise you to take your objection to our journalist here. The liberal American Press always welcomes the opportunity to champion a cause. Isn't that so, Mr. Tome?"

Wanting to reply, Tome was unable because of a bite of the sandwich he had yet to chew. Instead, he found himself measuring each of the two men to determine if he could side with either. Across from him was Drake, a man raised in Bingham County, yet his ambition made him eager to sell every square inch of the region. Sell it to whoever was interested and for any purpose. Lill, on the other hand, did not want the county to grow, and this made it difficult for other businessmen to listen to his point of view. Recently, he had been discouraged from Rotary gatherings, and he now performed any civic acts on his own. Lill had moved to Bingham County from the eastern city of Warminster, and the mountains that were the essence of his new home suited him just as they were. "In need of change neither here nor there" as he was apt to state. He might have been a flatlander once, but he waxed indignant when any native to the area insisted that nothing changed with time. Tome guessed he stood somewhere between the two. But the inclusion of conjecture in his self-assessment told him how unstable the position truly was.

Away from their table the singers broke off. They had returned to the imbiber's polka following their harmonies of a couple of Mitch Miller-style ballads, and running up the volume in the la-la refrain, their voices cracked. The sudden reduction in sound permitted neighboring conversations to be heard, and Tome eavesdropped on the bartender who was barking about the politics of antigun legislation. His name was Forster, and he was young and brassy and not from any college of mixology where a bartender learns to patiently take in the complaints of his customers.

Lill glanced at a clock face centered in a Seagram's plastic grouse.

"Getting late," he said. "I got to lock up." He finished his drink, then tugged at his jacket, tucked partially under Tome's thigh. "You'll have to excuse me, Meredith."

"Always thought the rebellious apothecary closed at six on Mondays," Drake said.

"When did you ever stare a gift horse in the mouth, Harmon?"

"Talking about you."

"So do it in my absence," Lill replied, grinning at Tome. "I'm leaving. Good night to you both."

Tome stood and Lill slid from the booth, departing without further word or gesture. A waitress came by to retrieve the druggist's empty glass. Drake, gazing through the window, watched Lill's departure even through the crowded parking lot before returning some attention to Tome.

"So, what's the latest news to hit your desk, Meredith?"

"Nothing much. Everything is pretty routine."

"All right, I'll try it this way. What is it that you find of interest nowadays?" Studying the stifling crowd when he had replied, Tome now transferred his gaze to the man before him and disclosed a trace of amusement at Drake's impatience.

"Let's see. My boy Jesse has taken up the drums. He's already got a couple of rudiments down fairly well."

"You don't say."

"Didn't think that would work. So what about this. Explain how you and Bill came to be sharing the same booth."

"We're not exactly enemies, you know."

"That's only because in the matters you disagree on, Harmon, push hasn't quite come to shove."

"I made an appeal to his business half. That 95-acre parcel which extends to his southern boundary is a valuable slice of terra firma. There's substantial profit for him there if he decides to sell. Unfortunately, what he said about a gift horse isn't true. All right, I've given you an answer to your question. Now how about help with one of mine?"

"What's the question?"

"It regards another parcel of land of about 400 acres. Over around Killdeer."

"AmeriCon Paper used to own it?"

"You have something?"

Tome could see that his instant knowledge of the matter surprised Drake. "Maybe six months back, a letter arrived at the shop inquiring if a morgue were in existence for the old *Upland Patriot*."

"Searching for evidence of a transaction, no doubt. What about it? Is there anything archived in the bowels of that old firetrap?"

"Hardly," Tome chuckled. "Old man Addy wasn't much for good organization and record-keeping, although had he employed his daughter even as a child, Mary probably would have had the place better organized than the Library of Congress. The only *Patriots* available I'm aware of are from its last years, when Mary started working for the old man. What's the intrigue with this piece of land?"

"Nothing but a question of ownership. AmeriCon Paper sold the land way back in the fifties, yet there's no record of the new owners."

"Who could be dead by now."

"If I can find the deed or some reference to it, I'll know for certain. Word is, they were local."

With a rattle of the ice in his glass, Drake abandoned the topic and abruptly gestured recognition in the direction of the far side of the bar where the owner of the local gun shop, Max Rayburn, had entered with his teenage son and another man, a thirtyish fellow dressed in blue jeans and jacket, both items held together by nickel-sized brass rivets. This man bore the same ridiculous visage now permanently framed above the jukebox inside the whitetail's anal sphincter.

"The way you're dolled up, Max, looks as if you went out first day after all!"

"Like hell!" Rayburn bellowed back. "Thing is, Studs, me and the boy joined the search for the old gunner that's missing up behind The Buckseller."

"Any luck?" Tome inquired.

"Naw. Had to call it off 'til morning. Rough area to be stumping the bushes for a man at night."

"Not to mention it's card-ee-ak country," piped in Studs who had come up to the booth a few steps behind Rayburn. The boy remained near the bar getting something from Forster, and Tome could see him occasionally staring through a side window into the darkness.

"Funny thing, though," Rayburn continued. "No sooner the party gets back to town and a fellow out of The Buckseller—"

"Fogger Dann," Studs said, while slapping two yellow boxes of cartridges against each other.

"Yeah, Dann. This piece of driftwood with the goofy name comes marching in and wants us to stump the bushes in the same goddamn area for a friend of his. Now get this, Harmon! The friend is our beloved Pig Chandler!"

Drake glanced at Tome and laughed.

"Take it easy on Chandler, Max. Meredith is rather fond of him. I understand we're to be treated to a feature on the man one of these days. We'll soon all be learning how to slop hogs."

"You like him, huh, Tome?"

"Obviously, Harmon's idea of a useful citizen differs from mine."

"Go on with what you were saying," said Drake.

"Well," Rayburn continued, "it won't surprise me if we find this old man wasted, his rifle missing, and his pockets empty."

"And let me finish it!" Tome offered behind a flourish of his hands. "Chandler is by now miles away and already looking for a new place to set himself down."

"Well hell, ya gotta admit," Rayburn said, harrumphing, "the sonovabitch wouldn't be leaving a thing behind that's worth a shit."

"Crazy," Tome muttered, "plain crazy. But you fellows will have to figure it out on your own. I've still a deskload of work tonight." He rose quickly, suddenly eager to be out of the company of these men, slipped into his parka and left. The first twang from the tune-up of a country band noted his exit.

Chapter 4

"Sure, I like comin' here. But living here?…That's another question."

"You don't think you could appreciate a quiet way of life then?"

"If you want to live quietly, you're not putting much into life."

Little remained of Chandler's head. Two hunters from eastern Ohio discovered him one hour after Emil Carter's search party had located the big foreman of the steelworking crew. They spotted the Buckseller man's body at the edge of a remote thicket of thornapples in a high flat area that shouldered many of the shabby dwellings below. Locals knew the area as Devil's Den, and its sole inhabitant was a female recluse who had made her home in a spacious tent for longer than a great number of people cared to remember.

The preliminary reports on the bodies by the county coroner, along with the close proximity in the location of their deaths, immediately drew the interest of Bingham County's prosecutor Eddie Rusack, a balding and small but solid stump of a man, who lived on a patchy farm north of town with his wife and four children, and who was inclined to shun the suit and tie in favor of country wear and heavy waterproof boots whenever he could get away with it.

Around the middle of the afternoon, a crowd of businessmen and elected public officials from across the town and county gathered in the D.A.'s offices on the second floor of the stone courthouse in response to an impromptu meeting he had arranged. Along with his dislike for professional apparel, Rusack enjoyed a reputation also throughout Bingham and surrounding counties for his economy of speech which included both what he allowed of himself and what he permitted from others.

"This meeting may strike you as out of the ordinary, and in fact, it is," the D.A. began, while toward a later purpose he drew open the shades on a window at the rear of the office. "This morning, two men were discovered dead above The Buckseller. Indications at this hour point to something more than a mere coincidence of hunting accidents, which most of us might have concluded. Frankly, I don't have all of the details sufficiently straight to present the matter to you in the most orderly of fashions. However, if you'll bear with me...."

Silencing himself, he stepped to the front of the room and took a standing position behind a large walnut desk. Several sheets of paper with handwritten notes littered its surface.

"The first individual, a William Weatherby, hailed from a Pittsburgh suburb, but he was hardly a stranger to our neck of the woods. His companions say they've been coming here for nigh on forty years. He was shot through the front of the throat, and the entry and exit signs suggest a high caliber weapon. Next to the body Emil Carter and his men retrieved a white handkerchief and a flashlight. A rifle was also alongside, but neither was it loaded, nor had it been fired recently. It seems apparent that Weatherby didn't shoot himself, accidentally or otherwise."

While Rusack paused to scan his notes, others took advantage of the time to sweep the various faces in the room. Insofar as Tome could judge, most seemed already absorbed by the few statements to which they had listened and even appeared fascinated by the fact that their D.A. had summoned them to his office to apprise them of the details surrounding the deaths of two hunters. No questions formed on any of their faces, not even in the usually inquisitive features of Drake. Yet it occurred to Tome he himself had a question and a very important one. He was the only member of the press on hand. Why was that? Tina Orleau, the *Olean Herald's* outlying districts correspondent, where was she? Her lithe young figure and disarming voice were always a blessing to those gin-dry council meetings and C of C get-togethers, and she wasn't but a twenty-minute drive away. The *Morning Era* out of Bradford, where was its local fellow, Jerry Drier?

"The second body, whom we all knew as Pig Chandler," Rusack resumed, "received a bullet in the side of the head, just above the ear, and it caused a great deal of damage. Now the slug that felled him may have been recovered. A hunk of lead was dug out of a nearby tree and preliminary identification makes it out to be a thirty aught-six. There was nothing beside Chandler save his rifle, and although the piece was loaded, like the rifle belonging to Weatherby, it had not been fired. It doesn't appear that Chandler killed himself either."

"Then it's the usual scenario. A couple of remiss hunters are responsible. If the wound of neither man was self-inflicted—"

Rusack cut off the youthful, outspoken councilman. "Remiss hunters haven't a thing to do with this! I don't think that either victim caught a wild bullet. I equally discount the theory that either man was the recipient of a slug fired from a hunter who mistakenly identified him as a buck, then vanished after realizing his error. Now I'm aware a few of the adventuresome ride their SUVs and pickups up the timber roads at the southern end now that AmeriCon's men and equipment have left. Some hunters, in fact, walk the Den on opening day, I'll allow that. But by and large, The Buckseller, its flats, the Den, they all remain remote. Ask Rums. The number of people who hunt it, you can count on both hands and still have a finger or two remaining to scratch your ass."

"He's right," Sagerville's District Game Protector Harry Rumsey drawled.

"In that case," Nicholas Popov spoke out bluntly, "you're telling us that both of these men were murdered!"

"Wouldn't it seem to you, Nick, that you're telling me the same?"

Rusack's odd reply to the popular businessman was not immediately comprehensible to everyone, and certainly not to some who were disappointed the baker had not supplied a tray of Danish as he sometimes would at other meetings; but Tome and a few others nodded their agreement with the District Attorney.

The freshman councilman Sherman Coppersmith spoke again. "So these two men were murdered. It's a crime and no doubt a terrible tragedy for their families and friends. But what's that have to do with any of us present in this room?"

Drake, who had been leaning against the rear windowsill, straightened and advanced a couple of steps. "It would seem there's a great deal more buzzing inside our D.A.'s head."

"A great deal for certain," said Rusack. "You care to hazard a guess, Harmon, or do you wish to hear it from me?"

"Unless I missed something, the suggestion is that we have a killer at large. A sniper, to be exact."

"More importantly," Rusack added, "he isn't finicky about his quarry. If the impact of that statement isn't immediate, gentlemen, I invite you to turn your faces to the window and let your minds brainstorm awhile."

Many of them complied. At the bottom of the window they could see the limit on their tiny hometown with its carbon and plastic factories, its new communications center, its cemetery, and a long line of old housing. But beyond there was only an endless, blue-gray series of decreasing undulations, each densely spiked with standing timber.

"A field day," muttered Rusack. "The bastard's going to have a field day."

There followed a period of silence as the question of a sniper started to attract thought.

Tome asked, "Are you certain one individual is all we're talking about?"

"No," said the D.A. "Except I think we'd have more dead bodies on our hands today if that isn't the case."

Drake took another step forward. "Satisfy my curiosity, Ed. How is this office managing things?"

"That, Harmon, is the reason behind this meeting." The office was becoming hot and the D.A.'s forehead glistened with moisture. "At this moment in Bingham County there are about seventy-five thousand additional people who are predominantly hunters. Add a few resident sportsmen—men, women, and children—and we've a fairly accurate idea of how many people are mucking about our land."

"Then he'll have an impossible time avoiding a witness," Coppersmith offered.

Rumsey emitted a short laugh. "Son, as the D.G.P. here for going-on twenty-six years, I can assure you the saturation level for hunters in the county is barely dampened by that figure you heard Eddie give. Bingham could absorb another hundred thousand in its woods and who would notice!"

"Try the merchants," grumbled a merchant.

"What are you recommending?" Drake asked.

"I'm not recommending a thing, Harmon. The story they're to get at the *Era* and the *Herald*, that's up to all of you."

Thus the answer to my question, thought Tome.

"These next two weeks for Bingham County are bustling times. About as bustling as they ever get around here, I think most of us would agree. I'm uncertain what effect it will have, someone out there in our mountains picking off unsuspecting hunters. But whatever the effect, each of you has a stake in the area and its communities. Consequently, deciding what is to be done is to rest on your shoulders. You may want to inform the dailies that a serial killer, psychopath, madman, lunatic, sniper, homicidal maniac—call him whatever you prefer!—is running the slopes and hollows. Or you might elect to make no mention of the threat. What this office knows, you've been informed of. What you say to the public... that I am presently placing in your bin."

If he had ever been in on a conspiracy, Tome knew he was lending an ear to one now as discussion broke out on how much the dailies already knew and wouldn't they be sure to suspect something the moment they heard about Chandler. He regarded Rusack, whom he had known since his earliest days in Sagerville and with whom he on occasion shared a drink, as the D.A. waited patiently behind his desk while the others talked among themselves. Frankly, it did not matter if they left his office in accord. He had assembled them not for the purpose of designing a clever scheme for public deception, but simply to reveal a situation he considered touchy and highly volatile. Sort of an insurance policy he created for himself against being a scapegoat in the event anything should blow.

Since the presence of a woodland sniper first entered the D.A.'s mind, it became clear there was no easy course of action. True, he had been involved in other cases where a hunter was shot. The one out at Flowing Well four years back ended in death. Historically, any shooting was written off as an accident. Officially, a misdemeanor. But for a long time now there had been a foreboding maxim: *Take a boy hunting if you want him a man. Take a man hunting if you want him dead.* It was that simple. The inclusion of a sniper, though, that was something altogether different, yet not an entirely novel thought. Moreover, there was this other concern, what Amidon, the county coroner who also ran an antique shop, had referred to as "economic crippling," the potential to rob the entire area of its timely and vital tourist trade. It was in this Rusack had instantly realized the political mousetrap and consequently decided that the handling of any public disclosure would be the affair of all business and officialdom. If matters failed to evolve in the manner he was hoping, he wanted an equable distribution of the forthcoming blame.

Tome quickly came to understand that his friend Rusack had called the meeting to protect himself against possible censure. As an elected official he was vulnerable and, lately, falling under ever-increasing fire. Early reports indicated that in the coming year's election the long-serving prosecutor would be up against the fiercest opposition, a fiery white knight from Killdeer with an old name and old money, who had entered the legal life of the county less than a year ago. For all of it, though, it was still a kind of conspiracy, and Tome wondered how long before one of those around him would realize the press was already in their midst.

It wasn't long as a county commissioner, a bulky, hoary-headed man beyond his sixties, nodded his way. "Gentlemen. Please note that our own Mr. Tome is present among us."

"Karl, Meredith will do the right thing," Drake said reassuringly. "He's fully aware of the editorial restraint required in a delicate matter such as this."

The manipulative vote of confidence flabbergasted Tome, forcing his eyes to widen with objection.

"You're a reputable publisher, Meredith. Your readers like you, they respect you. They count on your paper to protect their interests in this small community in the same way you must count on them to protect yours."

"Their lives aren't a part of those interests?"

"Carry on, Harmon. You stick to what you were saying," urged the Commissioner. "I want to hear the rest of it."

"I think we should hear what Meredith has to say," urged Popov.

"Go on, Harmon," said the Commissioner, ignoring the local pantryman.

"We all know that this county is reputed by a great many hunters to be the deer capital of the country! A lofty reputation as that isn't achieved overnight. A lot of people worked long and hard to be rewarded with that label. But start publicizing that we've got some deranged personality moving through our mountains and hollows, and we'll wipe the claim from everybody's mind, along with all the dollars spent by those seventy-five thousand visiting hunters, which are substantial!

Don't think for a moment they're not. This economy that most of us are employed in who live and work in Bingham County…" He broke off, momentarily unsure about the merits of what he was about to say. "Let me be frank. We're not the host as most of you high-mindedly think. It's the visiting hunter who's the host. We're nothing but a breed of economic parasite. Some of you might think that's unfortunate and are probably offended by my choice of words, but it's a fact no matter what you think or how you feel. Like it or not, a lot of us feed off the sportsman." He paused briefly, lifting his head back so that his eyes were peering down at the others. "There's something else, too. Something which I suspect moved our District Attorney to be sociable this afternoon and invite all of you to this office. This decision *is* ours! If we make it incorrectly, be sure that down the road there will be a lot of people demanding answers to their questions."

The Commissioner laughed abruptly, unexpected by everyone.

"Could this be the year, Harmon? You might have yourself a scoop tonight, Tome."

Unmoved, Drake continued in the same tone of voice and he even pointed a finger. "It's you that I'm addressing, Commissioner. You and the others who are—"

"Hold it, hold it. Hold it one goddamn second!" the senior official objected, flagging a big hand out front. "There might be merit in what you're about to say, Harmon, but your old commissioner has been around a long time and has weathered dumping threats from the likes of a crazy Beryl Victor to the noblest of them all, Cliff Addy, Tome here's predecessor. I'll say one thing for you and your paper, though, Tome. At least you get the names down correctly. Took two terms before Addy finally realized all the letters in Aufderheide and another term before he put 'em down in the proper order."

"Probably the reason he was never partial to you," Rusack joked quietly from behind his desk. "Too difficult a name to spell, Karl."

The Commissioner snorted. "You could have something there, Ed. Say, if I'm not mistaken, didn't yours show up in print the first few times as 'Rucksack'?"

Some of the others laughed, those who remembered the former publisher and were now prompted to recall his egregious recording of proper names.

Annoyed by their lack of focus, Drake remained controlled, yet raised his voice. "Addy is writing and misspelling the names of saints. Meredith isn't Cliff Addy. And maybe you are securely implanted in the politics of Bingham County, Karl, that you won't ever be unseated. But that isn't the case with Sherman and a number of others present. If we shut down this county after going public with this, are you intending to be the one who will accept all blame? I wouldn't think so. I don't imagine Ed asked those of you here to lend an ear for any reasons other than you were the ones who came to mind, you were near the phone, and this office won't accommodate any more. But rest assured those uninvited will hold us all accountable if we let this matter get out of hand."

"I think he's running," the Commissioner said in an undertone of comic acquiescence, and he winked at Tome.

On Drake's admonitions, the remainder of the officials began to discuss quietly amongst themselves the impact of the hunter. As they had been earlier, so were many now reluctant to express commitment, their eyes set to impress without revelation as they hoped to glean the popular opinion from the faces of others. Some, it appeared to Tome, looked as if they now wished their district attorney had not summoned them to his office at all. They did not want to argue that others should not be informed of what was out there, out beyond the office window they glanced apprehensively at from time to time. But neither did they want to contest what Drake had said. It was incontrovertible, wasn't it? There were a lot of hunters and they did bring a lot of money into the county.

"Regardless of anything, by not letting this out, you're putting the hunter in serious jeopardy," Rumsey cautioned.

"I'm assuring you he'll return next year and the year after," Drake countered, "which you might agree, Harry, is likely to be more in line with your Harrisburg employer. Besides, one very important matter remains to be substantiated."

"Which is what?" Rusack asked.

"That both men were actually murdered."

"Take my word."

"If you've no objections, a few questions. Their clothing, what were they wearing? Was it easily visible?"

"Weatherby wore the recommended coverage of fluorescent orange—a square patch on the front and back of the traditional Woolrich Mackinaw. As for Chandler"— he made a short motion with his hands toward his own attire—"similar, but considerably worn and soiled, and no orange at all."

Like a proper student for whom he frequently acted as a substitute teacher, Coppersmith raised his hand with the fingers spread wide. "You said a white handkerchief was picked up next to the old fellow from Pittsburgh?"

"That and a flashlight. Plus a few other items on his person. Thermos, hunting knife, so on."

A boyish grin stretched across the face of the freshman councilman. "Isn't it a popular practice for hunters to shun a white handkerchief when they're about to spend a day in search of deer? Red and blue maybe, but not white. Not something that when pulled from the pocket can too easily be mistaken for the tail of a deer. Whitetails, when alarmed, flag their tail upward, exposing the white underneath. Seems logical the first victim pulled out his handkerchief and was shot by another hunter who didn't insist on positive i.d."

Patiently, Rusack listened, aware of the flaw. "That's it?"

"It's logical, isn't it?"

"The flashlight was on when the man was discovered. No light was emanating, but the switch was in a forward 'on' position. The batteries had gone dead. I think Weatherby was shot before the opening hour of deer season and even before sunrise. He never reached his intended spot to start his hunt. According to his friends, they dropped him at The Buckseller before five. It's my contention he had the flashlight on and was trudging up the mountain in the dark. Those who hunt will bear me out that it's preferable to arrive at your spot early so that the sight and scent of your body have a chance to blend in with the surroundings. At one point he paused to wipe his brow or blow his nose, keeping his light on, and that's when he became the target. The fact that the rifle was unloaded strongly corroborates that the killing occurred before the initial hour. He was shot, he died within minutes, and the flashlight stayed on till the batteries gave out.... Plus, if I didn't already mention it, his thermos contained coffee to the brim." Rusack gave a quick, impatient glance at everyone in the room. "Anything else?"

"All very well for Weatherby," said Drake. "What about Chandler?"

Like a LCD screen under pressure, there was a reactionary shrinkage of the prosecutor's eyes. Tome recognized its meaning, having seen it before. Its meaning was that such a question should not be asked because there were no answers other than the D.A.'s hunches. They showed an outstanding record before the bench. But until they reached the courtroom, they remained speculation.

"The analysis isn't as easy," Rusack confessed.

Filigreed lines of satisfaction slowly settled in the handsome face of the broker.

"In that case I'd say sufficient reason to publicize this matter in terms of a woodland sniper doesn't exist."

"I don't know about that," said Popov, shaking his head.

Drake ignored the owner of the local diner, who had become the talk of the town because he was losing noticeable amounts of weight, and moved confidently into the very center of the group.

"Let the story appear anywhere. There isn't one of us who doesn't believe that newspapers, radio, and TV stations, especially those in the southern half of the state, will pick up on it and inflate it with more air than it deserves. As far as what is known at this moment in time, Chandler could have been shot accidentally. There's no reason to assume one murder from another. I say print it as that and nothing more!"

Tome surveyed the office when Drake became silent. He saw heads, nodding, slowly at first, but then with more and more vigor.

Too many heads, he thought.

Chapter 5

"....Except what would I do?"

"Besides, she's seemin' happy and contented behind there, so forget hers.... Honey, you get any complaints from the natives when you became barmaid?"

"Some."

"Well, you know, I've heard it from others like yourself. Live here for the rest of your life and on your headstone they'll want to write 'Flatlander.' "

The temperature had dipped. An icy wind now stroked Sagerville as Tome left the courthouse and made his way across the square. Intermittent sheets of snow fell, but the flakes were small and disappeared instantly.

Inside his office, the afternoon mail lay stacked atop his desk, some two dozen envelopes included, one of which, he could discern from the outside, was yet another rejection from an insurance company for libel coverage. He took to opening the remainder, less out of interest and more in an attempt to swing his thoughts away from the disturbing consensus that had concluded the meeting. He was under no order that forced him to go along with the decision. Neither did he feel obligated, despite all Drake had said. Even so, the threat of a small-town backlash was a reality for anyone attempting to push his way in a matter that affected many others. Rusack, afterward, had admitted to him the possibility of an accident in the case of Chandler. And although the D.A. stated that he would only take odds on such a conclusion and not give any, it was sufficient this moment to curb the uneasiness Tome was experiencing in the pit of his stomach. He knew already what this week's edition would report. Tomorrow's issue would carry the news of two deaths, but only one murder. Quite simply, he hoped Drake was correct.

Near the bottom of the mail pile, he hesitated before opening an envelope whose logo had become all too familiar. A well-antlered deer stood before a hunter who had his gun barrel raised. It reminded him of the ton of photos he had seen in the many hook-and-bullet publications, except that the end of the barrel broke apart and each splinter circled back to the hunter's head. Three gold letters, FGC, lay underneath this audacious design. Spelled out, the abbreviation became Friends of God's Creatures, an anti-hunting organization, whose increasing notoriety made it clear why its acronym had never taken on much priority as a tactic for being remembered. Headquartered in New York, the organization had a woman for its top administrator, an extremely beautiful woman, Tome thought, and if the pictures he had seen of her could be believed, it was another reason the group was widely known.

Letters arrived at his office drenched in the most vitriolic venom imaginable. Usually, the target was the hunter and his sport. Infrequently they attacked the State Game Commission. But when the group tired of both, he found himself the target. Scorching denunciations, one after the other, came hurtling off the page against his editorial policy of printing photos of successful hunters posed behind their kills.

At first he had chosen to scrap the letters, humorously reminding himself he wasn't advertising for an editorial consultant. That hardly stopped their arrival. In the end he surrendered and published one of the more vituperative mailings. The decision boosted circulation as the first published letter had sparked a steady war of attack and counterattack from hunters and their castigators. And there was still no end in sight.

He ripped open this latest.

Consisting of two pages on equally bold letterhead, the letter was an absorbing denigration of the hunter, casting him as a modern eunuch in pursuit of a surrogate masculinity. The elegant scrawl at the bottom read "Nila Ellenger."

He pushed the letter aside as a bundled-up farmer stomped in. "Ya got some 'No Trespass' signs, do ya?" the farmer drawled.

"Paper only. Thinking of posting your land?"

"All through on the thinking end. Yesterday one of the cows was shot. Ol' Doc Thomas, he sez she'll be okay, but I don't want anymore of it. Can't much afford it. I'm beginning to think I'm paying for his paper he writes all our history down on. You wouldn't think a pint-size town like ours would have all that much history."

Tome smiled while pointing to the adjoining room. "See Mary. She'll get you what you need."

The crusty farmer nodded and left the office. Tome scribbled a note regarding the injured cow for his own column of miscellaneous items that bore mention, if not occasionally a feature. Yet the story was neither fresh nor surprising. That moment he could have tallied dozens of injustices or accidents, or whatever they ought to be called, by hunters. Last season a prize-winning Charolais steer ready for market had stopped a bullet. Thousands of dollars dropped in an instant. The hunter responsible admitted mistake, but added that he was honestly trying to strengthen the gene pool of the deer herd by ridding it of an albino. Neither were horses, dogs, and cats exempt from the roster of targets. Nor was the land. He remembered yesterday's unexpected visit by Jim Roman and Emil Carter's wife, Suzanne.

Mary Kiel approached his desk.

"Out of signs?"

"Mr. Orcutt has been taken care of. I thought you might be wanting this."

She dropped a folder on his blotter, indexed "Features (Killed)."

Irony in the label of a file folder.

"Thank you, Mary."

Before opening the folder, he checked the clock against an appointment on his desk calendar. The first of several important meetings was to begin shortly in the neighboring community of Killdeer, named for the bird, although few visitors would have guessed it, on a new dam and reservoir complex that was already three and a half years under construction. His opposition to the most important issue, a proposal to make the recreational state park a prototype for other parks across the Tier and open it to corporate enterprise, was the reason he had decided to cover the meeting himself and not assign it to his staff. The clock told him it wouldn't start for another hour, allowing him to thumb through the material in the folder until he reached the feature on Seneca Chandler.

Tome had written the piece the past summer. Paperclipped

to the sheets was a black-and-white photograph he had snapped during the interview. The pic showed the agile man outside his shanty, sitting on a rickety wooden chair. Both hands with their conspicuous, fortifying wrists rested on his knees, and his intense eyes peered out beneath a rigid forehead lined with dirt and sweat. Behind him and slightly out-of-focus grubbed a sow and her farrow. Tome remembered the lot of them incessantly grunting and rooting in the earth like angry miners.

He stared at both copy and picture. Good stuff, he thought. There was no excuse for this one, the piece should have run. Yet he had listened to his employees and at the last minute had squelched it. But it shouldn't have mattered that the previous features in the profile series had been of prominent citizens in shirt and tie. So what if they would have received it badly? What was the worth in condemnations that Drake and Rayburn and others like them had to offer?

"It's just that his nickname doesn't imply his animals alone," one of his typesetters had explained. "People feel his entire way of life is implicated in the name."

True, Chandler had resided in a hovel. His odor, too, had been suspect, what with all his clothes badly worn and in urgent need of washing. But inside the person, the name was inaccurate. Frankly, Chandler had struck him as a man who had won a settlement with himself, and in some small way that he himself did not understand, Tome had envied the Buckseller man because of it.

It was easy for him to recall the interview. In spite of the alcohol floating off the swine-handler, Chandler had spoken lucidly as he boasted of extensive travels through South America and Alaska before settling in the bottomlands outside of Sagerville; as he talked effervescently of a favorite year, during which he had audited several agricultural courses at the state university. Whatever had led him to his ultimate mode of living, self-neglect, despite his appearance, had not appeared to be at fault.

Tome salvaged another memory, this from the bits and pieces in the days following the interview. A second charge leveled by his employees. Chandler, some had scoffed, was a reliefer. Yet the smallest effort of investigation had proven the accusation false. Although he would have qualified in an instant, Chandler had not received one cent from governmental welfare programs. His meager income had resulted from his animals and from the cutting and selling of firewood. Then why had there been so much disdain for the man? That Tome thought attributable in part to Chandler's own admission that he rarely performed favors. Always he sought compensation in some form or other. Money. A tool. A case of beer or home-canned food. Maybe only a promise of reciprocal labor.

He detached the photograph of Chandler and his brood and replaced the copy in the file folder. He should have ignored what the community thought. He should have run the piece.

Through the walls of the old print shop whistled the wind as it boxed with the alley. He shivered, and it occurred to him in a retrospective way that it might be something responsible apart from the wind. The clock said it was time. He rose from the desk and readied himself for the drive to Killdeer.

Because of the chilling decline in temperature, he found the side locks to the window van frozen. He tried the rear doors and climbed in, scrambling over boxes stuffed with not-yet-delivered print orders, a half-empty case of 10W-30, two tires, a smashed cooler, and an unopened glass bottle of apple cider... cider. Still another way by which Pig Chandler had supported himself.

He'd made use of the fruits from the apple orchard out behind his place. Apples wormy or lacking in size, he dropped to the ground so that deer and other animals might get at them. On Chandler's insistence, Tome had taken the jug as late payment for a copy of the photo. But no one in the family much favored the beverage, and so the bottle remained where he had first set it down. Inside a tire. Now dirtied, and still unopened.

Chapter 6

"What I've heard?...No one knows. For that matter, no one knows if that's her real name."

"How old is she?"

"Hard to say. But some who've seen her say if you bring her down out of that tent and clean her up, she won't look too bad. What'd you say, Forster?"

"...Is that right? No one knows who it is?"

"Maybe you all oughta watch to see who goes hunting up that way."

"Yeah. Maybe somebody's eliminating competition."

Having learned from Tome that another party was inquiring about the lost acreage out at Killdeer, Harmon Drake made up his mind to solve the matter and to do so quickly. On the second day of the deer hunting season, about the same time the Ohio hunters were showing the body of Pig Chandler to Emil Carter and his searchers, Drake descended into the bowels of the old Bingham County Courthouse. Its packed shelves contained every land transaction for the past hundred and fifty years, in addition to the sketchy records of still earlier sales.

Confident that he could verify the ownership, he pulled ledger after ledger from the shelves. Combining experienced conjecture with the facts available on the questionable parcel, he scanned the long columns and spot-read the tedious paragraphs of dry legal syntax, cross-checking frequently for signatures, addresses, and dates. After four hours of this painstaking work which included a barrage of telephone calls to AmeriCon Paper in Roanoke, Virginia, and to some relations of the attorney who had handled the deal, he was close to confirming what he had suspected. He might have traveled to Killdeer at once for confirmation, except while exiting the courthouse he observed the trail of public officials and fellow businessmen ascending the wide staircase to the D.A.'s offices. They invited him to accompany them and thank God they had.

But immediately after the meeting, he drove to Killdeer where he broke into the cellar of a defunct train station that had provided office space decades ago to a Killdeer attorney. There he discovered the answer that was true to his expectation. The large-acreage transaction had never been completed. The deed, never recorded, continued to lie in the attorney's boxed-up, eaten-up files underneath the musty, yellow bedding of mice. The man long dead, the purchaser the same, and certainly generations of mice as well. Both attorney and buyer had died within days of each other before the closing was a week old. AmeriCon Paper had taken it for granted everything was in order. Consequently, the acreage, large by itself but minuscule in contrast to the hundreds of thousands of acres the company owned in seven states, was lost even in nineteen fifty-six because of a general office incompetence. Or so he concluded. The possibility that an attorney in the tiny community of Killdeer might not have had office help in nineteen fifty-six did not occur to Harmon Drake.

But if he felt satisfaction from solving the puzzle, it had not endured longer than the time it took to drive from the old train station to the high school auditorium.

The open meeting on the Killdeer Dam and Reservoir, despite breaking all county records for length and the minutes it would generate, did not turn out according to the expectations of many, and certainly not to Drake's. On his return to Sagerville he found himself mimicking the concluding words of Karl Aufderheide, the evening's chair:

"'I wish to thank each of you for coming to the meeting to voice your concerns. As your commissioner, I would like to see Killdeer and all of the county develop, but as the means under discussion here this evening are not suitable to a great many of you, I will abide by your wishes, my friends. I will strongly fight any movement to the contrary.'

"Great, Karl. Just great," he shouted at the windshield. "Put a sign up at each end of the county why don't you, that reads 'GET LOST!'"

According to the Upstate section of *Downstate Magazine*, of which Drake bought a copy because the writer had quoted him, Killdeer was *"warming up to become a real municipality and not just another countrified hamlet with overalled people who, when an auspicious change is proposed for their way of life and they are opposed to it, respond with a harsh, confusing, and always uncooperative non sequitur."*

Even the town's newest promotional leaflet, sporting four-color, claimed that more than deer and timber had been discovered in the hills. It boasted pride itself had at last been unearthed. And the meeting itself with its grand panoply of charts and graphs and water tables and artists' renderings in assorted bolds and pastels, all highlighted by a three-dimensional replica of the flood-prevention playground complete with water, sandy beaches, simulations of dynamited rock moraines, and hundreds of tiny plastic trees throughout the assigned areas for the proposed businesses—the meeting had been much more than anyone would have expected of a community so small.

So what went wrong? Why hadn't he seen this coming?

Switching on the courtesy light of the Buick, he unlatched his briefcase sitting on the opposite seat, and while darting his eyes back and forth between the materials inside the case and the night highway, he withdrew the recent issue of *Downstate*. Perhaps he had missed something.

He positioned the magazine between himself and the steering wheel and, after locating the article's opening page that was part of a spread which carried a high-altitude aerial photograph showing both Killdeer and Sagerville as two tiny splotches on a vast landscape of forested mountains, he began to read. Yet he could not shake from mind those hundreds of voices that had entered the auditorium to release some small shred of consuming bitterness against anything that might alter their lives. Or the other voices that railed against those bitter, claiming they wanted change but were prevented from having it.

Momentarily left to steer itself, the Buick with a bang slipped off the high shoulder of the road, and after returning it to the pavement, Drake thought better of reading behind the wheel and tossed the magazine back into the open briefcase. Then he turned off the light, switched on the radio, and punched the first button that delivered only static. WMMO at the county seat bragged about the wide territory that it covered, but it could pipe no audio down the center of the highway, and the vehicle passed through several mountains and valleys before a single note was heard. In the dark of the car, Drake found himself momentarily scoffing at the station's A.E. The ad man was persisting in his attempt to sell the agency expensive advertising that would run during the "high traffic of drive times."

Passing within narrow range of an electric transformer, or something highly charged, the radio suddenly grated on his hearing, and he instinctively fumbled down the volume knob. In the same instant, he saw the man at the end of his headlights waving him to the other lane. On the road beside the man was a small bundle. He was too late with turning the wheel, and the luxury sedan ran off the shoulder and into a soft ditch. He flung the steering wheel back to jolt the car out before it became mired, but he only managed to swing the vehicle to a perpendicular with the highway. Both rear tires had cracked the icy crust and were now embedded in mud.

The man came running over as he let his window down.

"Y'okay?"

"I think so," said Drake.

"The car's just stuck. I'll push you out in a minute."

"What is it?" Drake asked, meaning the bundle in the road. But the man had already turned away and was crossing to the other lane.

Drake watched as the man knelt in the edge of the vehicle's headlights. The bundle was an animal, a cat. And it was dying. The small body heaved and trembled every few seconds and then lay quiet. He recalled seeing the heart of a snapping turtle act the same for well over an hour as it lay on a paper plate atop the bar at The Buckseller Inn. A couple of turtle hunters responsible for the tasteless exhibit, by far the filthiest and most fetid human beings he had ever encountered, had poked it with toothpicks each time it appeared to have stopped for good.

The man on the road straightened and raised the animal by its hind legs. He held it a little distance from his body and glanced up and down the highway. Then, in one monstrously violent motion, he swung the dying animal over his head and whipped the tiny skull to a final spongy impact with the pavement. Drake turned away while stifling an involuntary urge to vomit. The man waited to see if any life remained in the small body before carrying it off the road and leaving it.

Getting hold of himself, Drake got out to examine the car. There didn't seem to be any damage. However, the wheels were sunk halfway to their wells.

"You did seem to be flying," the man said, returning.

"If I had known you were planning on bashing the brains out of that cat, I could have saved us both some trouble."

"Rabbit," said the man. "I might have let you, too."

"Looked like a cat."

"Rabbit. Want me to retrieve it and plunk it on your dash for study?"

"I'll take your word."

"I thought you might.... So get in, straighten your wheels, and then accelerate on and off to help me get her rocking. If you feel the wheels grab or I holler to go with it, then just power out. Let it scream. Don't go running off either! That's my truck you passed about a mile back. I don't know what kind of monkey's got into it."

"Who are you?" Drake asked coldly.

"Name's Fogger Dann."

"You're without a car?"

"I told you. That's my pickup back aways. And it ain't going nowhere. You got a problem?"

"I keep a spotless automobile. I don't want it smelling like a dump."

The man, who had tangled blond hair and slightly pitted skin, regarded Drake from head to toe and laughed. "Yep, you're my size," he said, grinning.

Drake tensed. The thought that he might have to defend himself against this vermin frightened him.

"Nothing like that," said Dann, reading Drake's reaction. "I was thinking maybe it'll be me that gets behind the wheel. You do the shoving."

"Forget it!" said Drake. But Dann continued to grin at him, and he knew if he were to get the Buick out of the ditch, he would need this man's help.

"Shucks, it's mostly the jacket," said Dann. "I'll leave the rag along the road if it'll make you happy."

The big car had to be powered out with Dann spreadeagled on the trunk lid, jogging, like some fierce fornicator, the rear end up and down for as much traction as possible. Afterward, Drake waited on the highway with the car running as Dann hurried across the road and retrieved a rifle that he'd earlier leaned against the post under a speed limit sign. He opened the bolt and set it against the front seat. Then he slipped out of the offending jacket and, rather than discarding it as he had offered, knotted it to the mirror on his side where it flapped noisily as they soon sped along toward Sagerville.

About a minute into the ride, Drake asked, "Where do you want off?"

"You got yourself a woman waiting that you're in a hurry? The turn-off for the Buckseller will do."

Drake glanced at the darkened profile that was thin and grizzly. He might have guessed.

"That was some meeting, wasn't it?"

"You were there?" Drake said, surprised. He wondered why the pungency of the man's jacket hadn't permeated the auditorium from front to rear.

"That was some speech you gave, you know."

"Does that mean you liked it or you didn't?"

"To be honest, I'm not sure. Those restaurants, grocery stores, motels, and arcades you talked about having inside the park would produce some jobs, like you said. Fellows like myself could use the work."

"So what part aren't you sure about?"

Dann had been looking away from Drake as he talked, often gazing out the window on his side into the darkness. Now he turned and stared directly at the agent's profile. "That part about 'the non-polluting industry of tourism.'"

Drake looked over and met his gaze.

"You knew that was a lie when you said it. But it's understandable. I mean, all those that stood up, there was many that were telling lies. Remember the woman who feared turning Bingham County into the Poconos? You think she was ever there? Or how 'bout our councilman Coppersmith: *'Those opposed to the introduction of business into the park are being extremely selfish.'* Pshaw, as they say. Then, too, there was that banker man who threatened the region's rapid decline if tourism were hindered in any way. Where is that fellow living? In some upscale part of the county that none of us know about? Not to overlook that other fellow who told everyone that he was some kind of promoter and that he was listening to 'the shallow reasoning of a backwater people.' I'll give odds the boy grew up here. Of course, I did appreciate the one farmer who swore 'there's no need for the goddamn dam itself.'"

Drake heard his passenger chuckle to himself and repeat the

words, "goddamn dam."

The radio's static came in and out as they moved along, until they were fewer than ten miles from Sagerville, whereupon it came in clear and without break-up. The time was on the hour, and the station rolled its familiar tape to lead into the news. The names of a half- dozen towns and hamlets were sounded off at short intervals above the continued pounding of a tympanic drum, as the station announcer boasted coverage of a hundred miles. This was followed by a spot from a sponsor, and tonight it was the Drake Realty ad, contracted at the run-of-station rate.

"Sounds like you," said Dann, following the tag at the end of the jingle.

Drake made no reply. Instead, he listened as the news began. The announcer delivered the story of the killing of William Weatherby, "a dedicated sportsman from Braeburn, Pennsylvania." Facts were few, notwithstanding the story's length. Then, without a tie-in to the first account, he reported on the death of Chandler as a typical hunting-related fatality. A commercial for Graff & Aufderheide's Memorials followed and when the announcer returned, he summarized the day's hunting for the region. No one had been killed or injured. No one was reported missing.

Drake switched off the radio, satisfied. What he'd wanted to hear. It would be Tome and Rusack who would look like idiots.

The first car lights since leaving Killdeer flashed in his mirrors. He glanced at his unwanted passenger who was kneading his left palm over the top of the rifle barrel.

"I hope you don't mind my saying it, but you don't seem very upset by the death of your neighbor."

"It's not my way," Dann said matter-of-factly, staring straight ahead.

Drake flicked on the car's blinker and coasted to a stop in the middle of the turn-off. The tractor-trailer behind him and two cars dogging the truck rushed by, shaking the Buick. Dann got out and worked the frozen jacket loose from the mirror. He mumbled something unintelligible, then folded the stiff garment and tucked it under his free arm. He ducked his head inside the car door.

"You know they pay their rent."

"What?"

"Those folks in The Buckseller? They pay their rent. Every one of them. You should keep that in mind."

Closing the door, Dann moved off and disappeared into the darkness. But the piercing malodor of the Buckseller man's jacket had entered the car, and it stayed with Drake over the remaining distance to Sagerville and home.

Chapter 7

"Say, Sport, whatsa time?"

"Three in Missoula, four in Reno—"

"The time here, Sport, if you will?"

"Check the grouse."

"Says seven-thirty-eight, but that's nowhere right."

"Welcome to Sagerville."

"All right, which of you was messing with the clock?"

It was midnight when Tome returned from the meeting in Killdeer. He parked the van in the alley so his workers could load it with the new edition at daybreak and deliver the newspapers to their sales-stand destinations throughout Bingham and surrounding counties. Another worker Monk, a facially disfigured veteran of Vietnam who lived alone in the tiny settlement of Gunther, chose to load up his car with his own portion of deliveries before he left work Tuesday night. That way he did not waste his time and gas by making another trip into Sagerville, but started the deliveries right from his house. When he finished, he headed back for home, or somewhere else that he wished to be. It wasn't a day off, but it wasn't bad, and he was glad his boss had agreed to the arrangement. He was there outside the darkened brick building.

"How are you this hour, Mr. Tome?"

"Eager to get home."

"Let me drop you."

"No, you finish up so you can get home yourself and catch some sleep. It's just a couple of blocks."

"I'm finished. I'll drop you. It's too cold to walk."

"Sure you don't mind?"

"Just get in. I won't be a minute. I have to lock the rear door."

"You have a loose one I can take with me?"

"There's three or four on the front seat."

Monk locked the door of the shop, got into the car, and started it. Out of habit he pulled cautiously from the alley.

"How's the remodeling on the house coming along, Monk? Who did you hire to do the work?"

"Are you still looking for a dog for your kids, Mr. Tome?"

Tome hesitated, and almost said a disbelieving "What?" but then smiled to himself inside the darkness of the car. This man, who was several years his senior but still called him Mr. Tome, rarely volunteered information about his life, and he never answered questions. Tome had learned of the house remodeling and Monk's difficulty with finding a contractor while having a sweet roll at Popov's one morning.

"Mr. Tome?"

"Yes, I'm still thinking about it. Haven't done much in the way of looking. Why? You know of one who needs a home?"

"I do. Your friend Bill Lill stopped in while you were at the meeting. He said he's decided to give up his dog."

"He did? Then he must have just made up his mind. I had a drink with him Monday night and he didn't say anything. Never mentioned the dog at all."

"What kind of a dog is it, Mr. Tome?"

"Oh, it's an older dog. I think it was his wife's. It has some chow in it, some German shepherd. Kind of looks like a coyote. I think people fear the worst when they see that dog, but it's really a very gentle dog. What about you, Monk? You don't have a companion. Why don't you take it?"

"Naw, Mr. Tome. I'm away too much and I don't want to be taking care of no dog." Monk nodded toward the houses outside the car. "I forget which one it is at night."

"The only one with its porch light on. Pull into the drive."

"Naw, I'll just go around the block and see who else is burning a bulb at this hour."

Probably what happened to a man if he lived alone too long. Why wouldn't he want a dog? Tome wondered. But he knew better than to press the matter, any matter. He wished the best for his employee Monk, who avoided looking anyone in the eye because of the ugly cavity in one side of his face, but he didn't believe it was likely to happen.

"Be careful heading home," he said, getting out. "They're spooked good now that the season's well underway. Two leaped out in front of me coming back from Killdeer."

"I'll be real careful, Mr. Tome. Good night to you."

Tome watched the car move off before mounting the steps to the porch and going inside. He turned off the exterior light and made his way into the kitchen where he switched on a low-hanging lamp above the table. It cast a few dim rays on the face of his wife Irene, a lovely woman with soft rounded features that were wearing well through middle age. She was wrapped inside a yellow robe.

"You're still up," he said.

"I couldn't sleep, so I decided to boil some water for tea. Are you heading straight for bed? Or would you like a cup?"

"I'll join you. I want to look over the new issue first."

They talked softly to avoid waking their two children.

"So how did the meeting go?" Irene asked, filling a pot.

"An extravaganza of sorts. Lots of people, and from all across Bingham and its neighbors." He pulled a chair out from the table and dropped into it.

"For or against?"

"Mostly against. Corporate development isn't likely to exist inside the park for some time, if ever."

"That's too bad," said Irene.

"For whom?" he asked, surprised.

"For you, of course. I thought you were in favor of it, Meredith."

"You never heard that from me."

"Maybe not, but—"

"Then why would you think I was in favor of it?"

"It would have attracted more people to the area. Wouldn't that help the circulation? Wouldn't that be another step in getting the paper back to what it used to be?"

Restoring respect to the *Sentinel* would take more than a boost in circulation. It would require something from deep inside himself he wasn't sure he had anymore.

"Just make the tea," he said.

"It'll take a few minutes."

She went over to where he was sitting at the table and set down two cups with teabags inside.

"Can I sit down?"

"Don't get ridiculous. Of course you can sit down."

He unfolded the newspaper. The photo of Chandler on the front page, surrounded by black type, jumped out at him.

"Meredith, if you were opposed to it, why wasn't I aware of that. I *do* continue to read the *Sentinel* but, anymore, you don't take a stand on anything!"

He looked up from the paper, stared at her across the table, and was about to tap out a paradiddle on its edge, as he sometimes did when he desired to alter the tone and direction of a discussion, but she reached across and squeezed his fingers.

"You don't. All you report anymore is how attractive the numerous county festivals are. I'm told Cliff Addy did more than that."

"Cliff Addy never argued for land regulations."

"An exception, Meredith. We both know that."

"It's been a long day, Irene. I'd appreciate it if you didn't start."

"It used to be you had the paper come down somewhere on everything, every issue, big or small. Even when you were unable to make up your mind about a matter, your indecision was nonetheless informative and even provocative. The people were assured you were thinking about them. Now what can they be assured of?"

She stopped, regarding him for a time, and finally decided to let the matter drop. She went over to the stove, grabbed a potholder with an Amish hex sign decoration, took hold of the pot, and returned to the table where she filled the two cups.

"I was at the Market Basket this evening. Suzanne Carter was there with her mother, talking to some friends about somebody who's killing hunters. Apparently those two men who were found dead this morning were murdered. And by the same man. Is that what you understand is going on?"

"The first hunter appears to have been murdered, the one from out of town. They can't be sure what happened to Pig Chandler."

She glanced at the inverted picture of Chandler and he could see that she was reading some of the upside-down copy.

"That's not what she was telling her friends and everyone listening. She was insistent, Meredith."

"Suzanne Carter is insistent about everything! It's not her saving grace."

"She and Emil are inseparable. You know she got her information from him."

"She wasn't there on the search!"

"And you were? You and the others at this morning's meeting in Ed's office? I heard about it, Meredith. Emil led the search. He's led a hundred of them. And I would think he's more capable of interpreting what he sees than any of you."

She put her hand on the newspaper and spun it about so that it was rightside up for her vision. He watched her read quickly now, her eyes focused and intense. When they looked up, they were unable to contain her disappointment.

"You let them talk you into bending the truth, didn't you? For some reason they didn't want it reported that a crazy is after hunters, and you went along with it." She paused, letting her tone soften. "What's happened to you, Meredith?"

He didn't have to ask what she meant.

She pushed her cup of tea across the table next to his own. "Here. I have a feeling you won't be coming to bed until I'm fast asleep, and I doubt that's going to be any time soon."

Her disgust with him was throughout, and he could see it

plainly as she rose and left the room.

What happened was that a school board member from a district in the southern half of the county had sued the paper for libel and won. Two sources, who assured Tome that his story on the board member was correct and said they had proof, denied their comments in the end, leaving the *Sentinel* and its editor hanging on hearsay. Monetarily, the judgment had cost him nothing, as insurance had picked up the tab. But the underwriter dropped him immediately afterwards and he was unable to replace it with another. Nowadays, he took a stand on a matter only when convinced that the publication was not likely to be named in a similar legal action. That was the reason he had freely endorsed the land regulations. Disgruntled property owners would file their suits against the county and the town, not the paper.

It upset him when his wife sounded off, but not in the same way as when he heard the identical complaint from others. Because, with Irene, he believed it was the very thing that had saved the marriage and kept her from leaving him and returning to her family in Pittsburgh.

There had been no children when they moved north, and there would not be any for the next ten years. Bingham had always worn the crown of all the counties stretched across the Northern Tier, and he recognized its outstanding beauty from the moment he had first set foot in Sagerville to inspect the print building, the old Heidelbergs and Cords, and to examine the financial records of the shutdown business. Spring had been in abundance then, and in spite of the rejuvenation it ushered in, he had found the tempo of life in the upland terrain still far removed from the demanding chaos of the city. To doubting, city-minded relatives and friends *(What are you going to do up there?)*

he later likened it to sliding behind the wheel of a battered pickup truck that would not travel faster than 35 miles per hour, no matter how you teased it, until finally, he concluded to them, "You settle back, inhale deeply and slowly, and accept it. In a little while, you learn to love it." Oh, he had learned to love it all right. Rather quickly, too. Not so with Irene! For, what had appeared to him as a region of order and quiet, she saw as isolation from cultural pastimes, cornucopian supermarkets, and family and friends *(We'll never get to see either of you anymore!)*

At the time the marriage had yet to see its second anniversary, and she repeatedly punctuated the altercations that followed with threats of divorce. But learning the townsfolk knew of their troubles and that a rumor was spreading which said Meredith would quickly remarry his attractive and intelligent secretary Mary Addy Kiel who, Tome knew then as now, was quite content with her potato farmer, Irene Tome brought into play a quality she had been unaware she possessed. She was not about to let others dictate a future for her or for her husband. She would have forever stayed married against her wishes if the rumor had persisted, even if she had not discovered just how much she liked calling the shots in the small town and sparsely populated county. She right along had read parts of the paper. Now she began to read it all, and at home she discussed with her husband the stories with issues to be settled.

Together, the pair began to set much of the agenda for the area and this brought her a great deal of satisfaction. The rumor eventually died because neither his secretary nor himself complied with the community's divorce decrees. But the scandalous story needed a compatible ending all the same. For Mary Kiel it became a case of knowing where her bread was buttered best. For Tome, the continuation of his marriage was interpreted as a protective cover-up, an effort to prolong the healthy image that was vital for the success of a new owner in an old business. The explanations did not trouble Irene. She became happy with her life and she remained so until a month following the libel judgment, when she saw the change in her husband.

At two in the morning Tome nestled into bed alongside his wife, but he slept poorly; and during the night a castigating cinema, starring himself, played itself out.

One end of the press extended through a wall of the print shop into infinity while the other end butted against his desk. Numerous employees stood alert at various points along the press run, only they were not his workers. He saw, instead, they belonged to many of the familiar businesses throughout the county. As the paste-up of the paper filed by, each of them scrutinized it. Magically, with a swift rub of the hand for erasure and a drumming of the fingertip for correction, they changed whatever headline or segment of copy was not agreeable. The press was stopped again and again in order to accommodate these changes, and it seemed the edition at hand would never be printed. But then Mary Kiel rose from her desk to confront these people who were taking liberties with the news.

"Stop this!" she scolded them. "This is a newspaper for everyone. You can't make your own personal alterations to it. The editor will not permit such a thing."

"The editor?" an old man standing beside the press repeated. "Are you becoming daft already, Mary? Need I remind you that your father is dead?"

"Not my father."

"Then who? Certainly you're not speaking of *him*." The old man pointed a damning forefinger at Tome behind the desk.

And as though the pointing finger were a cue, the press began to roll and without interruption. Copies shot off the end of the press across Tome's desk to hit him in the chest. The newspapers came at him rapid-fire and continued to slice against his chest before they began to collect and were forced to the sides and off the desk where they littered the floor. He had time to read only the headlines, and these stunned him. Each copy carried a banner different from the one he had assigned, and he wondered how the people stationed along the run had done it. It was uncanny and worthy of compliment. But the copies kept on coming to inundate his desk and the uneven wooden floor about him, and slowly he came to realize that the major headlines only appeared to be different from each other. Instead, they were all virtually one and the same. And when he looked up this time, Irene had joined Mary Kiel, and together they were staring back at him with scorn and disgust rotting their lovely faces, and each was shaking her head. He lowered his eyes and the papers did not stop. They continued to assault him with their bland, puffy headlines, and the words in their thick black ink all ran together.

THOUSANDS ANTICIPATED FOR BUCK OPENER SPRING GOBBLER ATTRACTS THOUSANDS CANOE REGATTA WILL BE GRANDEST EVER FOLIAGE OBSERVERS FILL ROADS AND BYWAYS NEW RESERVOIR WILL BOOST ECONOMY SLED RACES EXPANDED, BIGGER PURSE THOUSANDS ATTEND RATTLESNAKE FESTIVAL TROUT OPENER WEATHER TO BE GOOD, THOUSANDS EXPECTED... and there were more and more, and they came to him faster and faster, until they blurred at last because of the mind's frustration arising from its sleepy recognition of the weakness of will....

The following morning at the print shop, before he had time to pour himself a cup of coffee that Mary Kiel had brewed, Ed Rusack phoned.

"There's something I need to bounce off you, Meredith. What are you doing for lunch?"

"No plans."

"Look, I have to run over to McKean County this morning. What about meeting at the farm around noon? I'll call Peg and tell her we're coming."

"What's it about?"

"Just what you're thinking."

At twenty to twelve, Tome left the shop for the farm. Rusack's Landrover was already back from McKean County when he arrived. Tome pulled in behind a couple of horses who watched him from the lee side of a run-in shed. The D.A. was at the door immediately, holding it open and waiting for him to get out of the car.

"Mary Kiel get herself a new vehicle?"

"About a month ago."

"Looks like it'll go anywhere."

"Dale's influence. What's up?"

"Let's go into the kitchen."

Peg Rusack had fixed them soup and sandwiches. Before putting it on the table, she removed several boxes, a stack of old newspapers, scissors and tape.

"I've family overseas," she explained. "I'm trying to get their gifts out on time this year so they'll have them at Christmas. Have you got Irene's present yet?"

"You want a beer, Meredith?" Rusack asked.

"No, thanks. I'm anxious to hear what's on your mind."

"Meredith? Have you?"

"Thanks for lunch, Peg. And no, I haven't gotten Irene her gift."

"Okay, you've been warned. Don't let it slip your mind." Peg Rusack smiled at him and left the room.

"Sit down," Rusack ordered, and he immediately launched into what he had to say.

"First off, Meredith, I had to prove to myself that Chandler was murdered. So after everyone left my office yesterday, I drove out to The Buckseller. I talked with several men who live out there and who knew Chandler well. Some had hunted with him. I didn't have to suggest anything. They said there was no way he would have let himself be accidentally shot. There wasn't one who had a doubt that he was murdered the same as Weatherby. According to them, Chandler was one terrific hunter who owned a spectacular vision. They said he never missed seeing anything. He saw the owl in the tree, saw the bobcat, the weasel, the tom that sat tight, the bow hunter in his camos. There wasn't any way a man could have come up on him without his being aware, according to them. That made me think for the moment that he must have known his killer, except he was shot from some distance. So I asked if any of them could explain it, and one of them had absolutely no trouble doing so. We both hunt, Meredith. What do you do when you discover that some hunter has you in his cross hairs?"

"Besides mumbling to myself what an idiot the guy must be?... I wave my arms frantically in his direction."

"Right. That's just what the man said. I would do the same, and so would most others. Soon after the hunter lowered his rifle, we would feel relieved, and we'd return to the business at hand. That was Chandler's mistake. This fellow said he must have presumed what any of us would have in similar circumstances, and once he did, he was murdered. I've been thinking about the shootings all hours, Meredith, and I believe we have it wrong. All of us, myself included, thought the obvious. That this individual is after hunters. That with all the hullaballoo from the animal rights groups, what happened is what was bound to happen. No longer just a threat, but a kind of fact that was being held in escrow, and now it's out. Someone has taken up the annual slaughter of the deer and is seeking vengeance. Except, why didn't he kill more than two?"

"I asked you the same question, remember? You answered that might have happened if there were more than a single person involved. Which made sense."

"No, it doesn't. I was wrong. Think about it. A serial killer could have hiked anywhere in the county for three or four hours and knocked off a dozen hunters. He could have gone road hunting and covered much of the county in a day. Who knows the number Emil Carter and his searchers would have discovered dead had that been the case!"

"What are you getting at?"

"This guy doesn't want to kill, Meredith. He wants to send a message."

"A message? So why didn't he send it with one and leave the other alone?"

Rusack widened his eyes as a signal to Tome that the publisher already knew the answer to his own question.

"What? Are you telling me there's something in the numbers?"

"Think about it, Meredith. If he knew one death would be viewed only as the typical hunting accident...."

"I've deprived him of his message. That's what you're getting at."

"That and something else."

Tome suddenly felt sick from the thought that tore into him. "You think I've set up a situation forcing him to kill again."

"If he wants his message to have any chance of getting across! He was counting on you to report Chandler's death as a murder."

The two men continued to sit, staring at each other. The steam from their soup circled upward between their line of vision. Then each took a bite of their sandwiches and chewed slower than would have been normal.

"The problem, though," Rusack finally said, "is the message. What is it?"

"I'd like that beer now," said Tome.

Chapter 8

"Wasn't Rumsey. Was one of his deputies."

"Bobby Talbot. He's some relation to the mayor."

"Right. He's the one who done it."

"But what's your problem? In this state, if a dog's chasing deer, you're allowed to pop it. Not only a game warden, but you, me, anybody. It's legal."

"What's my problem? I'll tell you what my problem is. One of the dogs he shot, its belly dragged on mother earth like a grounding chain. That pup no more could have bit into the hindquarters of a deer than you could kiss your own dick. Another beer, Forster. All the way around. I'll tell you something else too. That law's a trick. Some dumb bunny feels like shootin' something, he shoots a dog. All he has to do is say it was chasing after deer. He's home free."

The two men had returned from afield and now wanted to head for town. They stood before their young friend who lay in bed, covered like hot rolls in a basket.

"Let's go, Skeets! Get it out!" The glossy scalp of the taller man brushed against the room's rough center beam. He hunched to avoid taking a splinter. "Two nights you been runnin'. All you doin' today is pumpin' up b'loons." He gave a sharp kick to the metal cot that Lill had carried in from the garage to complete their accommodation.

From under the blanket a sleepy voice mumbled a series of barely coherent profanities. The men nodded in conspiracy, then moved closer to the cot, one on each side.

"Any human being who can deliver a spate of expletives with such natural facility," pronounced the other man, "is feigning fatigue and deserves to be on his feet."

"Up your skinny ass, Pendleton!" came the smothered reply. "Hustle on back to the university. Don't forget to take the redwood with you."

Pendleton signaled to the tall man. Together, they heaved the cot upright and positioned it on its footboard.

"There. You now have the best of two worlds," Pendleton proclaimed. "In bed to relax. On your feet to be about. Baron von Leibniz would have admired you."

Skeets swivelled his head around and folded the blanket under his chin. "Von who?" The face, soft and smooth, was not at all suggestive of the uninhibited voice. His bright eyes, which disclosed no hint of their being recently shut, caught sight of the tall man who continued to laugh gently at the bed prank he and Pendleton had pulled off.

"Do you big men always amuse so easily?"

"Let's go, man!"

"We're headed for town," Pendleton said. "The man says he needs a whetstone."

Skeets popped a laugh. "A whetstone! You must be feeling good about something. You come close?" Skeets raised his head.

His eyes narrowed in sportive suspicion. "You see anything today, big boy? Drew, he see anything?"

Pendleton could not suppress a grin.

"The redwood blow a shot? He did, didn't he? Come on, rat on him."

"A beauty of a buck. Seventy yards at the most and quartering right, like a statue."

"Oh man!" Skeets screamed in a fit of horselaughter and the metal cot was sent toppling backwards. It jackhammered against the floor with a racket causing a window to vibrate.

"Too much of that," Pendleton warned, "and we'll present your bones to Bill for fertilizer. Now come on. Roll on out of there."

📖

The Highland Gun Shop housed a diverse inventory of outdoor equipment and during the hunting season Max Rayburn took many items out of their boxes and put them on display, cramming them into whatever space was available. The store operated inside the long and narrow bottom floor of a two-story building. Exposed pipes of several diameters ran along the walls and just under the low plaster ceiling. Winter garments and boots of various types hung from these pipes, and a patient effort of indoor hunting was often required before a customer found the object of his search.

The guns remained on exhibit at the rear of the store. Legions of shotguns and rifles stood upright like sentries, as though watching out for the smaller firearms and knives on display underneath the cash register in a glass-encased counter. A small group of local people clustered out front and to the side of the counter while Rayburn stayed behind it. He leaned on its glass beating a thick, calloused finger at the front page of the *Tier Sentinel*. He was a sizable man in chest and neck, absent of fat. A high waxed brushcut made him appear taller than he was. His voice had a sanding quality to it, achieving the same undercutting penetration a foghorn does in a crowded harbor.

"Close down the season, that's what they voted to do in so many words, the whole worthless bunch of them. And this s.o.b. who calls himself a journalist, this sonovabitch apparently favored it the most! Yet take a gander at this. Although I'm sure I'm not showing any of you something you don't already know." He wet a finger and flipped through the pages of the newspaper to those which carried most of the advertisements. "Every bar and restaurant in Sagerville has an ad. Check out the number of real estate ads. Must be two dozen if there's one. This week, even yours truly took out an ad. Prepaid, no less! The entire business community feeds the guy and his family, pays his mortgage, and still the sonovabitch wanted to publish a story that a sniper is running about the hillsides, just waiting to flatten the ass of every hunter who moseys by.... Big sniper, huh? Three days already gone in the season and what have we got? I tell you, if this Tome had gotten things to go his way, right now Sagerville would be about as lively as your cemetery on the hill."

"So what happened?" asked a man in a three-piece suit that made him appear out of place amid the outdoor motif.

"What do you mean what happened?"

"What changed their way of thinking, Max?"

"Harmon Drake! He's what changed their minds. Just luck, too, he happened to be in the courthouse when he was. The D.A. hadn't thought to include him on the invitation list."

At the front of the store a bell tinkled and a young man in

his twenties came through the door. He held the tiny hand of a toddler, and they made their way slowly to the counter at the back. Some of the people greeted the young man, and a woman knelt to baby-talk to the child. Rayburn merely nodded at the man, as he was still thinking of Tome and the sniper.

"Sniper. In a way it's amusing," drawled Studs, a burly thimble of a figure. "If you think about it, it could be anyone. It could be you, it could be me. It could be that little feller there in a few years."

"It's asinine," Rayburn snarled. "Nothing amusing about it. A fat steelworker and a useless bum catch a couple of slugs and the do-gooders are ready to hold it over everyone. That reeks of the Kennedy mentality."

"So how do you figure it?" the man in the suit asked.

"How do I figure it? District Attorney Edward Rusack, that's how I figure it! My guess is, he figured to make it a big deal so when he got it to court, there would be a mountain of publicity and he'd be the man remembered for calling the shot from the very beginning. Next fall, he'd be a shoe-in."

"Pol-i-ti-cee-ans," Studs said, articulating each syllable, as he often liked to do. "How is one supposed to argue with them?"

"Awfully tough," said the man in the suit. "Awfully tough."

"We ought to rid the country of all those sonsabitches!" declared another man wrapped in a red hunting jacket. Beside him was his wife. He transferred a fawning gaze of pretentious fortitude from her to Rayburn and back again, all the while half-nodding his head.

The bell tinkled again, several times. Someone left without buying, and four other customers entered. Rayburn recognized immediately the rawboned man by the Robin Hood hat. It was orange and white and beautifully crafted from the finest felt. A wild turkey feather extended from two small holes on one side. The man lived with several rottweilers on a farm in Corby Hollow, and he did a lot of shooting and his own reloading of ammunition. Rayburn called to his teenage son, who was in the back storeroom, to bring out the man's order.

"Only trouble is…" Studs started and trailed off.

"Don't trail off," said Rayburn. He turned back and greeted the man in the Robin Hood hat. "Max is bringing it out."

"Only trouble is what?" the man in the suit urged Studs.

"The trouble is that someone might have poot a slug into that dude from The Buckseller."

"On general principles alone," said Rayburn, "it wouldn't surprise me."

"Sounds like *thee* discussion for all of Sagerville this evening," chipped in the man in the Robin Hood hat. "All this discounting a sniper, that's only because there's no one missing. But have even one of you considered how some flatlanders drive up and spend a week or two alone in their camps? Now I ask ya, who's going to report them missing?"

"That's so," Rayburn allowed. "I can't argue the point. But I wouldn't place a bet on it, and I don't think you would either."

"I don't know about that!" said Robin Hood, cocking his head.

Rayburn folded the paper and set it aside as his son hastened from the storeroom. The large cardboard box was obviously much heavier than the teenager preferred because he let it drop to the counter glass. A singing ping was forced out of the tight upper pane.

"For Chrissakes, Max! Ain't I got enough to do around here? You want me to start replacing glass?"

"It was heavy," complained the teenager. He was a virtual

double of his father, except the boy liked to laugh and often did.

Rayburn unfolded the carton's flaps and started recording the prices of the enclosed items on the cash register. "It looks like it's all here," he said to Robin Hood.

The next tinkle of the bell went unheard and no one at the counter turned to see the trio of black men enter.

"So any of you get lucky yet?" Rayburn said while he read prices and pushed the corresponding buttons on the register. "Anyone wasting shells? I got to sell to more than just Robin Hood here if I'm to stay in business."

The man in the red hunting jacket brightened and he put an arm around his wife's shoulders. "The boy got one today," he proudly informed the group. "He stayed home from school and went hunting instead. Took 'at bugger right behind the front shoulder." He raised the other arm and pressed the finger into his jacket, just to the rear of his armpit.

"He hates school," said the woman, beaming. "But he says he can't wait 'til tomorrow."

"That's all right," Rayburn said in a congratulatory tone. "You can be proud."

"What's the boy use?" Robin Hood wanted to know.

The man's face became gravely serious. He turned slowly toward each person in the group. "Cal says he won't use nothing on deer but an aught-six. He says his mind is made up. An aught-six or nothing."

The woman nodded her agreement regarding the firmness of their son's decision.

"A good deal of firepower there," Rayburn said. "It's a popular choice."

Two hunters left the right aisle and approached the counter to pay for a blaze orange hunting cap and a pair of leather laces.

They placed the exact amount on the glass. One of them asked the group as a whole for information about the doe season.

Robin Hood answered. "It runs on allocation. Each county is allocated so many."

Both men appeared nonplused. "We're new at this."

"He's talking about permits," said Rayburn. "You got to apply for a permit if you want to hunt doe. Each county is allocated just so many. But you have to make application early, and I'm afraid you fellows are out of the ballgame for this season."

"I heard talk next year they're going to run the seasons together," said the man in the suit. "Buck and doe all in one. Anyone else hear that?"

"We'll see," said Rayburn. "That'll be crazier than ever."

The young man with the little boy had been stooping in order to gaze at the display of revolvers and semi-automatics. As the two novice hunters turned to leave, he rose, hefting the toddler with him and hugging the boy close to retard his impatience.

"What about you, Max? Didja get your deer, didja?"

"Christ, haven't found the time. Max there was out opening day—wouldn't listen to advice—and I hope to get out with him this Saturday. The dickens thinks the ol' man can't keep up with him."

The youth had not returned to the storeroom. He had overturned a waste can in a corner and was now sitting on it. Robin Hood called over to him. "You see anything, Junior?"

"Lot of doe," the boy replied. "Not much else."

Rayburn totaled the cost of Robin Hood's order, then picked up the exact amounts the two hunters had left for the hat and laces and put the money in the drawer while it remained open.

"So what about you?" he addressed the young father with the child as Robin Hood was writing out his check. "What's your story? You venture out on the opener?"

"I just took what I could. I settled for a spike the first hour."

"What the hell," said Rayburn, for the moment forgetting the presence of a woman. "Who eats the rack and balls anyway?"

He took the check offered him, placed it with the bills, and shut the drawer to the register.

"Now the time's approaching, I can see. But before you all leave, there's something you must feast your eyes on."

Swinging away from the counter, he disappeared into a closet next to the storeroom, only to reappear as quickly modeling a hip-length jacket that was tailored from deer hides.

"Eighty dollars from an outfit in Michigan," he announced. "You supply the hides." He spun himself around for a moment, showing the fit at the shoulder.

Each person approached and took a turn at running a hand over the supple texture with its network of shallow canals. The woman caressed the jacket's surface the longest and commented to her husband that it was nice and soft and that she could appreciate a thing like that.

"How many hides are needed?" the husband inquired.

"Depends," said Rayburn. "Depends on the size of the wearer and the size of the pelt. This one needed two, wasn't it, Max?" The boy shrugged. "But they do everything. Treat, stretch. All you got to do is get it to them. Eighty bucks isn't bad."

"Last of the bargains, I'd say," the man in the suit remarked. "I take it you're handling it?"

"I can order for anyone, sure."

The young man with the child felt the jacket a second time. He pinched it, trying to determine its thickness.

"Really is nice, Max. What's it lined with?"

Rayburn opened the jacket wide. The woman reached out and skimmed her hand over the smooth lining.

"I'd think pile," Rayburn said. "Either that, or they shaved the heads of a band of bush niggers, huh?"

Blended laughter followed. The man in the red hunting jacket repeated the slur for a retelling among others later on. The man with the toddler laughed only the awkward half-measure of a liberal who, after finding himself aligned with a conservative on such issues as hunting and gun control, is awakened by his bedfellow's indiscreet attitudes on other, more fundamental matters. But the laughter died quickly, except for an overly hearty howl persisting out of the corner.

"Now what the devil, Junior," Robin Hood said. "It's not all that funny! You're gonna bust a gut."

"From where I'm sitting, it's funny!" the boy said emphatically, tossing his head about.

During the following seconds the handsome black Skeets moved from behind a haphazard display of camo overalls, while Drew Pendleton and the tall man also appeared.

"I see you found the stones," the tall man said to Skeets.

"I found 'em, yeah. But you sure Bill doesn't have one of his own?"

"He might. I never asked."

"Let's check." Skeets flipped the whetstone into the air and caught it.

"Is something happening under our nose of which the Redwood and I are unaware?" asked Pendleton from behind a frown. "What's going on, Skeets?"

"I'll tell you outside, man."

Skeets continued to flip the stone. Only the toss had become higher, nearly grazing the low ceiling.

"Think twice," Rayburn warned.

Skeets dipped and feinted an underhand loft of the gray whetstone in the direction of the glass-encased counter. When the woman and her husband jerked their upper bodies back, and as Rayburn threw his hands up to intercept, he smoothly spun the stone from his fingers like a frisbee. Rayburn partially blocked the stone, but it fell against the glass nonetheless with a sharp dissonance. Yet the counter remained intact.

Rayburn exploded. He ripped the hide jacket from his arms and hurled it over the counter. "It's missing a collar! But if you're aching to volunteer!" He dropped his eyes to the knives below.

"Are you taking this any further?" the tall man inquired of his friend while keeping his focus on Rayburn.

Skeets also kept his eyes glued to his antagonist. "I can't speak for him," he said.

"Fine. Let's get out of here," Pendleton advised. "Come on."

"You better get your asses out of here!" Rayburn growled.

Near the door, Skeets paused and turned. He seemed about to say something to the others standing at the rear of the store, but Pendleton nudged him on.

Once they were gone, Rayburn carefully pressed his fingertips at random spots in the counter's top pane. Like magic, a hairline crack shot across its diagonal.

"Goddamn you, Max! You're as much to blame for this as that sassy spade."

Chapter 9

"Every so often they run the 'Kill Bambi' editorial."

"The edge in your voice says you got some objection to the Game Commission doing that. I like that magazine."

"Sure, and I used to like it myself. Until I saw the hypocrisy. They belittle anthropomorphism and anyone who takes to it. Yet in every monthly issue the reader is treated to at least a dozen tidbits from their wardens, complete with cartoon illustrations of every animal inhabiting the state, each with a balloon above its head."

As he did every weekday morning, Max Rayburn, Jr., squeezed into his beat-up Volkswagen Rabbit and pointed it in the direction of the high school. But instead of turning right at the intersection, the senior classman traveled through it and stayed on the main road. Several miles out, the gray primered car swung left and bumped along a narrow, frost-subverted road. He made another left into the tiny settlement of Gunther which brought him to the mouth of Corby Hollow. There, he made a right, drove a little ways, then steered the compact automobile onto the dirt switchback that sidewindered several miles up to a bleak, logged-out section of Devil's Den.

The deep ruts in the switchback channeled the small car at will, causing it to rock endlessly, and Max drove slowly, all the while searching the forest on both sides of the road for sign of a buck, acting more like foraging bug than human. If one were sighted, the plan was to brake, then crawl out unseen on the opposite side of the quarry. The vehicle made a good blind, plus the low roof offered comfortable support to steady a rifle.

Of course, Rumsey and his deputies were on the lookout for road hunters— already a pair of his classmates had been ticketed and fined—but so what! It was an easy hunt. Why soak his puppies slogging through miles of woodland if there wasn't a need, he argued to himself. He continued searching, his eyes alternating from switchback to woods, but eventually he concluded what he had already known. It was too late to find deer hanging out along a road. No getting around it, he would have to get out and walk.

So at a high spot in the next turn, he coasted the vehicle into a hidden chase below the roadbed. From a scattered assortment of items on the rear seat, he fished out a cap and some gloves, a warm coat, and finally his scope-mounted rifle. Checking the knots on his bootlaces, he started his hunt soon after, walking much faster than he would have preferred, but realizing it was just too cold to dawdle. A red fox scurried across his path before he had covered a hundred yards, and Max was suddenly moved to wonder what trappers were getting for this year's pelts. His father's equipment continued to hang unused in the basement and lately he had been contemplating trapping coon and fox.

He waited a while in the hope the animal might reappear, but the expectation was futile as the fox had seen him, and so he pushed on, only occasionally pausing, and then it was to read familiar sign—you didn't have to be Chief Cornplanter to recognize turkey scratchings! He ran a boot, making an X, through one of the bare spots he came upon, as big as those found in a corridor runner subjected to heavy traffic. He cursed the game bird's elusiveness. Here it was deer season and they were leaving tracks of themselves. But during their own, you had to search all over to find even a dropping!

In time he reached a level dip in the forest and the residence of Clara came into view, urging Max again to stop. A female mostly forgotten by the region's inhabitants except, oddly, when they boasted to visiting friends and family that Bingham County had a recluse who had resigned her life to the solitude of the forest, the mysterious woman had lived in her tent remote from Sagerville and everything else for as long as Max could remember. The tent's size, too, had always amazed him. Twenty by thirty, if not bigger. A stovepipe in the center of the soiled white canvas pointed skyward. Faggots of cut wood surrounded the outside of the tent, each swaddled in sheets of plastic to keep it dry.

As Max looked on, the woman emerged from the tent and shuffled to the firewood. A heavy brown coat hung to her ankles, causing him to think of Yukon Jack, one of his father's whiskeys. Bending over, the woman gathered a few logs. When she straightened, she looked in his direction, then smiled. Next, the tent flap lifted and a hooded man appeared, and the man also looked his way. Although the man stood in the shadow of the tent where features remained hidden, Max was sure he had seen the figure before.

The hooded man next shuffled around to the rear of the tent, but he reappeared in Max's field of view pulling a cart of some type, a homemade gizmo, a cross between a toboggan and a wagon, for it had not only wheels, but also a rounded skid plate. A tarp secured with bungee cords covered the top. Max waited until the woman went back inside the tent, and while the man was withdrawing a tool or something from under a corner of the tarp, he slipped off to another section of the Den.

By noon the temperature had warmed and Max could feel his own heat seeping back into numbed appendages. Time to rest, he told himself. So far, the morning was proving satisfactory. He had already seen a lot of game, including a horned owl and an ugly turkey vulture. Just for the fun of it, he took a crack at the latter, but missed.

Looking behind him for a moment, Max estimated he was now two, three miles from the Rabbit and the switchback. No sense tramping any deeper, he decided. Best to circle back. Besides, the stomach was growling like a starving cat. Why hadn't he packed along a lunch, or at the very least, a Snickers or two? *Stupid. Stupid. Stupid.*

Hastening across the woodland, he came upon a tangle of brush that hugged the cleared ribbon of earth about a hundred feet wide above a natural gas pipeline. A well-traveled deer path angled from the line, passing within yards of the brush. A perfect spot to post, he told himself. And since there were so few hunters about to push deer, it seemed the wisest move—if the cold didn't get him first! Although the temperature had risen, Max was aware the margin of comfort would diminish with each passing minute during which he remained motionless.

With his body now collected against the base of a large tree, every few minutes Max would snake up the bark to scope the open area of the pipeline. For another countless time, he lowered the gun. Only on this repetition he was puzzled.

He slowly brought the rifle back up and put his eye to the scope. Was it?

It was difficult to identify the entire animal because usually only an ear, or tail, or part of a leg was showing. He was unsure of what he was seeing. Even trees sometimes resembled deer, and vice-versa. He studied the spot for a very long time. Then, as the upraised rifle began to weigh heavy on his arms, the magnified image stirred. Max instantly felt the violent drumbeat deep inside his chest.

The single deer padded onto the pipeline. A doe—and he suspected the animal to be the lead doe for other whitetails—she moved cautiously, bobbing her head, whirling her baldness, sniffing each passing wisp of breeze, seeming never certain about any move. She ventured forth. When she neared the center of the pipeline, other deer emerged like ghosts and shaded the edge.

Max peeked above the scope, wishing to avoid the narrow compression it afforded, and sought to pick out a rack. Then, as if the forest were opening her timbered womb, dozens of whitetails lolled onto the pipeline. He scanned their heads and estimated the distance at a hundred yards.

One bore a rack, a tremendous spread. He set his eye an inch lower and through the optics pried amidst the herd. The compressed and narrow field of vision effected by the lenses confused him; he was unable to isolate the buck in the scope. During the following minute, he peeked above it many times, each time finding the rack, but losing it when he raised the crosshairs to his vision.

The herd tired of lingering in the open and started to jog to the safety of the woods. The buck flashed across the magnification. With shaking knees and a pummeling heart, in one desperate move to prevent the animal from reaching cover,

Max whistled shrilly. The herd froze and gazed in his direction. Now familiar with its bunched image in the glass, he placed the buck inside the circle of the scope and pinned the intersection of gossamer on its heart. He fired, and the weapon's report sent the herd leaping frightfully back on the route they had come, along a path where they had not encountered danger. The buck crashed to the turf. With spine to the ground and legs jerking convulsively, the creature attempted to lift itself on air.

Max raced from the tree onto the pipeline, finally slowing as he neared the fallen beauty whose yearly symmetry was already scarred and festooned with dirt and sod from when its head had dug itself painfully into the earth. The buck rolled on its side, its chest and belly heaving in rapid futility. He chambered a second shell and stuck the barrel at the base of the animal's skull. The plangent slam terminated all movement with the body, but from its mouth and nostrils seeped a veil of hot steam.

He dropped the rifle to his side and gazed on the trophy buck. He counted the points on its rack. There were ten.

"Nice," he said.

A moment later, he whirled and fell backwards. Simultaneously, a crushing note shook the air about him.

📖

It wasn't the size. It wasn't the cockiness in the movement either. It wasn't anything but the single word. The tone of it, actually. But what it registered on the killer's mind came a second too late.

They were never part of the plan. And this was never part of the plan to stand here afterwards.

The feet went hesitantly forward. One step. Then another.

Don't be a fool. The boy's dead. If he isn't, he'll die soon enough, one way or the other. Turn around. Leave.

Another couple of steps. Drifting, uncertain steps.

So what if it's the boy. Do you think the old man will forgive you? It should have been the sonovabitch himself. Don't break your rule of keeping your distance. Do, and they'll find you. They'll convict you and kill you, don't think they won't. The old man will kill you himself. It's a good rule. Don't break it, no matter what.

Slowly, reason took over. The rifle came up. A steady eye peered through the scope and locked onto the silent prostrate figure in the distance. It stayed locked on for all of a minute. When it was allowed to drop, so followed the killer's breathing.

Chapter 10

"Ferm's brother's oldest boy was an aide. He heard Reamer say it during one of those politically frank moments that are often inspired by too much of this rotgut."

"'A hotbed of apathy.' Hmmm."

"'How do you think I get re-elected so often?' is something else he said."

Tome joined the search party for the Rayburn boy the moment he learned it was forming. He could not shake the thought that he would be responsible if another person were murdered. He hoped to God that Rusack wasn't right. It didn't make sense, anyway. If the man wasn't wanting to kill, then why had he? If he wanted to send a message, why not do as other people and write a letter to your congressman, or to the editor? Although perhaps he already had and it hadn't produced results. Perhaps he felt like some, that if change was what you wanted, then you had to do something horrific to effect it. But even that wasn't a guarantee. Often the resulting change was more restrictive than the one for which you bargained.

Tome wasn't sure why he had decided to go on the search. He knew only that if the teenager was dead, he wanted to see for himself.

"He could be shacking up!" Rayburn exclaimed. "It's part of growing up. Come on, Sheriff, the boy's going to graduate come May. He's his own boss. He keeps his .308 and hunting gear in the car all the time. So you tell me if he took to the woods. Just don't go laying that crap on me about a sniper! That's why you're along, isn't it, Tome? You're still crossing your fingers for a story, aren't you? Thinking it'll put some life into that dismal rag you call a paper."

"Why don't you give it a break, Max," said Emil Carter. "I would think you'd be concerned about your child. Hoping he isn't lying somewhere unconscious. Worried he might have busted a leg. In case you haven't noticed, Max, it's become downright cold over the past couple of days."

Rayburn drew back his head, letting a cynical smile spread throughout his features. "What do you know about kids, Emil? When did you stop shooting blanks? Suzanne and you make one that nobody in town knows about?"

"You got a reason to be upset, Max."

Rayburn quickly held up an appeasing hand. "That was uncalled for, Emil. Forget I said it, all right?"

When her son failed to come home, Mrs. Rayburn had become increasingly apprehensive and implored her husband to do something. Rayburn dismissed her late-night entreaties with the explanation that the boy had, in all likelihood, taken a couple of friends and a case of beer, and after school, buzzed up to Niagara Falls. They had recently discovered it wasn't on another continent, but could be reached in a drive of maybe two, three hours. There was nothing to worry about. The boy and his friends were merely giving in to their teenage wanderlust.

But not two hours ago, after telephoning the high school

and learning her son had been recorded absent for both the morning and afternoon sessions, she insisted on notifying the authorities, and thus a search party was mustered.

"Emil could be right," said Sheriff Fennell. "It doesn't happen all the time, Max, but it happens enough."

Rayburn softened at the speculation an accident might have befallen his son.

"Last season, when he took a doe the final day, he was truant. So I guess he could have done the same thing again."

There were over 1200 square miles in Bingham County, almost all of them thickly timbered. It made no sense to detail searchers into the woods because the Rayburn youth could be anywhere. Emil Carter pressed to send his team into the area where the earlier shootings had occurred, but Fennell and a detective from the state police substation dissuaded him, arguing it was best to put everyone to use in first locating the teenager's Volkswagen Rabbit. The detective had wanted to call in the Civil Air Patrol to aid in the search for the vehicle, but a dense haze prevented him from doing so. While a sense of urgency touched the mission, a handful of searchers scouring the county roads approached it with a practical measure. One automobile carrying three men and an equal number of rifles returned to the fire hall with a blood-spattered fender and a small buck attached.

The search this day failed to uncover anything, and as the sky darkened at an early hour, it had to be suspended until morning. Tome stopped by the print shop in the event he was needed, but then went home where he found his wife in a tedious conversation with a middle-aged woman from the community's charity club, abstrusely disguised as the Ellymosynaries. The bastardization of the word had something to do with the small group's founder.

"You've met Mrs. Collier, Meredith. She's brought over a release on their upcoming Christmas Ball."

"You weren't in your shop," the woman said, as if to beg forgiveness for coming to the house. "I thought maybe you had taken the day to hunt."

"You could have left it with Mary Kiel," said Tome.

He ran his eyes over the release. It typified the notices he received from other organizations around the county. Too many read like the flatulent yearbooks put out by the wealthiest schools. Mostly names accounted for the copy as each member wanted the community to learn of her contribution, however small. Quite often he deleted half and not because he had any arguments with charitable organizations. They were a good thing, of course. But many of the participants were too eager to reward themselves, rather than wait for an outsider's validation and expression of gratitude. Even worse, though, was that a few sometimes assumed what amounted to an almost ordained role into other matters of a social and, too often, educational or even financial nature. Oddly did they confuse a good deed with knowledgeableness. He set the press release on the table and brought his attention back to the woman.

"I was helping search for the Rayburn youth," he explained.

The woman nodded too knowingly for him. "I was telling your wife that a lot of the women feel it definite the boy ran off. I'm sure you know as well as anyone, Mr. Tome, that he hasn't been much of a father, Bertha's husband. He's allowed that child to do whatever he wants and whenever he wants. As for Bertha, well, she's just a tremendous woman—I don't think there's anyone who doesn't like her—but she's always been such a timid thing. I'm afraid she couldn't control the boy."

Tome glanced at his wife. Since the early hours of Wednesday morning, they hadn't talked much, but there was support in her eyes to endure this piece of small-town gossip for which they were acting as audience. Long before moving to Bingham County, he had heard of it. But to really understand both its bark and its bite, it had required living here. Like some drama without an intermission, gossip served as both nourishment and entertainment for the region. Sure, a small number of people talked of bestsellers, new music, and award-winning films, but too many others in the Tier also talked of other people, and not always with great amounts of love or kindness.

The weekly was proof of that! In each issue a half-dozen columns appeared in unchained English on the mini-migrations of individuals in Sagerville's neighboring, very sparsely populated townships. They were written by a resident from each area, usually housewives in receipt for minimal compensation— this, a few scant dollars and a belief they were journalists. Very reminiscent of the driveling one-liners that, before desktop publishing he had printed for the high school newspaper once every month, the columns informed the readership of visitations, marketing jaunts, and out-of-town trips to a distant movie, athletic event, or hospital. But had he permitted it, they might have reported on who was copulating with whom, for they had ideas on it, however erroneous. For a long time he had wanted to scratch all six of these carry-overs from the *Upland Patriot,* and on one occasion, he did exactly that. The resultant outcry from the intentional omission strongly indicated, from a businessman's point of view at least, that he had made a mistake. In the next edition, the columns reappeared with a short apology.

Listening to the gossipy tones from the woman of charity,

Tome found himself thinking of Chandler when the strange individualist had counseled a friend at The Buckseller Inn on how to live at ease in a small town. He had said it was necessary to sacrifice to the rumormongers one firm, out-in-the-open thing to talk about. Thus, if a man wanted to drink in peace, he might flagrantly live an adulterer. If to filch, a miser.

Irene Tome escorted the woman to the front door.

"I suppose I could believe like some," the woman said, turning back to them, "that the boy's been shot, either by himself or someone other. Because it's not unlike God to punish people by their mark in life. Those who sell guns sometimes die by them."

"It's the father who sells guns," said Tome, annoyed.

Once the woman was gone, Tome remarked to his wife: "How do they get that way?"

"At least she has a strong opinion of something," said Irene.

"Just how long are you going to keep this up?"

"Meredith, there's talk circulating that if this child is discovered dead, you'll be the one to blame. Are you ready to accept that?"

"Irene, do you think the hillsides would be empty if I had printed what I should have? I made a mistake, yes. But I don't need to be reminded of it, especially by my wife. A person's a fool if he thinks hunters will simply pack up and go home because a handful of their kind has been shot. That just isn't going to happen."

"But maybe the child would have been in school, that's what I'm saying. Maybe he would have thought twice about skipping his classes to go hunting."

Ed didn't get the message, and he himself didn't understand it either, except if he accepted his own inclination that it was still about an anti-hunter pursuing revenge against the entire sport-hunting fraternity. Either way, three killings wouldn't accomplish the goal and deliver the message. It would take more, many more. And it was only Tome's realization of this fact-to-come— or "fact in escrow," as Ed had described it—which now mitigated his guilt.

Chapter 11

"It didn't use to be that way! No, my sister and her
hub, they love it. It's the kids. There isn't hardly
anything to do up here, Uncle Jack."

As hundreds of campers and SUVs departed for distant
hometowns on the weekend, a new wave rolled in. Their
passengers numbered thousands fewer, a fact made possible
because a great quantity of buck had long been taken. Buck
remaining were fortunate, experienced, and clever enough to
have eluded the outset's onslaught. They required the patience
and honed conjecture of the hunter, demanded his stealth and
cunning. They also necessitated his footwork, for many padded
the woodland of remote slopes and hollows. The men who
pursued them, aware that if they dropped one they would need
to drag it a long exhaustive way, were characteristically fond of
the hunter's world, yet not dedicated blindly to the passion of the
kill.

The search for Max Rayburn, Jr., resumed Saturday
morning, and the icy haze was prevalent again, forestalling any
attempt at that time to discover the Rabbit from the air. Tome
rode in the patrol car with Sheriff Fennell.

"I've a summons to serve in Gunther first, Meredith. I told
Emil that's where he can expect us."

En route to the tiny settlement, they passed a small

subdivision on their right several miles out of town. Bulldozers had toppled all but a scattering of trees, and a blocked-out set of new foundations checkered the landscape. Tome recognized the construction site to be more business of Drake, and noticing that Fennell was surveying the area with a frown, commented that the developer was from Buffalo.

The Sheriff nodded. "Might be the same shyster who developed a similar piece in west McKean. Last season Rynes—the one who's on this with us from the State Police?—he said he arrested a pimp and five prostitutes operating out of the two completed bungalows. Beautiful girls, too, I hear tell. You don't think Drake had anything to do with that, do you?"

On the final downgrade into the tiny hamlet of Gunther, the patrol car turned into a narrow, rubbish-littered lane. The Sheriff drove to its end where a rust-eaten Ford Bronco was parked. Four scrappy dogs, short-chained to gray wooden structures which differed in size only from the human dwelling behind, rioted at their intrusion.

"What a pigsty! The crates in Buckseller Hollow are Swiss chalets compared to this."

Tome silently agreed, as he gazed at the dog shelters and at the larger house out back. It was impossible to pick out a straight line extending beyond a couple feet. Boards had been hammered together every which way, and there was no evidence that the owner possessed a crosscut saw, much less knew how to handle one.

"Who's the owner?"

"Perly Bechtel," the Sheriff answered, watching the shack. He thought better about where he had stopped the car. Putting it in gear, he backed up several yards behind a cluster of trees. "Can't be too careful with Perly."

"You expect him to come out shooting or something?"

"Stay awake, Meredith. I'm not joking."

Fennell pulled the folded summons papers from an envelope on the dash and slipped them into his breast pocket.

"What's it about?" Tome inquired.

"The summons? Ssss! This one would have been a candidate for that old tv program, *How'd They Do That?* Do you know Jimbo Johnson? Lives just a ways from here in Corby Hollow?"

Tome shook his head.

"Sure you do. Most folks call him Robin Hood because of the cap he wears. He's the plaintiff. Anyhow, just one week ago he had ten head of cattle, all Jersey. This week the number was reduced to nine."

"Perly's into rustling?"

Fennell sucked in his jowls. "There's no spunk in that for a man like Perly, Meredith. Plus, that would never have made the program. Nope! Robin Hood is claiming—and I gotta say I'm inclined to believe him—he's claiming that Perly quartered one of his heifers. Now get this! He says Perly did it while the animal stood in its stanchion."

It required more than a moment for Tome to register the scene just described to him. "Oh, for Chrissakes!" he finally blurted out.

"See what I mean? It's incredible, isn't it?"

With that, Fennell exited the patrol car and the dogs immediately ceased their barking. He glanced back at Tome as if to say "Go figure." Then he went up to the shack, mounted a series of broken steps, and pounded on its door. There was no answer, and he pounded a second time, harder, getting the same result. He peeked through a dirtied window, but didn't see anyone. When he came down off the steps, he first looked more closely at the dogs before he called for Tome to get out of the car.

"Lend a hand with these hounds, will ya? The reason they stopped barking soon as they saw me is they're hoping someone'll feed and water them. Perly's never been concerned with feedin' anybody but himself."

The Sheriff scooped up the water bowls, while Tome went searching for dog food. He found an opened bag in a shed behind the house and shooshed off a daytime raccoon that had been partaking. As he headed for the front of the house again, he noticed a figure moving at the end of a distant field to the left and called to Fennell.

"That's Perly all right. He must have known when we were in sight."

"You trudging out there after him?"

The Sheriff looked at Tome as if the editor had momentarily lost his good sense.

"You don't know Perly, Meredith?"

"I recognize the limp. There's something very distinguishable about it."

"Maybe you've seen him at a distance. You wouldn't forget him if you had met him up close. Perly got that limp from a big-ass tree falling on him. It was rotten at its core—sort of like Perly himself—and he didn't know it. It gave way while he was cutting and whipped back on him before he knew what happened. But that isn't the worst of it. The tree also hit the running chainsaw which flew up and struck Perly square between the eyes. Just about split his skull wide open. I'll give him credit. He didn't pass out, but managed to get himself out from under that tree, then drove himself in his pickup to the hospital. That's why I said you would remember him. He was never much of a handsome brute to begin with. Today, with that scar, he's downright scary."

Tome knew the Sheriff well enough to let go the hint of a grin.

"Oh, you bet I'm afraid of him. Only not for the reason you're thinking, Meredith. I walk out there and he'll fade into the cover. And very likely there'll be a loaded rifle within his reach."

"He's wild then. I guess the man would have to be if he's butchering cows in their stanchions."

It was the Sheriff's turn to grin.

"A number of townspeople think he's wild. I think he's downright insane. Does that stuff skip a generation? Because, you know, they put a straitjacket on his grandfather and hauled him off. Whatever, I'm not about to try and serve him out there in the field.... C'mon. Let's go back to the car."

Once inside, Fennell hesitated before turning the ignition key. "Hasn't your fellow Monk ever talked to you about Perly?"

"Monk? No. Why would he? Or do you mean because they both have faces that—"

"—That's what I mean. Only, again, not in the way you're thinking. Every chance Perly gets, he makes fun of Monk and his disfigurement. Does it right to his face, too. Monk doesn't like it and has threatened Perly a time or two to clam up. But there's nothing that affects Perly Bechtel, I can tell you." The Sheriff then looked at Tome with a quizzical expression. "It seems to me, Meredith, you're not up on things, and being a newspaperman, I'd expect otherwise."

After leaving the Perly Bechtel property, the patrol car traveled over several unpaved roads which cut through the mountains surrounding the sparse settlement below, before it entered into Corby Hollow and tried the switchback leading up, high and deep into Devil's Den. From an opening in the first rise, the Sheriff pointed out the farm owned by Jimbo Johnson who was known also as Robin Hood. Tome could see great lengths of its fence line and judged the farm to be made up of maybe a hundred acres. It was a pleasant spot—a squat, one-story house with a new barn and another building, much smaller, that was probably a garage. The Jerseys were outside, their heads down. Four dogs, penned near the barn, were lying couchant in the dirt.

Although rutted badly, the dirt switchback posed no obstacle for the lumbering patrol car. Fennell took the ascent slowly, nonetheless, and eventually stopped along one stretch next to a farmer astride a tractor that was trailing an empty wagon. The tractor was headed down to the hollow.

Fennell shouted out his window over the clatter of the farm machine: "You haven't seen an old Volkswagen parked along up here, have you?"

Bundled in heavy work clothes, the farmer feverishly rubbed his hands together like a squirrel pawing an acorn.

"I haven't seen one on my piece," he shouted back, a thick white cloud shooting from his mouth. He reduced the tractor's idle and the noise abated. "You're hunting for the Rayburn child, no doubt."

"Hunting for his car."

"Gotcha. This is a long stringy hollow, and this road underneath and a few others'll lead you smack into the next county if you want. Mebbe that's not news to you. You keep in mind if you don't want to get stuck, that this switchback isn't hard-packed every inch of the way."

"We'll keep that in mind," said Fennell, nodding.

"Awright then. When you get up here aways, look close. There's a channel runs alongside and this time of year it's fairly dry. A hunter who don't want his wheels mussed with, I've seen 'im park it there. Though I confess it's rare I've ever heard about them thievin' in their own ranks. But Sheriff, it mighta been a Blazer full of searchers that already tried this yesterday."

As the farmer fed fuel to the tractor and moved off, Fennell rolled up his window. "What do you think, Meredith? Cover it again, or should I turn this vehicle around?"

"It's thick along here. They could have passed by the car without ever knowing."

At the next bend the switchback began to writhe like a timber rattler, and they soon spotted the unmistakable tire tracks of the tractor that had come onto the logging road from a treeless swath which cut through the forest to an open field below. The haze was thickening with the elevation. Fennell slowed the patrol car to a crawl as they came upon the beginning of the gouged-out chase. At each turn in the switchback the channel was lost to view, and the Sheriff put the vehicle on the edge to give his passenger a chance to look without stopping and getting out.

Tome put out his left hand. "Stop."

The Sheriff braked and leaned in front of Tome. The gray-primered Volkswagen lay hidden by a sprawling web of laurel twine.

"No wonder they didn't see it. I'll call it in. You clamber down and check things out, if you don't mind."

Inside an hour, a train of vehicles weaved up the long switchback and emptied its human payload of searchers above the channel. Detective Michael Rynes, a watery-eyed state trooper from the Killdeer substation, consulted with Emil Carter, and together they plotted their search on a topographical map. Carter then briefed the scores of men, many of whom were new to his search team.

"Most of you know this area as Devil's Den. For those who don't, if you travel directly across its flats, you'll come out overlooking The Buckseller. But if you lose sight of the party and head in a too southerly direction, then we'll wind up wearing out shoe leather on you as well. In other words, stay in line, take it slow, take it easy, and make certain you understand what it is your eyes are focusing on. We'll climb to the flats and search due east until the elevation begins to dip. At that point, we'll banana north to strike the pipeline."

"What about Clara?" the Sheriff asked.

"We're bound to run across her digs," said Carter.

"We'll need to question her," Rynes said. "She could have seen the youth."

Underfoot, the earth gave way with a cushioned snappiness, and Tome felt his legs becoming limber. It had been a long time since he last stretched his muscles by trudging up the truly steep slopes of Bingham County, and it felt good, a kind of release he welcomed. On his right he could see the Sheriff who held a radio to his ear. On the other side was Rayburn. Impaired by fear of the worst concerning his son, the gunshop owner did not walk so much as plod, and his brazen manner appeared to have fled.

About a mile into the flats at the top, the searchers to Tome's left halted with the orderly intermittence of boxcars trailing a lugging diesel. The line stood on a small ridge and peered into the flat area below. He traced the line of their eyes to the object of attention, and in a thinly timbered patch of forest he spotted the soiled tent of the wilderness recluse. Starkly outlined by its contrast with the surrounding landscape, it offered no sign of movement, other than the rising smoke from the black stovepipe. The scent of burning wood was strong.

Robin Hood, closest of the searchers, sauntered toward the tent. Pausing near the flap, he removed his hat and stroked the long feather. Then he swung his gaunt head behind him in the direction of the other searchers before calling out.

"Yo! Clara!"

A tawny cat asleep in a pile of leaves started at the strange voice and bolted underneath the tent flap. The faintest of human shadows arose on the canvas, gliding specter-like to the entrance. It materialized without Robin Hood's knowledge, as he was again clowning for his counterparts behind him.

"Yo, Clara!"

Turning back, he discovered the strange woman standing just a couple of feet away.

"—Jesus Christ! Don't do that, girl! You'll give ol' Jimbo a heart attack." He inhaled deeply in order to regain his composure which required several seconds. "Look, Clara, a kid's been missing since Thursday. Anyone come by your tent here? Did you see anyone?"

As if mounted on a turret, the woman eased her head left, then right, scrutinizing the line of men in the distance on the short ridge.

"C'mon, Clara, did a boy hunt by?"

Emil Carter left the line and joined Robin Hood, as did Detective Rynes. Carter talked.

"Clara," the rescue chief began with a coaxing tone to his voice, "we need you to tell us if you've seen this boy come by your home on Thursday or anytime thereafter. We fear the boy is hurt. You'd be helping him as well as us."

"If you've seen anyone at all, we'd like to know," said

Rynes.

The woman remained silent.

Carter turned his body part way around and pointed to Rayburn. "That man standing in that clump of alder, Clara, he's the boy's father. He's mighty worried."

It was ash, thought Tome, not alder; and for some inexplicable reason, he believed the woman also had noted the mistake. The woman followed the extension of Emil Carter's arm and pinned her gaze on the gun shop owner. A fragile silence held. Then her arms swept upward in a gesture both saintly and authoritative, as she proclaimed: "God's in His grave! All's right with the world!" Abruptly, she retreated back inside her tent.

"The poor gal's about as crazy as a leek-eater!" came a squawky transmission from someone's radio.

And on that, the search line re-gathered itself and pushed forward beyond the tent, joined shortly by a state police helicopter that experienced safety problems at the hazy treetop levels, but incurred no difficulty flying over the bare pipeline. On his initial pass, the pilot reported seeing the bodies of a boy and a buck.

The line of searchers instantly broke into a shapeless mass that charged through the flats and onto the pipeline to discover the surreal scene. Sprawled on the ground before them were the pair of cold stiff figures.

Rayburn knelt to touch the face of his son, much like his own, except for the natural claims of age that now would never be made. After a time, Rynes moved closer and with the help of others nudged him away. The detective then stooped to carefully inspect the earth immediately around the boy. The pipeline grass bore a smattering of impressions. He traced a finger around the perimeter of one.

"Bear."

The detective raised his eyes with more than a little curiosity to regard the man who had spoken.

"Bear," Robin Hood repeated the word. "One stopped by long enough to sniff their condition. To see if either was ripe. Doesn't appear they were."

Rynes half-smiled to himself.

Emil Carter moved next to Tome who was still staring from several yards off at the bodies of the boy and animal. "You got a story now, Meredith. I doubt it's what you wanted. But you got a story."

On the detective's order, Emil Carter's men dispersed into the cover around the open pipeline to comb for a boot print, an ejected casing, anything at all that might help to explain the teenager's demise. Robin Hood ignored Rynes, remaining beside the bodies of the youth and whitetail buck. Except for the boy's father and the detective, who had measured the diameter of the hole in the teenager's chest using the tips of his fingers like feeler gauges for setting the gap on a spark plug, no one had touched the corpse. Max Rayburn, Jr., lay as he had been found. His head drooped backward over the front shoulder of his kill. Numerous strands of hair brushed the circumference of the animal's fatal wound and stirred in the slightest breeze. The eyes were frozen open and stared at the underside of the magnificent buck's mouth and snout. Off to the side was the boy's rifle. The black scope had ripped partially free from its mounts because of the fall.

Robin Hood kneeled alongside the pair and studied them. Studs joined him and crouched opposite.

"Whoever killed Max's boy," said Studs, "it wasn't because

of no argument over whose buck it was."

"No, it wasn't over the buck," Robin Hood echoed, lost in another thought. His palms and fingers skied over the thick winter coat of the animal.

"You thinkin' about that coat Max modeled for us?" asked Studs.

Another man, much older and dressed in a plaited vest of fluorescent orange, edged next to them and lowered himself to one knee. He whispered almost secretly to Robin Hood, "Hey, Jimbo. You're not thinking what I'm thinking, are you?"

Robin Hood put his hands at rest and bent over the deer, holding his nose but an inch from the animal's hide. He sniffed sonorously at the dead odor, repeating the test many times.

"What are you doing?" the vested man inquired.

"Ol' Smokey don't like it anyway but rancid. It might be worth salvaging."

The man stared at him, revolted. "You want the meat? Forget that, I want the head! I don't want a thing to do with the meat!"

Robin Hood and Studs exchanged looks.

"It's been below freezing for a couple of days," Studs offered as encouragement.

"The kid, he's been missing just since Thursday, am I right?" Robin Hood bit his lower lip and trailed off in silent calculation. After a time he shook his head as a sign of futility and urged the opinion of the man in the vest.

"I want the head. I don't want the meat!"

"Screw it! If it isn't, it isn't. My 'weilers can decide for themselves."

The search for clues turned up nothing and the men returned to the clearing. Rynes continued to flick his eyes at the earth around his feet.

"No empty cartridges, no footprints, no nothing. This scum doesn't give a damn if his victims are dead or not. They can die a lingering death for all he cares. He comes no closer than the point from which he fires, and we can't even determine where that is. At least not without a battery of people who know what they're doing climbing all the way up here, and I can tell you that isn't going to happen."

"All that means what, Detective?" Tome asked.

"That means it's going to be extremely difficult to root him out."

"Too bad it hadn't snowed," Fennell remarked.

"Probably none of this would have happened if it had," added Emil Carter.

Minutes later, two of Carter's searchers lifted the frozen body of Max Rayburn, Jr., onto a stretcher and covered the boy with a blanket. The search party then retreated westward toward the switchback and their vehicles. Robin Hood, Studs, and the older man in the bright orange vest lingered behind.

Robin Hood straddled the dead buck like a buster and positioned it on its back. Pulling a knife, he slit open its belly to expose the vitals. The two men watching reeled backward from the pungent and offensive odor released with the pent-up body gas. But the man in the vest came back, bent over, and grabbed hold of the thick antlers.

"When can I have the head, Jimbo?" he asked, stifling a persistent urge to vomit.

"Soon as I remove the hide."

Robin Hood tumbled the deer's internal parts onto the ground. Then he reached into the forward portion of the cavity to blindly slice the esophagus.

The man's entire face shrank from the gore, black-red and congealed, like mixed licorice. "When is that?" he managed.

"Later. Stop by my place this evening. I live in Corby, where we came up. You'll see my dogs."

With a hand to his mouth, the man hastened through the flats of Devil's Den to rejoin the others in a ride back to Sagerville.

A half-hour later, Robin Hood finished dressing the animal and left the pipeline. Because neither Studs nor he had rope, they dragged the gutted buck behind them with their belts looped around its antlers.

From her world of aloneness, Clara had watched above a fold in the flap of her tent the search party's withdrawal: the still form on the stretcher and the uneasy gait of the parent alongside; the funereal formation of the others; a man in orange pausing to throw up; lastly, the sweating struggle of two searchers dragging the carcass of a majestic buck. To herself and to the bare timber that swayed in spite of standing tall, she repeated her strange pronouncement: "God's in His grave. All's right with the world."

Chapter 12

"It wasn't him, but he was around. Was an overzealous patoot. Paley. Had jurisdiction south of Killdeer. He's long gone. Picked me up for trying to shoot a second deer."

"Were you?"

"Hey, does the Pope crap in the woods? But you know, he wouldn't just write me. He insisted on taking me in. So check this now. Along the way, which was maybe eight, nine miles to his home, what do you think he was doing? How do you think he was spending his day? I'll tell you. He was riding his roads hoping to put an end to crippled deer."

"Why do you put up your hands like you don't know what for?"

Word of the senior classman's death, the revelation that he had died like Chandler and the steelworker, surged through Bingham County like new rain racing down a saturated slope. Suppressed hints of fear presently found a voice, and the word "terrorist" spurted from lips swollen with intrigue.

Saturday evening brought an end to the first week of buck

season. Attired in clean jeans and a new shirt, hunters jammed the county's taverns to exchange information, to fabricate tales of an incredible stalk, and to ogle waitresses, the demeanor of many falsely accused of deliberately stirring sexual appetites. For some hunters the time also became their first occasion to ponder themselves in the role of their quarry, having their tissue instantaneously shredded without the cognizance of a bullet on the wing. For others, three killings in view of the six days that linked them was inconclusive evidence that a killer was about.

"Big fucking deal!" was how several would describe it. Yet in spite of fears and skepticism, a strange game established itself throughout many circles of sporting friends. Hunters gathered around a table studied each other with artificially inquisitive looks and gestures as they bandied about names and personal qualities in a freakish attempt to determine which member of their group could most likely succeed as a woodland murderer. The results proved captivating. They seldom declared a winner. For emerging into clear perspective was the easiness and availability of random murder during the hunting season. Had the victims numbered more than three, the game by itself might have induced a paranoia throughout the region.

Rusack phoned Meredith Tome at six, wanting to talk, and they agreed to do it over drinks, settling on The Buckseller Inn, a primitively rugged stone building erected in the same year as the courthouse. The Inn, located a mile outside Buckseller Hollow, housed a showcase of perpetually staring animals that had perished before maturity. The majority were stuffed spotted fawns a foot or so in height, but a few pickled embryos also were available for viewing. These had been cut and preserved from the bellies of pregnant doe whose misfortune had placed them between the twin hypnotic lamps of nighttime cars and trucks.

The two men walked in together around nine, and there was standing room only. They made theirs at one end of the long bar, an uncomfortable location for the D.A as a narrow aisle ran behind him to the staircase that led upstairs to an apartment and rooms, and next to the stairs was a dart board with an intensity lamp above. Several people descending from the second floor jostled him as they moved beside the dart board, trying to stay clear of the game which had a drunken thrower who freed the darts only after winding up like a major-league pitcher.

At the opposite end of the room, a small recessed stage framed the entertainment. Tonight and throughout the year, this meant a one-man band orchestrated by a silver-haired, rotund individual with the name of Leopold. By means of a piano, a thumping bass drum, and two cymbals chinking against each other, he provided relief to some of the Tier's populace from the habitually slow routine, and most were grateful. But for others from the cities and suburbs, "men-about-town slick roosters" Tome once had heard the inn's proprietor label them, who favored the undisciplined decibel range of a shoddy nightclub's clamor, Leopold was a target for scurrilous jokes. At the peak of the stage and directly over the music-maker loomed the large head of a trophy black bear, its yellowed-through-age teeth bared in a timeless ferocity. It appeared a guardian with its charge beneath.

"Stay alert for a table," said Rusack, peering into every corner of the old bar.

A waitress wove her way toward a far table from which a man in a blue shirt had excused himself, slid around her in a dancing motion to the heavy beat of Leopold's drum, and propped a pair of broken sunglasses on the snout of the bruin. Between the stuffed animal's teeth, he lodged a twisted butt. It was a double joke not everyone saw or understood, but his friends hooted loudly at both the bizarre creation of their companion and his open slap at the tight law of rural conservatism.

The waitress reached the table with her tray waist-high and began placing the orders inside the ring of hunters. One man, sucking at his tongue, glided a hand up the length of her leg. She jumped back, warning: "Hey! You keep your hands off me, you hear?"

"Aw c'mon, Dolly. What say we dance?"

"Dance with yourself, but keep your hands clear of me!"

The men at the table laughed, giving no credibility to her objection. The hunter who had demeaned the bear returned and picked up instantly on what was happening.

"Now what are you getting so upset about, Sugar? You're a little rough, but attractive. My guess is you got a divorce or two behind you. Dance with this horny bastard, why don'tcha? His old lady cut him off, and I think maybe you wouldn't mind having something hard between those luscious legs."

"All right, creep. That kind of language we don't use in here."

"Who you puttin' on?" the man jeered with a flouting sweep of his hand. "This don't look like no fancy Holiday Inn to me!"

Again they all laughed, and another man, obviously the oldest and with part of a finger missing, called her a "homely hick."

"You better leave," she said. She started to confiscate their drinks.

"Whoa now!" said the hunter in the blue shirt. He laid a hand on her arm and squeezed. "Now you hold on a minute,

Sugar. We're gonna finish our drinks. Don't you think we're not."

She jerked herself free. "I said to keep your filthy hands off and I meant it. Why don't you paw each other? You all seem to be the kind that would enjoy it."

"You talk tough for a cunt," said the youngest.

"Easy, Sonnyboy," said the old hunter with the shortened finger.

"We get you alone, you'll find out what we enjoy."

The hunter who had first touched the woman leaned forward in his chair, still sucking at his tongue as though it were a lozenge, and gripped the table. "Lady! The five of us have blown more than five hundred beaners in this dive so far this week. We don't aim to be leaving here just 'cause our lingo ain't suitable to you!"

"Right on," said the man standing. "The fact is, she's probably quite familiar with it."

She glared at them with defiance. "You think I give a damn what you spent? You think you can come in here for a few days out of the year, waste a paycheck, and do whatever you please? Where I'm concerned, honey, think again."

"Here comes your boss, Dolly. I expect he'll view things a whole lot different."

The owner, a portly older gentleman in a white shirt whose collar and cuffs were yellowed and tattered from age, slipped in front of her. "You fellows are going to have to leave," he said without any sign of entreaty in his voice.

"Hey, what sort of bummer is this, Doc! We've unloaded a lot of bread in your joint."

"And we thank you for it."

"What the fuck! We ordered these drinks and—"

"Look! Just go," the owner said politely, but sternly.

There followed a long silence as the men at the table agreed on something through mutual eye contact. The blue-shirted man standing then moved closer to the owner, put an arm around his shoulders, and said, "I don't think so, Dad. We're gonna finish what we started."

Rusack, who had been watching this scene unravel from its very beginning, elbowed Tome. "Here we go, Meredith. I believe we got ourselves a seat." Grabbing his drink, the D.A. swung away from the bar and hurried to the gathering at the other side. Tome followed several steps behind.

"Good evening, gentlemen," Rusack addressed the table, observing how they immediately regarded his shortness of height.

"Who are you?"

"Never mind that," said the man standing. "Are you here to stick your nose into other people's business?"

"I am," said Rusack.

"Now the reason for such suicidal behavior, what would that be?"

"Let's just say I want to fix up America."

"Nobody likes a smart ass," said the hunter who had first touched the woman. "A runty one, besides!"

Rusack threw a glance at the speaker who had four inches on him. The D.A. was short, but no weakling, and he could tell the man knew it, despite his words to the contrary. The tongue was switched to the other side of the mouth.

"Actually, I'm only after your table and a couple of chairs," he said, and then he turned to the owner. "You've made up your mind you want them out, Bob?"

"One way or the other. I tired of putting up with this

behavior a long time back."

"What is she grinning about?" the young hunter swore, thrusting a thumb at the waitress.

"Sonnyboy's right. You are grinning, Sugar. You know something we don't?"

"Plenty," the woman replied.

"Look, I really don't want to make this into a game," Rusack said, addressing each of them. "I'm the district attorney for this county."

"And I'm Perry Mason," said a man wearing a Cat hat. His eyes never blinked and no part of his body moved. It was the first time he had spoken.

The man standing and the insolent youth were measuring Rusack. The kid made a move to rise and Rusack blocked him.

"Don't do it, son. You'll be buying trouble that'll keep you busy for years to come."

The man standing said, "All right, so you're the big Bingham County D.A. Who's your friend? The village chief-of-police?"

Rusack flashed a grin at Tome.

"This man publishes the local paper."

"No kidding," said the man wearing the Cat hat. "This is Tome, who we've been hearing about? Then why don't you quit with us and arrest your friend for contributory murder, or whatever it's called. From what I've heard, everyone thinks that kid would be alive if he had done what he's supposed to do. If I was that kid's old man, Tome, I'd be hunting for you. I'd getch ya, too."

The oldest of them spoke next. There was mischief in his eye: "You might be interested to learn there, Tome, that early this week—"

"You sonovabitch!" The man who had felt the leg of the waitress shook the table violently and it was unclear at first if the man was truly so upset or just extending the private humor of the group into a new dimension.

"—that early this week this pitiful excuse for a hunter shot one the first day. Blew its head off, and the poor thing still had spots on it."

"I told you I was sick of hearing it!"

"Spots on it. Tiny golf balls all over its weety-beety hide."

The man under ridicule appealed to Rusack for understanding. "I take it home, the Afros'll buy it. It'll pay for my license and a few bucks in gas."

"All right," the man standing said to Rusack. "I'm gonna believe you when you say you're the D.A. I'm gonna do that." He momentarily sought confirmation from both the waitress and the owner, but received none. "But if I find out differently, that you've just been scamming us... well, let's just hope for your sake that isn't the case." He picked up his glass of beer from the table and guzzled the contents. "Let's get out of here, gentlemen."

The ring of hunters then rose and pulled their jackets from the backs of their chairs. The man who had just issued the order to exit turned to the woman. "As for you, Sugar, consider yourself fortunate. This boss of yours would rather play protector of a rummy waitress like yourself than make a buck."

The woman smiled victoriously.

Because of the long and hideous exchange which had finally come to an end, no one in the bar but Leopold had observed the removal of the broken sunglasses and roach from the bear head.

"Here. Take these. The bear's got no use for either."

"Jesus Christ! What have you been sleeping with?" the hunter exclaimed, recoiling his head. Rusack himself reeled backward a step from the man's offensive odor.

Fogger Dann reached out, grabbed the hunter's wrist, and slapped the two items into its palm.

"What is this, a big deal or something? He leaves me with this and walks away. Christ, I've seen this in a couple of men's clothing stores. Fancy places. It was part of their display, their... their...."

"Mo-teef," said the youth Sonnyboy.

"Yeah, motif." The hunter was shaking his head with amazement. "You know, you folks around here might have different jobs and all like everywhere else. I mean, here's a two-bit table-humper, a shrimp of a dude who claims he's D.A., and the fellow that just disappeared, he must roll in shit for a living. Maybe different jobs and incomes, but I'll tell you one thing. You, all of you, you fell off a pony one too many times. C'mon! Let's move out, compadres. Let's go try the Buck 'n' Doe."

Then the man in the Cat hat and Sonnyboy yelled out the familiar cry of hunters on a drive, "Whooee! Buck an' a doe, buck an' a doe!" and together the group rose to their feet, wound its way among several tables, and out the front door.

Once they were gone, Leopold resumed playing, pounding out a jaunty tune that encouraged a number of men and women onto the dance floor, or the small part of the floor that the sitting crowd surrendered. The music slugged at the ears of Tome and Rusack as they took their turn at the table.

They were delivered a drink on the house, and the waitress stayed a moment.

"Ain't that something! They spend a measly purse and think it buys your soul."

"I don't think they gave a hoot about your soul," Rusack teased.

The woman laughed good-naturedly. "No, and they wouldn't have fared any better, had they. Either of you need anything else before I leave?" Rusack shook his head. "Holler when you do." She left them for a table surrounded by six men in suspenders.

Rusack took a long sip of his drink as he eyed Tome across from him.

"Wake up, Meredith. There's plenty of blame to spread around. You're no more at fault than the rest of us."

"But I'm the only one who owns a paper. Or did you forget?"

"And you're going to keep on owning it, I hope. I heard you got a call from one of those outfits that make it a habit of buying up small-town weekly newspapers."

"Milestone Publications. I told them I wasn't interested. The first thing they would do is cut half my staff. In the end, the *Sentinel* would be worse than it already is."

"Don't club yourself over the head, Meredith. I know you and you'll come along whether you want to or not. It's not in your blood to put out a half-baked newspaper."

"Have you come up with any ideas about the sniper's message?" Tome asked, wanting to change the subject to something other than himself.

"Only one that makes any sense."

"And it isn't anti-hunting."

"Not in my opinion. Of course, hunting is a part of it, and a major part. But it's not the sole motivator of his action."

"So what is?"

Rusack waited a moment before he answered, measuring his words.

"Whoever's behind the killings, Meredith, is attempting to

discourage people from visiting and moving to Bingham County."

"That's what you came up with?"

"You don't sound impressed. But listen. Whoever is behind this feels his way of life is threatened. This is someone who's opposed to change, or at least the swift pace of it. Probably, he's a person who thinks globally, but knows he can only act locally, so that's what he's doing. Here he figures he can frighten people away. Scare the bejeezus out of them so that next year they travel to some other county that has an abundance of deer."

"He could be on to something," Tome said.

"Look, deer season is the most conspicuous of the events that attract others from outside the area. But if he isn't nabbed before the season is over, come April, it's my hunch Emil Carter and his crew will be out during the fishing season. I wouldn't be surprised if before the winter is over we also stumble upon a dead snowmobiler or two. All the attraction for the region lies beyond the town in its surrounding mountains and hollows, and this killer knows it. If he can make it unsafe and maintain it that way, he'll succeed. Hunters and fishermen will leave Sagerville and go elsewhere, as will the sledders, campers, backpackers, and everyone else who travels here for a dose of outdoor recreation. So the question, Meredith, is this: Who fits the profile?"

Somewhat shamefully, Tome thought immediately of the outspoken, antisocial druggist Bill Lill, but almost as quickly many others came to mind, including the man across from him.

"Me?" Rusack managed to laugh. "All right, I guess I do fit the profile."

"But fortunately, you're not much of a shot with a rifle. Or at least I recall that's what you once told me."

"It hasn't changed. Peg can still outshoot me. I imagine

more people fit the profile than either of us would like to admit."

Tome shook his head out of frustration. "How do we to put a stop to this, Ed? Whoever's behind it feels at home in this terrain. And the identity of those underneath the blaze orange doesn't seem to matter in the least."

"I called Dolf Meixelberger today," said Rusack. "I threw it out to Rumsey first, just to see what he thought since he's part of the same organization."

"Regarding what?"

"Termination. Closing down the season. Not everywhere, just Bingham County. It would stop the killing."

Tome was surprised. It wasn't a solution that he would have thought of. It seemed unthinkable, and he was willing to bet that the Executive Director of the State Game Commission felt the same.

"What did he say?"

"All that's required is a majority vote of the Commission members, but he doesn't think it likely. Especially since there's no precedent for such an action. He also worried over the State's liability. Some licensed hunter with a good attorney might sue the Commonwealth for a tidy sum because he was deprived of his recreational pleasure. Or worse, deprived of securing meat for his family. Of course, the same thing might happen from the other side. The merchants might win permission to sue the State. I can see Drake putting that action together. Nevertheless, he's driving up. He'll be here on Monday."

"If he's not inclined to act, what's he coming for?"

"Frankly, I think he's been rummaging for an excuse, and I gave him one. He labored my ear about two gobblers and a whopper of a cinnamon black that he took out of Flowing Well eons ago, but he's never—"

"—taken a Bingham County buck!" finished Tome.

Both amazed and amused by the power local whitetails had over many hunters, the two men shook their heads. Eventually, Rusack caught the attention of the waitress, pointed to his glass, and held up two fingers.

On the stage Leopold started another tune, and the chubby wife of the bar owner approached and tried to coax each of them onto the dance floor. She started with Rusack and ended by tugging at the arm of Tome. She yelled to Leopold to play a tune less bouncy.

Tome reacted vigorously. "No way, Myrtle. I was on the search and my feet are lead."

"Well it's a good thing, John Meredith, you got a good excuse. Otherwise, I'd have you and Eddie doing the hootchee-kootchee before the night is done."

"How come you're not helping Bob behind the bar?" Rusack asked.

Just then a languid housefly, partially heated out of hibernation because of the crowd, dropped from the ceiling onto their table. Rusack moved to smack it, but was interfered from doing so by Myrtle.

"That's a breeder," she said. "You never kill the breeders, Eddie." With a swift hand she brushed it from the table amid the feet of the dancers.

"You're crazy, Myrtle."

"You want to know why I'm not helping my Bob behind the bar? I'll tell you why."

"Are you two fighting again, Myrtle?"

"Aw, he was already getting into a snootful, and we started talking politics. He said he heard that Harmon Drake was throwing his hat into the ring for something big, and that he might vote for him, too, in spite of how he feels, just 'cause he's a hometown boy and that it might be better having him rather than someone from the other counties. I told him, 'Bob honey, you even think about voting for that no-good sonovabitch of a real estate bozo and you can just figure on working tonight's bar all by your lonesome.' He might be hometown on paper, I said, but he's no different than a lot of them I seen come here over the years, trying to find an easy buck. If there uz profit in it, he'd sell his mother, this Drake would. He gets in, and things'll change. I'll wanna dance, boys, and it'll have to be disco."

"You rest easy, Myrtle. We won't let that happen."

"You're right about that!" the woman said.

"First Aufderheide. Now Myrtle Faner," Tome said after the woman left them.

"I've heard it elsewhere. I'm surprised you haven't. It's fairly reliable stuff."

"Judging from what she said, he'll be running for the House. He's never held the smallest office. There isn't a snowball's chance."

"You're not thinking, Meredith. Piece it out. Reamer's been in for eight years and folks have tired of him. At the last congressional election, we Democrats slated Pennington to go up against him and the man lost by fewer than a hundred votes in a region that is two-to-one Republican. Pennington's already announced his candidacy for the coming year. As for Drake, the Republicans have always liked him and have continuously urged him in the past to get into politics. This year, he'll take the leap. He's got money and he's got looks."

"Aren't you forgetting Reamer?"

"Not at all. He's to announce shortly his decision not to run again for his seat. What's more, he'll declare support for Drake."

"He's getting out, just like that? That doesn't sound like Reamer."

"I didn't say he's retiring. I just said he wouldn't be running for the same seat. Reamer's a realist. He can't very well buy TV in this kind of an area to construct a new image, so he'll do the only thing he can. He'll enlarge his constituency. Reamer will run for the Senate, mark my words. Plus, in exchange for his resignation from the House, so to speak, where he can no longer win, he's extracted the support of every Republican county committee in the congressional district."

"If it works, I'll have to hand it to him."

"Nor is the timing bad," Rusack added. "This year's senatorial race is wide open. If he's never had anything else, Reamer has always had good organization. It's what got him elected in the first place and kept him there."

Tome's eyes narrowed.

"What is it?"

"I'm wondering if that's what accounted for Harmon's economic stand the other day."

"At the meeting I called? It accounts for that, and more, Meredith. It backfired on him. He blew it. He believed in the position, I can't say he didn't. But more importantly, he saw it as an opportunity to jell the support and the favor of a substantial group of area businessmen. That's the reason I said not to go putting the blame all on yourself. Drake's catching his share of the flak as well. Let me ask you. Once he declares, will you support him?"

"On that I'll dance with Myrtle."

"That would have been my guess. You can assume it's Drake's as well."

"Are you suggesting—"

"He's been punching at your reputation, yes! He plans to discredit you before he officially begins his campaign. It's your resourcefulness he's attempting to destroy, Meredith. Prior to the Rayburn boy, he made you out to be a kind of traitor to the county and its economy. But now he'll try to smear you as an editor and publisher who's lacking prudence, integrity, and even dedication to the principles of respectable journalism."

Tome felt dazed by the explanation of machination. It was not a kind of thinking to which he was accustomed and he said as much to Rusack.

"Maybe so, my friend, but I am. And more than you might think."

They stayed a while longer, enjoying another round of drinks, talking of other things. When they finally rose to exit, Rusack led the way. As he opened the door leading to the parking lot, he found himself staring into a pair of broken sunglasses. The voice behind them muttered an obscenity and a fist instantly followed, directed at the D.A.'s head. Tome, behind Rusack, caught the redolent smell of swine, and his own head was jerked slightly to one side as another arm extending a hand, like open pliers, reached forward and swallowed the oncoming fist. A crack followed, the broken shades went sailing to the gravel lot, and the hunter screamed: "You busted my hand! You busted my fucking hand!"

Dann never broke step, but continued unmenaced through the small band of the hunter's companions who had collected near their vehicles. Tome watched him get into a pickup and drive out of the lot before turning back to the others.

"This man *is* the D.A. of this county," he said emphatically. "Has been for quite a while."

"No lie," said the oldest man with boyish eagerness who

then separated from the group to approach Tome. "So that means he wasn't lying about you. You're Tome."

"The smelly dirtbag broke my wrist!"

The old man, using the hand with the partial amputation, took a rough hold of the complaining hunter's hand and twisted it all about before releasing it like a useless stick.

"There's nothing broken. He cracked a joint or two, that's all. So shut up and let me talk."

Finally, Tome was given the name of the hunter who had killed the spotted fawn, apparently with legal antlers. It was a difficult name and the old man repeated it and even spelled it out for him.

"You make sure you spell it correctly in the paper, too, you hear? No screw-ups! When he sees it, that boy is bound to go bonkers."

II
Buck Season
2nd Week

Chapter 13

"What I remember about him goes back to when we first arrived here and before they moved above the store. He heard New York and thought the city. We moved here from Speculator, up in the Adirondacks. We already knew plenty about hunting. The bear head above the fireplace? Everyone thinks that's mine. It's Virginia's."

"What did he do?"

"He was scolding her for walking about our property without some orange. Then to dramatize his point, he told her he'd had her in his sights, and he was smiling as he said it. So I told him it was a good thing I hadn't witnessed him doing that, because I love my wife. It was too subtle for him. But I can tell you, if I'da been on hand and carrying a gun, I would have put a bullet in that kid without a second thought. I mean, what are you supposed to do? Wait and see if he shoots? Oops! I was wrong.... Had her in his sights. Where does a kid like that come from?"

Across the northcentral tier of counties, Harmon Drake owned fourteen offices, but all of these served as the workplace for his agents. His main office occupied a large section of his much larger cedar home set on sixteen acres on the outskirts of Sagerville, and because he had money, it was hardly a typical home office. On Sunday morning, Nila Ellenger, the founder and chief administrator for Friends of God's Creatures, stood gazing out one of its many windows at the blue-gray, washed-out timberland that stretched to the horizon and beyond. She held a bloody mary in hand, as did her host. Her auburn hair was pulled back to defeat an attack of the harshest wind and other unpleasant elements. Her teal-blue eyes were as alert as ever.

"I seem to remember you telling me at the Convention Center last summer that this would be a sure thing," she said, swinging away from the window.

"What can I say. I was wrong. I'd forgotten something fundamental about these people I grew up with."

"It would have been the perfect thing to fund us."

"Yes, it would have been ideal. You would have had your administrative offices in Bingham County, and the park would have provided Friends with consumers year-round whose purchases would have sustained the organization far better than your contributions."

"What do you know about our contributions, Harmon? The membership continues to grow at a steady pace. People are fed up with these so-called sportsmen."

He elevated his chin like a shrewd cross-examiner, an action which left her unfazed. "Two questions, Nila. Why move the offices of Friends at all from the city to this area?"

"To be in the thick of it, of course. To be on hand when it's happening. To be in the house of the enemy and not outside it, which has always been an effective criticism of our opponents."

"They have an argument."

"They have a point. Which will be eliminated shortly if

you've done your job. What's your other question?"

"Why so tough on hunters in the first place?"

"Let me ask you a question. You have a lovely home here. When you awake in the morning and gaze out a window, what's your preference for what you see? A beautiful animal going about its business and doing what God intended it to do? Or some unfamiliar idiot wielding a gun? Strike idiot. Just a stranger. Maybe even someone you know but not well. Forget it! Don't answer! Because if you answer any way but correctly, I'll think you're still selling and I won't be able to stand it. Even the gun-toting idiot knows the correct answer. Everyone but a liar would prefer to see the animal."

"Don't be so sure. Some folks love their rhododendron and azalea bushes like you wouldn't believe."

"Anyway, Harmon, you're wrong if you believe we're critical of all hunters. It shows how indiscriminately you must read our letters. If you read them at all."

"In that case, discriminate for me," he said, smiling. "What sort of hunter does your wonderful organization have it in for? I used to hunt when I was a teenager. Would I have made your list?"

She left the area of the window and moved closer to where he was standing at a refinished sideboard, pouring himself more bloody mary. He offered her a refill, but she pulled back her glass.

"It's simple. 'Friends' opposes the hunter who shouldn't be out there, but often is, thanks to marketing and promotion. It's that group which brutalizes deer and other wildlife. I'd rather see a man, such as the one I read about in the paper, slaughter three or four deer than allow the killing of even one animal by this other."

"What's so special about the old-timer from Pittsburgh?" he asked, amused. "I must have missed something."

"Not him. The other one. If what his friends had to say about him in the paper were true, I would have had no objection to that man taking deer. He must have respected them before and after he killed them."

"Like the Indians. Excuse me, Native Americans."

"Your problem, Harmon dear, is that you have no respect for anything."

"My problem with 'Friends' is that there are other industries involving animals that are more brutal, and I don't hear any complaints coming from your group about them. Industries like the slaughterhouses and dog-racing, to name just a few."

"You have to start somewhere and hunting is much more in the public eye than is the killing of livestock and the abuse of greyhounds. Surely you know that. But enough of this. I can see you're a long way from becoming convinced of anything on this issue." She set her glass on the sideboard. "What about these alternative sites you've told me about? Do any of them match up with the Reservoir?"

"You'll have to judge that for yourself."

"How many are there?"

"Six. This is a big county, so it's unlikely we'll get to all of them. Today I'll drive you out to a place that was a mystery for the longest time. You'll want to see The Buckseller as well. Forgive me. Make that five instead of six. I couldn't persuade our local druggist to part with a piece of his land that is perfect for what you're after."

"The Buckseller? That's where that fellow Chandler lived, according to the paper."

"It's where a lot of riffraff lives. But there's one owner to all of it and with the kind of money you're willing to put up, he'll sell before I get out a dozen words. You can be sure we'll both end up heroes around here if we rid The Buckseller of its vermin."

Her face loosened, and Drake saw that he had amused her.

"People around here generally don't consider me to be much of a comic."

"Oh, I wasn't laughing, Harmon. Just that the underlying venom in your voice when you spoke of the inhabitants in The Buckseller made me wonder for an instant if it could have been you who killed this Chandler."

"For what it's worth, my dear Nila, the identical thought had crossed my mind when you were speaking of sportsmen who brutalized deer. Seems everyone, including myself, have been envisioning this killer as a man."

"Oh come now. You don't really believe I'm capable of such atrocity, do you? I was joking, what I said about you."

"I don't mean you personally. Your organization must have numerous women, though, who feel as strongly."

"You believe they would take to the mountains of Bingham County?"

"Some of them took to the mountains of New Hampshire. They and what's that other group?"

"B.S.F.F. 'Brothers & Sisters to the Flora & Fauna.'"

"Following hunters, harassing them."

She reached out, took his glass away, and set it on the sideboard next to hers.

"What are we waiting for, anyway? Are you expecting others to join us?"

"No, we can go any time. I just thought it would be nice to

have an early morning drink and chat a little."

"So we've done that, Harmon. Let's get busy visiting these properties. I'm anxious to see what you've lined up. Besides, I want to talk to you about your run for Congress. I want to take unfair advantage and it'll help my cause if you have to concentrate on driving."

"Obviously you're unaware I ran off the road a few nights ago. Whatever's on your mind, you might improve your chances for success by putting it forth right here in this office."

"Sorry, Harmon. As beautiful as your home is, I don't want to sit around here and sop up bloody marys all day. I'm sure you're curious about the effect that would produce in me."

"Sounds like you don't trust me."

"Of course not, stupid. I hardly know you."

From another woman, Drake might have taken offense, but he knew what she had said was merely a position she would take with anyone: Nila Ellenger never trusted anyone from the outset.

Drake drove her through The Buckseller first, as it was nearest. The time was approaching eleven and the bottomland was quiet. Most of the shacks revealed a smoking chimney, yet there was no one around.

"Nobody hunts on a Sunday?"

"Not permitted."

"A day of rest."

"Yes, and I support it."

He guided the Buick to the hollow's end, a cul-de-sac except for a narrow footpath that led up into the mountains and ultimately into Devil's Den. Then he turned around and started back.

"Do you want to step out and walk around?" he asked. "I don't mind stopping."

"No reason. It's not a house I'm buying." She flung her eyes about in all directions. "It's absolutely gorgeous here. Especially when I imagine these ramshackle buildings out of the picture. And it isn't too far from Sagerville, which could be a plus."

Drake told her about the landowner, Beryl Victor, and again assured her the property would sell at a fair price.

"But only if it ends up your choice. That goes without saying."

"Okay, that's one, Harmon. Take me to another."

He pressed on the gas pedal and the car accelerated through The Buckseller toward Route 6. He glanced in the mirror before leaving the area and thought he saw the man he had given a ride to the other night. The man was pulling a sled layered with split wood. He surprised himself by remembering the man's name so easily.

Later, the name Fogger Dann still lingered in his consciousness when he passed the point on the highway where the Buick had careened into the ditch. He looked briefly for the small animal with the crushed skull, but some other animal had already dragged it off or had eaten it. It remained in his mind that the small bundle had been a cat, not a rabbit. He started to relate the story of all that had happened during his return from the disappointing meeting on the Killdeer Dam and Reservoir, but Ellenger interrupted him.

"How far is it to the next site?" she asked.

"Maybe twenty minutes. Is Mother Nature on the line?"

"If she were, I suppose I'd have to ask you to pull over."

He glanced at her, wondering for the moment if she could really relieve herself along a country road.

"I want to talk with you, Harmon, about the race you're going to enter."

"Interested in making a contribution?"

"On the condition that you'll accept our endorsement, I am, yes."

"'Friends'?" He inclined himself toward her and raised his eyebrows emphatically. "Surely you jest."

"It takes a great deal of money to run a campaign."

Two logging trucks with dangerously precipitous loads rushed by them from the other direction.

"You haven't been in town long enough to hear, Nila. I already blundered once. I don't expect to do it again. Accepting Friends' endorsement in a region like this would be a blunder of the highest magnitude."

A third logging truck, piled high as the others and claiming a part of their lane, roared past them.

"So are you going to tell me?" she asked. "Or must I wheedle it out of you before we're hit by a truck. Why are those wobbly monsters allowed on the road anyway? Especially on a day when even hunting isn't permitted."

It was a magnificent Sunday in Bingham County. A bright sun stood alone in a crystal blue sky and the wind was gentle, according to the trees. It was warm and comfortable inside the luxurious Buick. He really had no wish to tell her how he had screwed up, but she wouldn't relent.

Maintaining his gaze on the highway out front, he finally muttered, "I'm simply one of those who doesn't expect a sniper to be in the middle of ten thousand trees where he might or might not find someone to shoot." Then he went on to tell her all about the meeting in the District Attorney's office and how he had opposed public declaration of a sniper in the woodland.

Throughout, she listened without interruption. When he finished, she asked, "What of Tome?"

"What do you mean?"

"Will Meredith Tome hold you accountable on this?"

"I don't see how. He was there the same as everyone, and although he might have felt pressure to go along, nobody, Nila, was holding a gun to his head."

"If he had followed his conscience, the boy I heard about when I arrived… he might be alive today? He was local?"

"Max Rayburn's son. Owns the gun shop."

"What I really was asking when I brought up Tome was whether or not he's a supporter of yours."

"Meredith would never support me, whatever the case."

"But will he remain in the background and keep his thoughts to himself? That's the important question. Or will he become an outspoken opponent of your candidacy?"

"Look, I throw a lot of money his way. What do you think? Besides, he's been running scared as of late, ever since the courts forced his insurance company to cough up a considerable sum. He doesn't like to show it, but it's there, and so I like to remind him where his money is currently coming from."

Meredith had always impressed him as the introspective type. The newspaper publisher and editor had never impressed him as a man of much cunning. Still, why take chances. But he thought it unwise to inform her of his efforts to discredit the man. "It wouldn't matter much if he did, Nila. We're not speaking of some influential daily here. It's a small weekly newspaper Meredith puts out. Many subscribers aren't even in this congressional district."

"All the same, it has a readership."

The automobile hurtled along the highway, in some sections shoulder-rubbed by steep mountain slopes thick with sun-obscuring pine and hemlock, pressing against the concrete berms, trying to recapture the smooth level strip; in other areas, flanked by pasture and farm ponds fed by a stream or spring. The first sign of ice was gradually spreading across these ponds' surfaces. It was wafer-thin and had yet to take on the cold white colors of a hard freeze.

"You know you allowed your political passions to get the better of your business sense, don't you? No one will close and lock their doors as a result of what has happened. That's the grandest hoax, the super deception, long perpetrated on a great number of tiny American hamlets—this iron, never-to-be-shaken belief that hunters, in their annual fly-by-night visit, are the economic make or break for every small businessman who lives there."

"You want me to believe you actually take issue with that?"

"I'm amazed you don't. On second thought, I suppose I shouldn't be. You've obviously advocated it so frequently, it's become an enduring part of your pitch. This isn't the early part of the century, Harmon, where a man in the woods meant that tree life and wildlife would soon be decimated for profit. In the event you haven't noticed, people today are immersed in a great many outdoor activities that don't involve the shooting of every living thing which comes their way. A promotional push to some of these with the same effort as that given to the promotion of hunting, and they would let out their own perennial roots."

"This is it."

He angled the Buick onto a narrow gravel road that appeared to head straight for nowhere. "It's another six miles from the highway."

She turned halfway around and gazed back at Route 6. Then she looked over at him, and he saw out of the corner of his eye that she was grinning.

"What is it now?"

"You don't give a hoot about most of these hunters any more than I do," she said. "Admit it. They've provided your agency with a multitude of sales, that's all. You must have sold acreage and cabins to thousands of them. I'm guessing, as a group, they're the easiest to sell to."

"You think so?"

"Let me think. What are the buzzwords? Rack, that has to be one of them. Scopes. The condition of the herd. Ah yes, talk to them about the condition of this year's herd. I'm sure you must do that. Most of them think they're conservationists, those who've bought into the government's promotional line. They believe that by removing any one deer they are actually supplying next year's animal kingdom with two. They're gluttons for camaraderie. Most must have been forced to play alone when they were kids."

Drake couldn't help but chuckle out loud as two bald whitetails crossed the road in front of them.

"You're only laughing, Harmon, because it's true."

"What if it is?"

"It's the reason to accept our endorsement."

He shook his head, still laughing. "Political suicide."

"You've already botched your chances. You've admitted as much."

"But it might stay contained to Sagerville. Besides, it's a ways to election day."

"You're counting on the short memories of your constituents? Lord, I don't believe it. What a strategy!"

"I'm counting on not blowing my candidacy apart right from the beginning. What I've done makes me only human. It was an error in judgment which will be forgiven. I accept the endorsement of 'Friends' and I might as well forget the whole thing. There's something else, too, that you're overlooking. I can't overlook it. Accepting your endorsement would be financial suicide as well. No pun intended, Nila, but anyone would be a fool to buck the sporting clubs and federations throughout this state, whether their membership roles are filled with real hunters or the kind you despise."

She was staring at the empty road, shaking her head at his adamancy.

"Things are changing in this country," she said. "One day, and it's not too far in the future, 'Friends' will acquire a strong voice in the federal government. The super pro-gun mentalities are already finding themselves on the defensive. You're making a mistake, my dear Harmon. There are plenty of congressmen out there who are running about in the hopes of finding some new aegis of righteousness to stand behind, some popular movement they can hook up with and take advantage of."

"So select one of them."

"No, Harmon. What we need, what 'Friends' and its companion organizations need, is a duly elected representative from one of the largest bailwicks for hunting in the nation. You could be the start of much."

"The start, the end," he responded cynically. "Just forget it."

"Your victory would be a solid statement and a major blow to every sport-hunting federation in this country, from the wealthiest on down. Inside a week you'd be scheduled to appear on every major news show there is. There'd be a book in it too, I'm certain. Who knows where it could lead."

He ignored her, hoping she would drop the subject. The hunting and gun federations all over had too much money at their fingertips, and in the legislative circles their power was furnished by flaunting it, not weaponry.

She took the hint, smiling to herself, and switched her attention to the surrounding landscape. She could press him only so far. A man like he was didn't end up rich and successful by being a pushover.

It was easy to recognize where the four hundred acres began. Because of the lost deed of many years ago, virtually all activity on the property had ceased. Most of the standing timber had not been cut for longer than half a century, and it struck the visiting eye at once.

Drake pulled the car off into a grassy area, offering a magnificent vista. They sat at the very top of a mountain and could see dozens of smaller mountains and hollows stretching away below, each bluer according to its distance. They got out and walked to the edge of the grass. Blue sky and bright sun filled the heavens around them. Only here there was a steady wind whipping their unprotected flesh.

"This is a distance," said Ellenger. "Who's going to trouble to come out here?"

Although she was sure he had heard her, Drake failed to reply. She saw, instead, that he was staring at something about a hundred yards beyond them, and it put him on edge.

"What's the matter, Harmon? You all of a sudden look nervous?"

"There's a vehicle parked up there."

"So?"

"I've driven out here several times before. It's rare to see another car. We're quite off the beaten path, you know."

"Yet you think this is a possible site?"

"Not for selling trinkets and postcards. You'd also

mentioned the possibility of opening a restaurant. Having that as your money-maker. Long as the food is worth it, people around here will drive the distance. They're always on the lookout for a good restaurant."

He kept his eye on the vehicle.

"Why is that car bothering you?" she asked, struck by his intensity.

"I told you why."

"Because of what's been happening?"

He glanced at her. She right along had been intuitive.

"You're not hunting, Harmon. Besides, it's Sunday."

"I still don't like it." He summarily swept a hand out over the land. "This is what the property amounts to, Nila. It would be a fantastic location for a restaurant. Of course, the company will log most of it before they sell it."

He moved quickly back toward the Buick, and she followed after a second or two, still amazed at his aberrant behavior. A figure then appeared at the other vehicle. The man was gazing in their direction, and he waved to them. Next the figure crawled into the vehicle and wheeled it around. Spitting up dirt and gravel, the vehicle, an old Ford Bronco gutted by rust, roared at them, stopping on a dime. Its driver's window came down. Emil Carter stuck his head out.

"Beautiful day, I'd say."

"What are you doing way out here?" Drake asked, feeling strange relief. He saw Emil bob his head to glance at Nila, and a crow flew over them.

"You thought I was Perly, Harmon. Admit it."

Drake couldn't help looking shame-faced. "You can't deny your Broncos do look alike. Same rust holes and everything."

Emil Carter nodded understanding. "I wouldn't be too keen

on meeting Perly Bechtel in these parts either."

"So what are you doing out here?" Drake asked again.

"I didn't realize it was you listing this property."

"Are you interested?"

"In a piece of it. Not no four-hundred acres. Couldn't afford it."

"What makes you think you can afford even a piece of it?" Drake said with good humor.

"Like you said. It's way out."

"Emil, there's no land in Bingham County that's cheap any longer. Those days are gone."

"And who do we have to thank for that, Harmon?"

Drake let the question pass with a salesman's smile.

"I have a client who might be interested in all of it," he said without any indication that he was speaking about the woman sitting to his right. "If that turns out not to be the case, I'll see what I can do for you. I've places listed a lot closer to Sagerville, though, that might be to your liking. They might fit your wallet, too. Why do you want land way out here anyway? Is Suzanne in favor of it?"

"I won't tell you what Suzanne thinks about it. But I've wanted some land away from the general crowd of hunters for some time now. Most that hunt, they wouldn't walk no ten miles in. Guys that come up from the city and a lot of those around here that we're friends with, they're lazy. They'd roadhunt every day if it was legal, or they thought Rumsey wouldn't catch up with them. Harmon, I gotta go. You real-it-ors always ask too many questions, anyway. You must have been private investigators in a former life."

Up went the Bronco's window as quickly as it had been lowered, and Emil Carter roared away. Drake raised his own window and turned the car around in the grass.

"I take it he wasn't the sniper."

"Emil Carter," he explained without acknowledging her gibe. "I went to school with him and his wife. Actually, he was a year behind us. Chief of the Volunteer Fire Department and Rescue Squad. Probably gives as much of his free time to our community as anybody. He was charitable with it back then too, but his classmates only made fun of him. Now, many of them do the same thing."

On their way out of the remote area, Nila Ellenger relaxed in her seat and gazed out the car's window, enjoying the scenery of Bingham County on this gorgeous, late-autumn day. Drake, too, remained quiet and punched at his cellular to listen to his voice-mail. The first voice resembled an aging, bucolic Dale Carnegie. It spun out its message with extreme rapidity and was absent of much punctuation:

"Harmon, Sonny Liottis. Hear tell you're running for sure and good luck, you got Tom's and my support. Anything we can do, way we can help, let us know no problem. No problem either on The Buckseller you tell your client, we'll give fair bid on whatever she wants. Tell her too no charge on the removal of those rat-infested dumps, some bulldozer muscle all that's needed. I figure one pass, they'll all fall. Be talking to you."

Chapter 14

"These are stubborn people who live here. They want things as they've been and they're unwilling to make sacrifices. But a sacrifice that must be made is surrendering up the idea they can do whatever they want with their land."

"Of course you understand the trouble there."

"It's ego. Stubborn ego."

"It's more than that. The land has always had the greatest magnetism for most of us. If in whatever sense it becomes owned by all, the value is diminished, and it seems only natural that all other possessions would follow suit. The bottom line? There would be little respect for ownership of any kind."

Dolf Meixelberger's flesh resembled the hide of an elephant. Tough and loose and grooved all over, it made others think that here was a man who *should* be an outdoorsman. Only he was enormously overweight and this fact invited the men assembled in the D.A.'s office to compare him to the murdered Pittsburgher. What business did such obese males have trudging up steep mountains? If they were searching for deer, they were making a big mistake. The fat old fools were setting themselves up for an early death is what they were doing.

If the head of the State Game Commission had known of these critics' thoughts, he would have shooed them away like a pesky bug. His mind was dead set on hunting for a Bingham County whitetail buck, and just as soon as the meeting adjourned he planned on a good steak with a few drinks, some bullshitting with whoever would listen, and then he would hit the hay early for a good night's rest. At the moment, he sat on the edge of Rusack's desk, joking with Bingham County's senior district game protector.

"A fin, Rums, says you haven't been writing many field receipts as of late."

Harry Rumsey, always in uniform like the Cuban dictator, grimaced and let out a grunt. "Getting to be too many headaches in this," he said. "I should have done as you. I should have got into the administrative end of it."

"My end?" Meixelberger extracted a cigar from a pocket and broke the cellophane wrapper. "There's no money here, for Chrissakes! Maybe you've been out-of-doors too long and breathing this cold mountain air has begun to freeze out your remembering faculties."

Meixelberger's rib alluded to the fact that Game Commission members served as unpaid volunteers. Although each of their appointments required confirmation by the state legislature, ideally they were to stay free of the pressures from political influence. The lack of compensation, the argument went, would guarantee their integrity whenever they were called upon to deal with a matter affecting wildlife.

The big man looked away from Rumsey and surveyed the

office, overflowing with people. This meeting wasn't his idea. What he had to say, he preferred to say to the D.A. and maybe a handful of others. Who needed a convention!

"What's he waiting for?" he complained to Rumsey. "Can't be anymore coming than is already here. There won't be any place to stack 'em. I hope they're not planning on asking a passel of questions either, 'cause it's my intention not to answer but a few."

On the other side of the room, Rusack stood near the outer door, waiting on Tome. When he saw the *Sentinel's* publisher ascending the courthouse steps to the second floor, he rushed to greet him, then pulled him aside.

"All those cars parked outside because of this?" Tome asked with mild amazement. "And what's with you? You seem anxious."

"My idea I related to you at The Buckseller Inn Saturday night—that this killing is about more than just hunters—have you repeated it to anyone?"

"Not a soul."

"Irene?"

Tome shook his head.

Rusack glanced back at the swollen office that gave off the distinct hum of restless men. Meixelberger waved the big paw holding the unlit cigar at him to come inside and start the meeting. Rusack lifted a finger to signal he would be there shortly.

"Good. Then don't!"

"What's this about?"

"Keep it to yourself. Don't tell anyone what we talked about. Last night two things occurred to me. First, what I told you doesn't make any difference at the moment. Because at the moment hunting is the only game in town this sniper can get a ticket to."

"What's the second?"

"He might soon realize that fact himself. If I'm right, Meredith, our friend will want it known that it isn't just the hunter that he's after. If his real game doesn't appear anywhere in print and he doesn't hear it in the bars or anywhere else, we can hope that he begins spreading the word himself. You understand what I'm getting at?"

"You want me to keep my ears open in case I hear it again. This time from someone other than yourself."

"If either one of us do hear it, maybe we can trace it back to its source. It's worth a try. There's not much happening with this case, as you're about to learn. Come on. Let's see how fast Dolf gets himself out of here."

Together, they left the area near the interior staircase for the D.A.'s office where Rusack went before the large assembled group. Before introducing the Executive Director of the State Game Commission, he summarized investigative results as they stood at present, making no attempt at positive spin. First, he told them that police had identified the bullet responsible for the Rayburn youth as a 30.06, but they had yet to successfully compare it to the other aught-six that had been extracted from a tree near the discovery area of Chandler. Second, there was a set of tracks from new automobile tires, still bearing their rubber whiskers, that police had stumbled upon and were interested in checking further.

"What about Cal Pollard?" someone asked. "There's word about this crazy kid is awfully fond of his 30.06 and that he spends more time in the woods than school."

"The boy was questioned," Rusack answered. "His alibis

check out. Howard and Rebecca Pollard informed us also of the altercation at the Gun Shop. The African-Americans check out as well."

"What you mean is, they'll vouch for one another."

"They always do," said a second man at the rear.

"Why don't the two of you move in with that group up north?" said another man while shaking his head.

There was more from the D.A., but it didn't amount to much: the interrogation of an AmeriCon Paper logger who had fired a warning round over the heads of two hunters trying to tag his deer; further questioning by Rynes of Clara. The detective had climbed the mountain alone, but reported no better luck talking to her than had Robin Hood.

"In other words, we're nowhere," Sherman Coppersmith remarked from the center of the audience.

Rusack pulled on the cuffs of his white shirt, ignoring the comment. He was scheduled for court later in the day and was dressed in a suit and tie. "Now I'd like to turn this meeting over to Dolf Meixelberger. For those of you who don't recognize the name, Dolf Meixelberger heads up our State Game Commission… Commissioner?"

Meixelberger removed his hulk from the desk and centered himself before the crowd. He continued to hold the unlit cigar.

"I didn't favor this meeting and so I won't be answering a lot of questions," he told them straight out. "Your D.A. telephoned me, while I was in Harrisburg, to explore the possibility of shutting down what is left of the deer season inside the borders of Bingham County. I told him flat out I didn't think it likely, just as I told him it wasn't a good idea. But those were just my opinions. Once we hung up, I put a call in to each of the other commissioners all around the Commonwealth. All told, I spent more than eight hours on the phone with them this past weekend and they concur. Gentlemen, the Commission will not render a pre-emptive termination to the remaining part of the deer-hunting season in your region. Now, had there been an epidemic of killings, I have no doubt we would have elected to do just that. But as it is, the others and myself believe the season should finish as it is scheduled. On Tuesday of next week, the second and last day of the doe season."

"Is the Commission aware that it's not a disease were contending with?" said Coppersmith.

"We don't need to close down the season!" someone else shouted out. "The Commission is right."

"Commissioner, sir? How many dead hunters does your board require before they call what is happening in this county an epidemic?"

Meixelberger merely waved away Tina Orleau from the Olean daily and her question. What was a woman doing here, anyway?

Tome scanned those in the room, wondering if, by their faces, he could pick out those in favor of early closure from those opposed.

"I said I wouldn't be answering a lot of questions, but I did expect a few. Let me address the young gentleman's concern," said Meixelberger, pointing the cigar at Coppersmith. "Let's suppose for a minute the season is abruptly halted. What's to say your dirt bag won't be satisfied simply to wait until next season and start his murderous ways all over again. Or let's take it the other direction. He objects to waiting a year. Termination angers him, means you're trying to put the screws to him. So he travels westward to McKean County or south to Cameron. In this scenario, all we'd be doing is expanding the boundaries of fear, not containing it. The only chance for nabbing your buddy is to keep the woodlands of Bingham County open." He raised the cigar to thwart another comment, this one about to come from County Commissioner Karl Aufderheide. "Yes, of course, that's slim. This isn't the Rocky Mountains where you can observe both hunter and quarry on bare rock for miles. Nor is it the prairie, where the same can be done. This is Pennsylvania and there's thick, heavy timber and brush on every mountain, drumlin, and knoll. Timber and brush in every hollow. Spotting a man from a distance... well, I'll admit, the chances aren't good."

Tome, like most others, would have preferred contending with a rooftop sniper. With that type of aberrant, there was a compression of fear and a suspension of time. The victims were like nameless, meandering ants, and the conscience of their killer was indisputably believed to be deranged. The urgency created from such concentrated terror was persistent, demanding immediate solution. But this, what Rusack and authorities and they all were dealing with, this with terror stretched in time— two killed on opening day, then rest on Tuesday and the next, then a shooting on Thursday, then again rest, rest, rest, and now today! Was someone dying while they were meeting?

In some sense it seemed to Tome a form of sick joke, as if there was no killer. And no victims! It was as if the man knew of a law or an equation involving time, murder, and fear. *Axiomatic! The amount of fear is inversely proportional to the length of time when multiplied by a constant number of killings.* If that didn't make sense, it was something like it. The fear created by this sniper endured only for a day or two and then subsided, not totally of course, but to a degree that was somehow cool enough to wet the hot intensity of community and regional concern. This was evident in his fellow townspeople. Common sense would have dictated they would ask many questions. Instead, they asked only a few.

Meixelberger, speaking again, was already wrapping things up: "I believe it's to everyone's advantage that we are done with the first week of the buck season. There are no longer the thousands of sportsmen tramping around the mountains." Smiling, he paused to light the cigar. "But there will be one more than was counted on," he said, raising his voice. "Wish me luck, gentlemen! I've said what I had to say, and now I'm going to rest up the remainder of the day so I can nail one of your magnificent Bingham County bucks tomorrow. Which merchant hosts the Big Buck Contest around here, anyway, and what's the prize money amount to? I plan on taking it home."

Chapter 15

"You remember Creighton Halthrop.... Yes, and he moved back to Philadelphia because of those looks. I interviewed him over lunch here for a piece on the Fall Carnival.... Now listen, Jerry, I'm serious. He was a great example of what you're talking about. He explained to me that the goal of his community involvement was to make the area grow and double its population. 'They would easily go for that,' he said, meaning us. But when I asked why he wanted to do that, double the population, he was stymied. Oh, he gave an answer, but it wouldn't qualify as a sample answer to a test question."

"Creighton merely wanted to be a big cheese, Tina, that's all. He apparently couldn't achieve it downstate, so he came here. But he didn't succeed with us because he thought the make-up of the area was that of dunderheads. He thought he was better and of course he wasn't. All of our party hosts serve cheese."

The busy activity of an early weekday was underway when Tome returned to his office. Mary Kiel hardly acknowledged his entrance as she sat before an old electric typewriter slapping paper, her eyes tensed to decode every kind of wild penmanship.

Another woman flung glossies onto a board and spun a reduction wheel to determine the required percentage of cropping for photos. From a distant room came the clack-clack of presses that stacked the cards and announcements for the approaching holiday events. And the pervasive odors mingled. The heavy pungency of inks. The sharp volatiles for cleaning rollers of the hugging blacks and blues. The papers, except for the sour atrophy of *Tier Sentinels* from the past that loomed high in corners and on out-of-way tables, each emitting an oddly pleasant fragrance.

All of it struck Tome as if he were a college freshman again, experiencing in actuality what made up the pride of printed materials, what gave respect to the creative and too often even the not-so-creative, the latter currently more likely to happen because of sophisticated computer software and laser printers. It was a profession he loved, and one he had elected. But lately, he wondered if he might be taking it for granted.

Ruts. Sometimes they were dug without the knowledge of the digger.

He settled himself behind his desk and leafed through the stacks of material that had accumulated on its surface, all possible inclusions in this week's edition. One pile was relegated to the schools and included the coming week's menus and a list of honor students. The chit chats from his home reporters in the outlying townships made up the second. Others provided reports on police patrols—Sagerville salaried only two full-time officers and a glance at last week's summary revealed numerous responses to sniper-related false alarms—plus hospital news, nuptials, obits, and scattered reminder pieces of the past in the Northern Tier. (Although few copies of the former *Upland Patriot* survived, Cliff Addy's many filing cabinets had not met the same end.) Thickest of the stacks and requiring the greatest attention was the hunting material. Through it he began a careful edit.

A pair of buck hunters had brought a wounded bear cub out of the woods, its hindquarters paralyzed by shot. Game officials, the report said, theorized the shooting as a deliberate act by a turkey gunner. For humane reasons the animal was destroyed. There was Rumsey's estimate of the buck harvest on opening day. Not the fat figure of other years, yet Tome wondered as always if the count of available whitetails wasn't padded. The old game officer once explained to him how the figure was arrived at, but the method had sounded simplistic.

Next, he uncovered a score of captioned photographs of successful hunters and their buck, all entries in the annual contest sponsored not by a single merchant as Dolf Meixelberger had assumed, but by the local Chamber of Commerce.

Spreading them out on his desk, he realized he had seen them before, dozens of times. Not the individual features, but each man's overall aura. Their look or mask or costume, call it whatever, identified mostly by the quick beards that darkened many of the faces, as their owners permitted whiskers to have their way until a return to wives and jobs. And identified by the hats, numerous and multifarious, a kind of enforcement of the wearer's individuality. Aussies, bombers, balaclavas, tams and berets, pork pies, bandanas, the cavalry hat, shapeless camo headgear from the military, rangerstyle baseball caps. Even an occasional furry Crockett with a flag of orange to warn the careless shooter and rabid novice. Hats of every size and shape. Hats made from a variety of materials. Yet the hunter's crown was not always the chief item of sporting apparel. The framed individual in one pic glared back at Tome from behind his slaughtered game. A pair of bandoliers weighted with unspent cartridges crossed the hunter's chest.

He re-stacked the prints and pushed them aside.

There were reports of accidental and self-inflicted shootings, reports of damage to utility lines and houses, and finally, the reports on the cardiac arrests of out-of-town hunters who foolishly believed they hadn't gone soft with age. To date, the topography had seized the hearts of five, relenting on two.

Drawing himself tighter to the desk, he compiled the next edition. When it came time for putting together the editorial page, Mary Kiel transferred a stack of material from her own desk to his and, picking through it, handed to Tome the latest letters.

"Here's a complimentary one from Ontario. It's rather long." She held out an accompanying check for a two-year subscription.

"To the bank," Tome said, then read the letter quickly before giving it back. "Trim it. What else?"

"A pair of reactions to the murders. Both are anti-hunting. One unsigned."

"Let's have the other."

"There's also a response to last week's Ellenger letter," said Mary Kiel. She placed this letter in front of him as he was already reading the antihunting letter that carried a couple's signature at its bottom.

> **To the Editor of the Sentinel:**
> For too long God's creatures have been slain unmercifully. They are helpless and they have not the guns with which they can fight and defend themselves. But lately we have

witnessed an Almighty God dealing out punishment to those that kill our wild animals with not so much as a thought to their actions. We did not wish to see a young boy die, but God does not seperate the murderers in the world by age. His concern lies with the guilty and a boy can be as guilty as a man. God rules justly! Those that died received their punishment from a God who is warning others against the massacre of more wildlife. It is wrong and GOD CANNOT BE FOOLED! He protects his creatures and will continue to smite those who kill them indescriminately. The people of Bingham County should realize this. There has enough been done to the deer and other animals. There has enough been done to God's beautiful land. He cannot be fooled and He is losing patience. If no further people are to be killed, we must all realize this. WE MUST!

Mr. & Mrs. Milford Dwyer Pelfry

He scanned the letter a second time, corrected the misspellings, then extended it back to Mary Kiel.

"We'll go with it," he said with a raised brow.

"Martha Pelfry is a very nice lady, Meredith. I can't say the same for her husband."

"Good enough. As for the Ellenger rebuttal, mark it for

next week." He leaned back in his chair and glanced at the clock. "Have you eaten?"

"I've a lunch to finish."

"Put it aside."

She shook her head. "I want to leave before seven tonight. Dale wants to use the four-by-four to do some spotlighting in an area he's never hunted. But you can pick up something for me. Where are you going?"

"Popov's."

"Something sweet then. The gooier, the better. Popov *is* still selling pastry, isn't he? Dale said he's been running twenty miles a week and losing weight like crazy."

"Between you and me I think he's doing all that just so he can keep on eating the stuff."

Outside, a dismal cloud of darkness had crashed into late afternoon and heavy snowflakes started to fall. Without wind, the snow attached itself to Tome and he relaxed in it as he strode along the sidewalk, rapidly whitening, until a burly farm woman confronted him. Bundled under a heavy coat and scarf, the woman gripped a large manila envelope.

"My son shot a wolf," she blurted out. "There was three of them on the farm and we been watching them who knows how long, but we never got a chance to shoot until this last time, and my son, he got him one."

Tome found himself being herded underneath the awning of the hardware store. The woman slid a photograph from the envelope.

"Ferm, well he shot too. Ferm's my husband, and he hit one we're pretty sure, but he dint kill it and the thing it ran off. Only our boy got one. He's proud. Why, we're all proud! Here! Here's a pitchur. A fellow lives down the road from us, it's his son 'at took it."

She pushed the photo to him at the level of his neck, causing him to strain his head backward. An enlargement, it was lacking contrast but had good detail nonetheless. He judged the woman's son to be about fourteen. The boy was wearing a quilted vest over a rather dowdy jacket that might have been a regular item in his apparel for school, as it was colored with tiny bright checks and had a shoestring cord around the waist. A faint smile on the boy's face suggested the photographer had tried to loosen up his subject a moment before the shutter was released. The animal, with its coat thick for winter, wore anything but a smile! Its visage was ludicrous and insane, as the youth held its ears and forced its head toward the camera's lens. With the ears stretched, the eyes were drawn and the lower jaw had dropped open to bare its icicle-styled incisors. Tome was briefly led to see an indistinct flash of a movie, which he doubted he'd even once recalled, involving kamikaze pilots during the Second World War. The dead animal appeared to be a coyote, or maybe a coydog, the latter carrying the strains of wild, free-roaming dogs.

The woman seemed to have read his mind.

"That's no wild dog, I can tell you that. It's no pack of wild dogs we seen. One o' dem had a rabbit in its mouth but dropped it quick when Ferm and Boyd started shootin'. That cottontail's head was chewed up terrible. When you see somethin' like that, that's no mistakin' a wolf."

Tome extended the photograph back at her.

"No, you keep that. I got me another. I thought mebbe you might want to use that in your paper. There ain been no wolf seen around these parts for some time. Thirty year, says Ferm, anyway. Just a shame, isn't it, we dint git the other two? You think you might use that pitchur?"

"Depends if there's space," he said. Cold had infiltrated his clothing and he found himself shivering.

"You ain gonna find no better news than that. And Boyd, he'd like to see his pitchur in the paper. That ain never happened. Think you'll use it?"

"Maybe if there's room."

Tome started to move out from under the awning, but the woman again cornered him. She switched the tone of her voice from one of proud excitement to that of secretive gossip.

"You hear who's busy again?"

Tome repeated the last of her words as if he didn't believe the conversation was about to continue.

"They found two more," the woman whispered to him. "Shot just like the others." She pointed a stiff finger at the shop behind him. "Heard it in there, as a matter of fact. Ferm needed a new rule for a job in the basement. He's a carpenter, you know."

"Two more. Did you hear their names?"

"Dint hear that."

"What about where they were found?"

"Dint hear their names, nor that either. You go on inside, though. You tell them you're a newspaperman. They'll talk to you, they wouldn't me. They wanted to sell me the rule, that's all."

He gladly took the woman's invitation to excuse himself, then turned and pushed open the door on the hardware store.

"You use that pitchur, Boyd'll sure 'preciate it."

He gave her a not altogether superficial wave of farewell.

Inside the store with its distinct aroma of thinners, Tome waited for the clerk to be free. The man could not elaborate on the information, except to say that both victims were males and were related. He had heard it from a customer, he said. He told Tome also that he had been listening to the radio ever since and nothing official had come across.

"Maybe if we had a scanner."

"These men were accidentally discovered?" Tome inquired. "Emil Carter and his crew weren't called out. Is that your understanding?"

"That's my understanding," said the clerk.

Tome picked up a roast beef club from Popov's Pantry and two chocolate crullers for Mary Kiel. No one there had yet heard the news, including fifty-two year-old Popov who, Tome had to admit, resembled a totally new man now that he was exercising regularly. He went back to the print shop afterwards and started dialing. No one had information to give him. There was nothing from Rusack's office, nothing from the Sheriff, nothing from the State Police, although when was that ever a surprise? The desk sergeant did not consider the weekly to be a bona fide newspaper and he always disseminated any news under his control to reporters for the dailies first. Lastly, Tome called the home of Rumsey who, according to the game protector's wife, was somewhere out in Berks Run to the north, checking out a report on poachers. Several times over the next couple of hours he made the same calls, but clearly nothing was being released.

Mary Kiel left for home as she intended at seven o'clock, and the rest of the staff followed at the usual early weekday hour of eight. The long Mondays and Tuesdays compensated for the much shorter working hours at the end of the week, and the staff, very loyal to Tome and the paper, were appreciative of the steady forty hours. The uneven work week had originated following an auto accident that claimed the lives of three high school students. The fatalities had occurred within an hour after the dismissal of school on a Tuesday, but the new *Sentinel* was already in print and readied for delivery. To learn of the accident, readers were forced to buy a daily. Because the paper was assembled and printed in their hometown, Tome felt he had cheated them, taken them for granted. Now, since the establishment of the uneven work week, he had actually scooped the *Morning Era* more than once. On occasion, his staff without complaint had remained at the office well into the early hours of a Wednesday morning. They formed a good group—Reecy who was a great aunt to Councilman Sherman Coppersmith, Cindy Wilson who was Suzanne Carter's niece, Tanya who drove down each day from the northern part of the county and brought along her stories of the neo-Nazi compound, Monk, and of course, Mary—and he had not once hoped for better.

Apart from the many materials that would be compiled into a newspaper tomorrow, there lay also about the shop dozens of print orders awaiting boxing. He decided to band some of the larger orders and slip them into their cartons, leaving the labeling for a typist. But first, he put identical notes on Mary and Cindy's desk to hold on any front-page material.

It was getting on eleven when he finally left for home. He locked the front doors beneath the exterior masthead, then climbed into the van. Weary and anxious for sleep, he nevertheless pulled the van into the economy station, open until two a.m. during deer season, to fill the depleted tank. Inside the station the attendant was sitting half-turned around with his head slumped against the wall. Tome eased the long box of a vehicle into the outside pump aisle and the van's lights slid across the expansive windows, stirring the man from slumber. Seconds later, Studs stumbled out holding a bucket, and scattered halite, like chicken feed, over the glazed asphalt. The snow had ceased and the temperature had fallen. The wet pavement had swiftly become ice.

"Fill her," said Tome through the lowered window.

"I don't know why you can't fill it yourself, Mr. Tome. I don't think you have plans to run off without paying."

Studs and attendants working earlier shifts had been ordered to pump all gas by the owner of the station because some out-of-town hunters were filling their vehicles themselves and then quickly driving off without paying.

The LCD on the pump zeroed out and Studs shuffled his legs about as he held the pump trigger tightly for rapid flow.

"At this hour it must start to get a bit dull in there," said Tome.

"Does," said Studs. He hesitated, then glanced over at Tome in the captain's seat before adding: "Sometimes nobody for hours, and then a convoy. Everyone's in a rush."

"Makes you wonder if they're headed anywhere."

"Might you," he said, "doesn't me." Studs checked the changing meter numbers frequently. "Many buck being *harvested?*" he asked.

Tome heard the stress on the final word. "A few."

"Renooable resource," Studs muttered. "I get a laugh out of that. None of us ever *kill* a deer anymore. We bag them, drop them, and the one that really goads me is we *harvest* them. Harvest them, like they're timber, corn, or cotton. As if I'm some farmer with boo-koo crops he's gotta tend to before they spoil in the fields."

"Euphemisms," said Tome. "Language that turns the sour thing to sweet, the unacceptable to acceptable."

"Then it *bee* the language of the century," Studs offered in a conniving pirate's voice.

"I take it you don't think deer should be thought of in such a way."

Studs fluttered the pump trigger briefly, then replaced the nozzle and read the amount of the sale. "$17.75."

Tome didn't want to wait for a credit card transaction. Instead, he drew a twenty from his wallet and hung it out the window. Studs screwed in the gas cap, then went forward and took the bill.

"No matter to me how it's thought of, deer and hunting and all of it. But don't forget about people. That word, it don't in any way change the fact."

"It hides the fact," Tome said. What in the world was he going on about?

Studs rubbed his hands together briskly, then fished for change in a coat pocket, extracting a wad of assorted bills. "Too cold," he said. "Seventeen seventy-five, eighteen, nineteen... twenty.... You just missed Mr. Drake and that fine, two-legged fox he's been running with these past few days. She's that woman that writes you all those letters. I wonder if Mr. Drake be bangin' her?" This last statement Studs said more to himself than Tome as he walked away and toward the building.

Just for a moment, Tome considered calling him back and asking Studs if he had heard any news concerning the day's killings, but then decided that he would now rather learn of it in the morning. The truth was, he didn't want to exchange any additional words with Sagerville's strange little man.

Chapter 16

"Gag me with a spoon! You think because he shows a little social conscience in that rag from time to time, he ought to get a pat on the back? He could show a lot more social conscience is what he could do. All these upstate weeklies are the same. If their publishers didn't print up business cards on the side, they'd all go hungry."

"You're a hard man, Charlie Brown."

At the feeder outside the kitchen window, the jays were harassing the juncos. Tome took no notice of the noisy sunrise row. He sat with his first cup of coffee, absorbed by the front page of the *Morning Era*.

BROTHERS SHOT HUNTING; KILLER'S TOLL MOUNTS

Sagerville (SC) — Two victims have been added to the list of sportsmen shot and killed this hunting season while walking the thickly timbered lands of Bingham County. Thomas Liottis, 44, and brother Robert "Sonny" Liottis, 42, both of Gunther and general contractors well known throughout the north central counties, are the fourth and fifth persons to have been slain while hunting whitetail deer. The frozen bodies were discovered by a team of natural gas workers in Nyger Hollow, about seven miles southwest of Gunther.

According to police, both men were fired upon and struck from an unspecified distance by a high caliber bullet. Slugs from the 30.06 caliber have been linked to a pair of earlier killings.

Local officials at this county seat expressed fears that the death count may rise as a week remains in the statewide season for deer. Earlier this week, the governing State Game Commission denied a request by Bingham officials to terminate the season within their borders.

Some authorities are interpreting the latest slayings to mean that the killer has decided to widen his area of operation. Until yesterday, the discovery locations of victims were confined to Devil's Den, a flat area of 25 square miles that connects some of the loftiest mountains in this part of the state.

Sagerville authorities are reluctant to comment on possible motives for the slayings. Yet a popular suspicion, according to councilman Sherman Coppersmith, is that the killer is a self-appointed vigilante opposed to sport-hunting and is committed to carrying out a vendetta on behalf of slaughtered wildlife everywhere.

Coinciding with this view is the presence in Bingham County of Nila Ellenger, chief administrator for an anti-hunting organization based in Manhattan. Ellenger could not be reached for comment.

Complete obituaries on Thomas and Robert Liottis, along with related stories, appear inside.

Tome read the piece again. Until now, there was a hook to this villainous affair that had failed to cross his mind. Who could guarantee that the murderer of Chandler, the downstater, and the Rayburn boy, who could say that he would not turn into a scapegoat for other killings? So what if it was determined that the Liottis brothers were silenced by a 30.06. Unless the slugs in question were located and identified through ballistics, it meant nothing. The aught-six was ubiquitous. He owned one himself. Rusack, too. And as for Tom and Sonny Liottis, they were not without their serious detractors, which included everyone from homeowners dissatisfied by shoddy workmanship and cheaper, surrogate materials to, more recently, a large group of loudly complaining subcontractors who had accused the traditionally low-bidding brothers of holding back on payments long reimbursed by the government. It was conceivable that someone might have taken the opportunity to avenge a wrong and gun them down.

Then, too, there was the mention of the woman who marshaled the troops of the nation's most vocal animal protection group. The *Era's* Sagerville correspondent Jerry Drier seemed to be suggesting her involvement in the matter. Was that really possible? Tome asked himself. Could this woman have a connection to the cold-hearted dispatching of deer hunters?

A junco slammed into the window, attracting his attention, and Tome set the paper aside. He watched the bird gather itself slowly as the morning gained definition, becoming gray, still, shadowless. Irene appeared in her yellow robe and fixed them a breakfast and for a while they talked, avoiding the killings. A short time later, Tome climbed into the van and headed for the shop. A generous dispersal of salt from the highway crew had turned the town's streets into glistening black borders around the numerous squares of white lawns. An occasional tree stood piebald from a barrage of snowballs hurled by students en route to school.

At one of the stoplights in the town, he caught the red. While he waited, someone standing beside a car out front of the fire hall beckoned him. On green he moved the van through the intersection in the direction of the beckoning arm, which he soon learned belonged to the owner of the acreage on which he had hunted turkey in November, just a few weeks earlier. The man was a nephew to Commissioner Aufderheide who was also on hand, as the white-haired official loomed up from behind the car, pulling tightly on a rope to better secure the carcass of a very large deer. Each man was roomily garbed in a one-piece camouflage suit. Aufderheide wore also a green tam-o'-shanter with a flourishing orange pom-pom at the center.

Tome got out of the van and walked toward a small group of children too young for school. They were gaping at the buck, but they opened for him. He saw the animal's impressive antlers, six very long points on each with the sharp curve of an eagle's talons, and thick like tree limbs.

"Whattaya think, Tome? Is it one beautiful whitetail, or isn't it?"

"It is indeed, Karl."

"Unfortunately, it isn't mine." The Commissioner moved beside his nephew and roughly squeezed the young man's shoulder. "He's been bummed out since the season began. Scouted out this big fellow right up to the opener, and then nada."

"I remember you're telling me," Tome said to the nephew. "He definitely is one mountain of a deer."

"Just over 200 field-dressed," the nephew said. "He edges out that flatlander who's been at the top of the list since day one."

"No question. Should win heaviest deer. Maybe points as well. You have your photo taken?"

"Your man Monk was here."

"What's the matter?" Tome asked, detecting a note of displeasure in the response. "Monk's no Ansel Adams with the camera, but he does all right."

"Maybe most times, Meredith. Not today. He could have cared less. If you don't mind, I'll drop off one of my own pictures after the film is processed."

"Tome, I'm going to take it up with the Chamber that they

ought to double this year's prize money," the Commissioner boasted loudly. "Next year's too. What about it? Won't hurt, in my opinion, to beef up everything that keeps the hunters coming 'round."

Tome offered no reply. Instead, he watched a little boy with blond hair stroke the ears of the dead deer. The boy's head was cocked like a robin's in repast.

"I never knew this nephew of mine was so damn lucky, Tome. Get out with him and you see tons of game, all kinds. Getch your buck?"

"Have yet to make it out," he answered, dropping his eyes off the blond-haired boy.

"Don't fret none! Plenty of freezer meat around for Monday and Tuesday. But if you want a buck, trek along with my sister's boy here. It's sin, how he attracts the wildlife."

The nephew rolled his eyes for Tome.

"Yeah, he thinks his old bleach-headed uncle is full of it. But let me tell you, Tome, I've lived here all my life and though I've seen a bobcat on occasion, or think I've seen one—you've heard how the saying goes: if something flashes by you and you think you just saw a bobcat, then you have—but this morning marks the first time I've ever seen one *standing still!*"

"It wasn't a bobcat," the nephew droned.

"The hell it wasn't!... And he wouldn't shoot," the Commissioner added for Tome's benefit.

"So why the devil didn't you shoot?"

"You little fart, you were in my line of fire."

The children all giggled. Tome had the thought that the bobcat season did not run concurrently with deer.

"Well, it wasn't a bobcat. It was an oversized housecat."

"The hell it was."

The little blond boy said, "Don't you like cats?"

"He hates cats," said the nephew.

"I hate everything!" the Commissioner shouted, then pretended to snarl and growl at the children who all giggled before running off and kicking up snow. Tome had listened to his own children tell of the Commissioner's funny antics that included an imitation of Clara the recluse, who apparently did not vote.

"There is something that bothers me about the two of you," said Tome.

"Only one?" said the Commissioner. His tone of voice was still for the children even though they had left. "God'll gitcha for lying. With me alone there's gotta be more than one."

Tome gently smiled at the repeatedly elected official. If the old man's sense of humor often focused on others, it focused also on himself as well.

"I'm staring at the camo. Are the two of you striving for a permanent layoff?"

"Helllll!" The Commissioner drew the word out and let his eyes course over the nephew and himself. "Tome! Listen up! Now you were on hand yesterday the same as me. Dolf Meixelberger didn't mention a damn thing that would help the hunters any. Some joker is out there hoping to fling a slug in my direction, I'd be a fool to assist him."

Tome eyed the bright pom-pom accusingly.

"I've always hedged my bets a little. You've been around here long enough you should at least know that about Karl Aufderheide!"

The nephew ran a hand slowly along the curve of one of the big buck's antlers.

"I've never believed in that color-blind claim," he said. "If I had been wearing blaze orange, I doubt I could have stalked within a hundred yards of this fellow."

"Five hundred for that bobcat," said the Commissioner.

"I spotted him long before he took that first and final look at me. The men who go in after this sniper, they won't want to be wearing it either. Don't look surprised," the nephew said to Tome. "It's the only way they'll apprehend him, if they do at all. They'll need to catch him in the act."

"They'll be needing a ton of luck just to find him," remarked Tome, thinking the nephew was probably correct in what he was saying.

"He's right, you know," said the Commissioner. "Scum like that, you have to take direct action against. Sitting on one's ass won't get it done."

Tome left the two men before long and on the remaining drive to the shop, he noticed a parade of moving lights on the other side of the commons. The funeral procession for the Rayburn child. He counted nine vehicles in the deliberately slow moving line, but then corrected the number to eight. The last car was passing without its lights on. It carried the dead twelve-point.

Throughout the day and into the evening he and his staff worked steadily to produce the new edition, knowing they had no scoop on anything, but taking steps nonetheless to compile a story as completely as was possible on the shooting deaths of the Liottis Brothers. Thinking, too, that the killer might be accelerating his murderous tempo, Tome held on rolling the press for as long as he could because Emil Carter might be mustering a search party at any minute to go out after a missing hunter. But at 6:30 he could wait no longer and ordered Monk to put ink to paper, at the same time musing on what the commissioner's nephew had said earlier in the day about his employee. But Monk, as always, turned his face away when people spoke to him and Tome was unable to determine if the military veteran was under any kind of stress.

Soon after, he walked to the Buck 'n' Doe for the usual beer and sandwich, but returned to the business within the hour to continue with the boxing of Christmas cards and other orders. A copy of the new edition lay on his desk. He snapped it flat.

There staring back at him were the halftones of the hunters and their kills.

Ruts, he murmured. Dug without the knowledge of the digger. Who was it who had warned him of that? Whoever it was, it must have been a long time ago. Maybe a professor. Perhaps a reporter from his hometown paper where he had been employed for a summer. He couldn't remember.

Three photographs dressed the front page and there was at least the same number on the inside where he had placed the week-old results of the Killdeer meeting along with the photo of the young shooter named Boyd and his "wolf." Except for the front-page story on the latest killings and a shorter one on the Rayburn teen, there was hardly any real news contained in the paper. The masthead and banner appeared as limp as the tongue on the dead buck he had gazed at in the morning. There still were moments of course, although nothing like the reporting that had led to the three-hundred-thousand dollar libel suit against him. But once in time, the *Sentinel* had unfurled every week as a triumphant Argus of the communities throughout the county. A steady, dependable organ underscoring its readers' importance and contributions to the slow but emerging changes across the Tier.

As for the pictures themselves, for some time now they, too, had been the same. The bricks of the fire hall formed the background. Not a hint of the wild where the animal had lived. Just bricks with their weathered mortar lines matched impeccably to the pictures' borders. Never askew except for the times when Monk or another member of his staff was requested to take the picture. The photos cost him nothing. Year after year a part-time shutterbug had been shooting them as a favor to the Chamber and as a source of revenue to himself. The proud hunter was always glad to pay the modest fee. The photographer's work was clean, he had to admit. Never a tongue exposed, it was always rolled back behind the teeth. Never a patch of dried blood on the animal's snout. Occasionally, the dead deer resembled a living dog, pleased to be cuddled by its master.

Ruts. Yes, there had once been news, and lots of it. Maybe someday there would be news again.

At nine that evening, Nila Ellenger opened the door to the print shop and stepped inside. The place was lit but quiet, except for the muffled thumps of the press under operation in a back room.

"Is there anyone here?" she shouted without embarrassment and, then, letting her voice drift, added, "or am I talking to myself?"

"Can I help you?" Tome said, emerging from a corner stacked with dozens of cartons.

"Yes. I'm looking for Meredith Tome. I was told he often works this late."

He identified her at once as there was no mistaking the woman's attractiveness; the photographs hadn't lied. He plunged several large staples into a box before weaving his way forward around several tables and filing cabinets.

"Meredith Tome," he said, extending his hand. When she

did not immediately take it, instead glancing back at the corner where the cartons were piled, he explained, "It's a small shop. Everyone does what needs getting done, including myself."

It was the answer she wanted. "Nila Ellenger," she said with a smile and offered her own hand.

"It's a pleasure to finally meet you. What can I do for you? Are you perhaps stopping by to drop off a new letter?"

"You must admit," she said charmingly, "they haven't harmed your circulation."

Tome briefly laughed. "I'm sorry, but I can't really confirm that, as it's been some time since I've seen a doctor."

She smiled again, in appreciation of his humor, and said, "I intend to buy a piece of property in your area, Mr. Tome."

"Really?" he responded, unable to restrain his surprise at the information.

"Looking to escape from the city on occasion? It's beautiful around here, as I'm sure you'll agree, and the best place in the world in my opinion to relax and collect your thoughts. Are you intending to build, or buy one of the camps already on the market?"

"Forgive me. I misspoke. It's Friends of God's Creatures that is buying, not me personally."

Tome threw back his head a little. "I don't understand. 'Friends' isn't a conservancy. Why would your organization want property in the Northern Tier?"

Instead of acknowledging that he had asked anything, she turned her attention to the items in the office. "Do you have any coffee by any chance? I could stand a cup."

"In another room. But it's not exactly fresh."

"I'm quite used to drinking old coffee. A little cream or milk too, if you have it."

"I'll be right back," he said; then added, "and I'll want an answer to my question."

When he returned delivering coffee for both of them, he saw she was moving among the tables, admiring samples of various printed materials that were stacked on their surfaces. She picked up a Christmas card and inspected its cover of snowflakes and blizzard swirls.

"Do you print only the inside greeting or the entire card?"

"Whenever possible, we do everything ."

"It's very nice. The register is perfect. And four-color?"

"Capability, yes. Profitability, no"

He set both mugs on his desk and pushed over Mary's chair. "Here. Sit down. Take the card with you. Take some of the other designs, too."

He circled around and stood behind the desk until she came over and settled into the chair. She grasped the mug and sipped its contents.

"So explain to me now, Ms. Ellenger. Why is 'Friends' desiring to buy property in Bingham County?"

"Mr. Tome—"

"—And call me Meredith."

"Very well. If you'll address me as Nila.... What I've decided, Meredith, is to move the main offices of FGC. To move them here, to Bingham County."

Tome waited before responding to see if there was more to her opening statement. However, it seemed she wanted something out of him before proceeding.

"Okay, I can see how your operating expenses will lessen," he said.

"To be honest, it's what started me thinking."

"I can't imagine running an organization like yours out of a major city. Although that environment has its upside, the basic expenses must be absolute murder! But you could have decided on a thousand other places, Nila, and all of them larger than anything in Bingham County."

"But what purpose would that serve apart from the one you mentioned?"

"So you want to be where the action is, is that it?"

"Also, I'm making plans to open a business, a restaurant, that will help to support the organization's goals."

"The goal to eliminate hunting and hunters. How well do you think such a restaurant will do in this area? Forgive me, but it sounds foolhardy," he said, unable to resist a grin.

"It's the reason I stopped by, Mr. Tome." He noticed her departure from the more friendly address, but let it go. Enforced informality didn't always work. "Your interpretation of our goals, that is."

"What's there to interpret? 'Friends' hates hunters and hunting."

"I'm sure you must have read this morning's paper. And if I'm correct, then you saw where there was an attempt to smear my organization. You see, the media for these large hunting areas never miss a chance to discredit us. Now if I had remained in New York, then you and others might have awakened this morning to read about some Pennsylvania Bigfoot in possession of a gun and able to shoot like John Wayne."

Tome primmed at the lips. It was a half-truth he could appreciate. "But I don't see what you're getting at."

"We are not like our sister organization, Mr. Tome. We do not hate hunting and all hunters. Your friend, Mr. Drake, presented a viewpoint essentially the same as yours, which got me to thinking that I need to educate a few people."

"Then I'll need you to define for me who the hunters are that 'Friends' is opposed to. Is it perhaps only the men that your organization can't stand?"

"Only the men? Aren't they about all that do hunt? Men and little boys who believe they'll become men just as soon as they spill some blood that isn't their own?"

"Much the contrary. Quite a few women are taking up a rifle and entering the woods nowadays."

"Really!" she said with a faint guffaw. "Quickly, name me three from your hometown."

"I can name you more than three."

"Three will do."

Not to be baited so easily, he first sipped his coffee. Was she uninformed of the extent of women's involvement in today's hunting? Or did she think that he was? Quietly, he delivered a small directory of Sagerville's women who were known to shoulder a rifle or shotgun: "Let's see, there's Peg Rusack, Donna Sweitzer, Virginia Lasky, who once killed a very large black bear, Suzanne Carter, Tammy Forster. Myrtle Faner and Muriel Higgins in their day. Candace Paley, Ruth Ann Davenport, Claire Lindstrom, Faith Aufderheide, before she had the accident. Tammy Moore, Ruby Davis, Karen Acres. Meg—"

"All right," she interrupted him. "There's more than I thought."

"—Meg O'Brien. Even my secretary Mary Kiel has been known to bring down a few whitetails over the years."

"Still, women remain a small minority. You won't argue that, will you?"

"I'm not wanting to argue anything. I just want to learn who the hunters are that your group is opposed to? Who don't you people like?"

She told him what she had told Drake, about marketing and promotion geared toward keeping hunters hunting and bringing more people into the so-called "sport."

"That's an interesting take on it," he said when she had finished. "You say it's in your letters?"

"You have only to read them. Our sister organization—and I'm sure you know to whom I'm referring—is working to eliminate hunting all together. To most of us in 'Friends' that's simplistic and overlooks the reality that deer and other animals will continue to die in large, and even greater, numbers on the highways. Without natural predation, there is little choice between killing animals with a gun and a car. What we are attempting to do—"

"—What Friends is attempting to do, it sounds to me, is to elevate the culture. It's a noble approach. All right, I'll go back and read some of your letters again."

The siren at the community fire hall sounded, commanding their attention. It started on a low sluggish note, but soon its ball bearings were seated, and the wail threatened to break the eardrums of every living creature within a quarter-mile. Tome gazed in the direction of the sound.

"Does that mean another missing hunter?" she asked, almost shouting.

"It could. Sometimes it's sounded, at other times not."

He opened the door to peer out and learn if he could determine the siren's message. Fogger Dann loomed there, a step away from opening the door himself.

"Looks like a house in flame on Walnut Street," he informed Tome. "You can see the smoke if you step around the corner."

Tome pivoted around at once and went to summon Monk from the press in the backroom. Dann entered the main office after a small ruckus of pounding his boots at the threshold to dislodge the caked snow.

Returning with Monk several steps behind, Tome turned to face the disfigured war veteran and to give him instructions.

"Monk, there's a burning house over at..." He stopped in mid-sentence, recognizing the abnormal behavior: the man was looking straight at him.

"Monk, what's going on? What's the matter?"

Monk transferred the gaze of his mangled face first to Ellenger, then Dann, lingering on the second.

"Monk?"

"It's nothing, Mr. Tome."

Tome glanced at his visitors, both of whom were staring at his employee.

"What is it you want done, Mr. Tome?"

Tome continued to hesitate. What was going on? Monk wore a look like he was about to kill someone, and he never looked anyone in the eye, never gave anyone a chance to see and study the ugly disfigurement that had shaped the left side of his face like a deep crusted crater. Tome remembered, too, what the Sheriff had told him about Monk and Perly Bechtel. Was something going on with that?

"I'm going back and watch the press," declared Monk.

"Grab the camera," Tome ordered. "I'll watch the feed and bundle your batch. Ever shoot pictures at night? Set the film at three times the recommended speed. We'll push-process it."

Averting further gazes, Monk marched to a cabinet along an outside wall to retrieve the camera.

"I hope he's all right," said Tome to neither visitor in

particular as Monk hastily left the building. "I've never seen him that angry."

Dann said, "I suppose you can read that face as well as anyone, seeing that he works for you. But are you sure it's anger?"

"You think it's something else?"

Dann shrugged.

"You're entertaining some idea. What is it?" asked Tome.

"It's just a thought…. Tom and Sonny."

Dann could see that Tome didn't get it.

"Your man who just left has been having some remodeling done on his house. You know that, don't you?"

"And he's had some problems getting the work completed, yes. Are you saying the Liottis Brothers were doing the work and giving him a hard time?"

"Not exactly. But they were responsible for setting up the contractor who is doing the job. Tom and Sonny, big as they were in the region, were known for that. And then they pull out the rug by demanding a little bigger piece of the action. Whoever's doing the work has to do the same, and your man wouldn't hear of it. So the work stopped midway and his house is a mess."

"If it's not anger?" fished Tome.

"Worry," Dann said.

Tome briefly switched his attention to Ellenger, not wanting to leave her out of the conversation. "You read this morning's paper, so you know something of whom the two of us are talking about."

Ellenger nodded. "Harmon Drake also mentioned one of them," she offered, but remained silent about the fact that she had listened to the recorded voice of Sonny Liottis as he spoke of razing The Buckseller.

Tome turned back to Dann. "Worry that, what? That he murdered them and he may not get away with it?"

"It's a possibility," Dann said, faintly grinning; it wasn't what he was thinking. "More likely that he might get accused."

"Oh," said Tome. "That could be a problem, couldn't it?...Who are you?"

"Most folk call me Fogger Dann."

Tome studied the face of the Buckseller man. "Monk's not one to air his problems. Certainly not at this office. And I doubt he does it anywhere."

Dann understood what was being asked of him.

"Sonny paid a visit to The Buckseller the other day. That's where I live. He wouldn't cough up why he was there."

"But he told you all that you just told me regarding Monk?"

"Just a little. You see, I worked for both him and Tom years ago. I know what they're like. It's not hard to paint the trim."

"Look. Why don't both of you come with me into the other room so I can remain near the press. They're old machines and want to fly apart if you glance the other way."

When Dann passed in front of him as all three moved into the back room, Tome asked, "Those men at the Inn the other night, did you know them?"

"I know their kind if that's what you mean."

Tome nodded. "So, what are you here for, Mr. Dann?"

"Pig Chandler was a friend of mine. I want to get hold of the actual picture that was in your paper. It was a good picture of Pig."

"It's probably still on the paste-up board."

Tome hurried from the press to the very rear of the shop and disappeared into a small storeroom to search for the photograph.

Dann gazed at Ellenger who was intrigued by the repeating action of the press.

"You're the woman folks are talking about," he finally said.

She raised her head and met his eyes on the other side of the press. "Does that mean, then, you know who I am?"

"I know who you are and what you do."

"Then might I ask you a question? To satisfy my curiosity, that is. Mr. Dann, is it?"

"Fogger Dann."

"Some of the people who hold important positions in your community, including Mr. Tome and Mr. Drake, have been confused on what my organization represents. Do you read the paper? The *Tier Sentinel?*"

"When it's in front of me."

"And the letters to the editor?"

"I've read a number of yours and I support where your group is coming from."

"Do you? Where are we coming from, if you don't mind my asking. It's where the confusion lies."

"I don't know why anyone would be confused," Dann said. "I understand your position to be this: There are too many people in the woods and many who plain shouldn't be there. Nor would they be if some other folks weren't always encouraging them that they ought to be."

Nila Ellenger couldn't help but smile. "And you're out of The Buckseller. Was your friend clear on it as well?"

"Pig Chandler was clear on everything."

Tome came hustling back to check the press, photograph in hand.

"You got something to put it in?" Dann said. "So it doesn't

get wet?"

Tome retrieved a discarded brown envelope from a waste can and slipped the enlargement inside, at the same time using his index finger to remove a splotch of rubber cement from the emulsion.

"There you go."

"Do I owe you?"

Tome waved away any consideration. "You know, if someone other than yourself is wanting a picture, your friend had one in his possession. He insisted on paying me for it, too."

"Yep. That was a fault of Pig I often criticized him for. He never recognized a favor done without strings attached. He always wanted to even up. What did he give to you?"

"One of those heavy jugs of pressed cider. I still have it too. It's in the cargo area of the van. The cap's never been cracked."

"He told you he wanted back that jug, too, didn't he?" He looked over at Ellenger as if the next thing he was about to say would be of interest to her. "My friend hated plastic containers, and so he was always on the lookout for those old glass jugs for his cider. He had about a hundred of them." He looked back at Tome. "You say it's been sitting in your van? Ought to be getting right wicked about now."

"What about his hogs?" Tome asked. "In fact, what about everything?"

"No one's touched his things," said Dann. "Buckseller folk'll just let it sit for awhile like he's never left us. Then one day we'll take inventory and divvy up what's there. As for the hogs, oh, I've been slopping them. I carried his cat over to my place too, but he's a loyal feller and keeps on going back." He turned momentarily back to Ellenger. "You like cats?"

"Very fond of them," she said. "I have three."

He nodded, as if he had made up his mind regarding this woman with whom he had been talking.

Tome said, "You said you're a friend, not family? You look a lot alike, you know. Except for the color of the hair, I'd have assumed you were brothers." Especially because of the wrists, thought Tome. That's what he remembered was most memorable about Chandler, and here were those same wrists extending out of Dann's undersized coat. The wrists were extremely hard and lean, looking like they were forever torqued; and during his interview with Chandler, Tome had scratched out the word "hornbeam" on his notepad because that small rugged tree had come to mind.

"Did you pay respects?" Dann asked Tome, who nodded. "Thanks. Few people are aware there's an old cemetery in The Buckseller. That's where we buried him."

Then the face faintly bunched up and at last Dann gave the shortest farewell to both of them and left.

The press continued to slap out papers.

"I should be going, too," said Nila Ellenger. "I fly out of Bradford first thing tomorrow morning. Mr. Tome? It's been a pleasure."

"I can say the same, Ms. Ellenger. And don't forget to keep those cards and letters coming."

"Letters you can count on. About the cards, don't hold your breath."

Chapter 17

"I recall reading a story like what's happening to us."

"You read a story?"

"Must be the only one ever, you think? You could be right. Anyway, it was about the formation of an underground army and because the government kept tabs on them, they accumulated their weapons by killing sportsmen year after year and taking theirs."

"Pretty silly, wouldn't you say?"

"For sure. Except when I think about that group north of Killdeer."

To Monk, she was beautiful. From the first moment he laid eyes on her up-close, he had thought so. More beautiful than Mr. Tome's wife, and when she occasionally stopped by the shop often dressed in summer's yellow, Monk could not restrain himself from staring at Irene when she wasn't looking back. More beautiful, too, than the woman fighting for animal rights. The truth was, despite the dark coat which hung to her ankles, despite the wild hair with its nest of tangles, despite all the extra age anyone would expect to see on a female living a rough existence, when Monk met Clara face-to-face at the end of the summer, offering her a ride and assisting her in toting several bags up the steep slopes behind The Buckseller, he considered her to be the most beautiful of all women. In little time he wanted her for himself and despite her actions to the contrary, he became convinced she wanted the same.

It was not unfounded conviction either. Her name, she soon confided in Monk, wasn't Clara, but Darla, and there was no one else who possessed this knowledge. Nor did anyone know that she had lost two boyfriends in Vietnam within six months; and when no one seemed to care, she packed some things and disappeared from her family in Maryland, ending up eventually in a tent above The Buckseller. Dreaming what he thought he could never dream after the terrible injury to his face, Monk began to nurse the thought he would someday have a woman all his own, that Darla would turn her back on what she was doing, walk out of the tent and down from the Den forever, and live with him.

During their initial coupling, without mentioning names, she had told him of others, wanting to be honest, and driven by jealousy he began to visit the Den at all hours and from all directions, watching those who came and went; driven also by a worrisome fear that another man would move Darla enough to share secrets, and then how special would he be to her? And then on a day which was to be his day, he accidentally discovered inside the tent what he wished he had not. A brass rivet, the kind that appeared on denim jeans except this one was oversized, had lain exposed next to the bed.

Except for the state trooper whose visit was brief, Monk hated all those he had witnessed leaving the tent. The old, the young. Those he knew and others who were strangers. He even came to hate Pig Chandler, a man who had been scorned like himself. He hated them all because of the fear they would soon call his woman "whore." But it was the realization that Studs was sleeping with Darla which stirred him like no other, that made his scenarios of killing almost brutal.

And so, when Tome had summoned Monk from the press room with instructions on how to shoot photos of a late-night fire, it was the knowledge of Studs, a man much younger than himself, that Monk carried and that had turned his face into a conflagration all its own. Studs, the buffoon. Studs, who wouldn't remove his picture from a deer's ass, instead letting it hang in the bar for all to see and laugh at. Studs, who sucked up to Max Rayburn and other blowhards like him. But also the other Studs, the momma's boy. The other Studs for whom women often felt sympathy, to whom they often shared thoughts they would not willingly share with other men. Monk had felt the threat from Studs start to grow deep inside and there it continued to expand like a malignant tumor, even as the house burned and crackled, and timbers fell, and the disconsolate family stared at the relics of their history wiped away before their eyes. Monk appeared hardly to notice the tragedy, barely moving out of one spot on the sidewalk as he snapped off the roll of film as if the camera were motorized.

And then, while standing there, staring with angry vacancy, a harsh voice, full of mockery, confronted him. "Hey ladlehead, you got any naked pictures of your lady in the woods?"

Not waiting for acknowledgment, Perly Bechtel limped his large body mere inches in front of the camera, inside Monk's space. More wrecked and uglier than Monk's, the face of the bull-chested man made no impression on Bechtel himself.

"Have I got to repeat myself?" said Bechtel, who pressed his thumb on the camera lens and pushed it to one side. "And don't go thinking I give any damn at all that you're some combat veteran. You try to walk away before I'm through talking and I'll squeeze the other side o' your head so you end up looking like a stupid hourglass." He stepped back a couple of inches. "She got any bowls in that tent? Or when she serves up soup, do you just dump your head on the table and she pours it in one side and you spoon it into the other?"

Bechtel grinned, but only another misfit would have known it.

"Did you corner me to do stand-up? Or is there something else?" Monk boldly asked.

"Yeah, there's something else. Perly Bechtel is aware of what you're doing."

Monk forced a laugh and looked away for a moment. "What do I care that you know I'm seeing"—he almost said Darla—"Clara?"

"You aren't listening," said Bechtel who screwed his eyes into tiny vortices. "But here's the good part, the part that'll keep you a happy man. Perly Bechtel, you see, don't care. So if you got any ideas for that little weasel you only learned about last week who's cuttin' into your time, don't go flushing them down the toilet on my account."

A period of silence passed, marked only by more crackling wood and flame, and Bechtel moved forward again into Monk's space. The two men's faces were but inches apart and each could feel the breath of the other mixed with the heat from the fire.

"There's one other thing," Bechtel said, almost in a whisper. "When I take my turn, I don't want you entertaining any of the same thoughts, you hear?"

"You stay away from her," said Monk.

Then Bechtel, not without some timing, grinned again and so apparently that no one would have missed the signs. This he followed with a guttural sound that was intended to be laughter.

"Take a pill, ladlehead. I was just putting you on. I won't be milking your cow, as I like my woman a little cleaner than myself." On that, an arm shot out, punching Monk in the chest, and pushed him off his balance for a stride.

The next morning, his car loaded with wired bundles of newspapers, Monk raced out of Gunther and over the county roads, delivering the *Sentinel* to the markets and convenience stores, as a winter storm, predicted earlier, was taking shape and intending to dump a lot of additional snow. When he finished, he directed himself toward the timber road that ran up the backside of The Buckseller. Stopping near its end, he got out and removed a rifle from the trunk. An unrelenting wind beat at him and raked a billion snowflakes across everything in its path.

When he reached the mostly level earth of the Den after a half-hour of climbing, he spotted Studs moving in a direction that was away from the tent. Already finished, Monk thought. Scared, too, he concluded, as Studs carried a rifle and was glancing about himself in all directions.

An old instinct came alive and Monk began to track his target. Minutes elapsed and Studs paused beside a large tree from which he surveyed the surrounding woods. Monk raised the 30.06 to his shoulder with a finger on the trigger. Across the woodland spread the reverberant explosion of a rifle shell.

Studs reacted to the deadly resonance by whirling himself in its direction. Catching sight of Monk, he scurried like a frightened squirrel, hurtling himself off the Den and down the slippery, snow-covered mountain, out of sight.

Monk remained where he was, not moving. Who was it?

Who had fired the shot? In the silence he wondered after a time if Studs had thought he was the sniper. Or maybe Studs now knew that he knew about his visits with Darla, and was afraid.

Time passed slowly, but Monk remained crouched like a ground bird at night. No one appeared and visibility was becoming impossible.

Finally rising, he started back down the mountain, along the same path as best he could remember it. Just for a moment he considered turning about, going back up and seeing Darla. But no, he had no desire to have her so soon after she had done Studs. That was out of the question, wasn't it?

Far above him, the wind in his face, the turkey feather threatening to blow out of his hat, Robin Hood shuffled onto the flats of Devil's Den.

Chapter 18

"Up here you're stuck with a couple of doctors and lawyers who couldn't make their way in the city, and I'm including our elected D.A."

"Shame on you, Mr. Hopkins. You sound like Mr. Halthrop who used to come in here once in a while."

"Halthrop? I didn't think he ever took a drink."

"He didn't. He'd bring a friend up from the city and he'd start saying things just like you were. And I haven't found what you just said to be true at all. I think it's very unfair of you to spread something like that."

Tome slept longer on a Wednesday morning than was normal. He woke around nine, in time to catch the last televised weather report until noon. On the kitchen table rested an opened cardboard box containing a crumpled out-of- town newspaper used for packing. A card lay beside it.

"It's from Uncle Rennie," explained Irene as she watched him pick it up.

"What does he mean, 'You can purchase drums down here, too'?"

"He never gives up trying to coax us to move back. He UPS-ed Jesse a percussion pad."

"He did? Well that was nice of him. Jesse use it yet?"

"What do you think." She took the card from his hand and stuffed it in the box. "Meredith, I heard the Wrabels lost everything."

"Everything except for their car and each other. As for the home, it was simply old. Clapboard siding and all. It didn't stand much of a chance.... Listen, I don't mean to sound callous, but did you know that Bill Lill is giving up his dog?"

"Ahhh, that's a shame. Now he won't have anyone at all to keep him company."

"He's forced to leave it at the house all the time, and he feels for the animal. He's looking to find a good home for it. Are we still interested?"

"I suppose, although the kids haven't mentioned it again for I don't know how long. But I thought it was a puppy we're considering."

"Realistically, Irene, it'll be you who has to take care of the puppy. This dog is much older and well behaved."

"Why doesn't Bill take the poor thing with him to the store?"

"He's tried that. Several people complained they're afraid of the dog. But see, I could haul him along with me to the shop where he could just hang out. It's different than a pharmacy where customers are always coming in. After the van returns from deliveries later this morning, I'm running out to his place to see the dog. You care to come along?"

"You're aware there's a storm coming, aren't you?"

"So it'll be a beautiful day to play hooky and ride the roads."

"More like dangerous."

"It'll be fun. Come on. Say yes."

He could see she was softening and he reached out to tickle her as a means of closing.

"All right, I'll come," said Irene.

"Perfect! I'm going in to make some calls, but the van should be back from deliveries around eleven. I'll be by soon after."

The calls went to authorities to learn if there was anything at all breaking in the sniper matter, but once again there wasn't much that appeared new. What was, was hardly worth mentioning. Amidon had dug a badly splintered slug out of Robert Liottis and, sure enough, it was from a 30.06. There was no ballistics report as of the moment and there wasn't much confidence that the slug could be matched to the others. Rynes told him the State Police had set up a hotline and the radio stations began broadcasting the number late last night. The detective said over a hundred calls had already been received and that each was being afforded proper attention.

The last call went to Rusack.

"No, they're not keeping anything from you, Meredith."

"Just double-checking. Hope you don't mind if I use you as my own private system of check and balance."

"What about our theory?"

"Haven't heard a thing. And I've been eavesdropping everywhere I go. Are you sure—"

"—No, I'm not. But it's a hunch that won't go away. Just keep your radar switched to 'on.'"

Some small printing jobs also required his attention before he could leave, and it wasn't until noon that he picked up Irene at the house. By then the temperature had dropped another eight degrees, the wind grown vicious, and snow was already inches deep to round off the edge of every outdoor item. It was going to be one dandy of a winter storm.

Outside of town where there were few buildings, the weather proved even worse as the wind drove the snow across fields and highway as if it were one thick unending blanket, and riding in the van, Irene complained about the absence of heat.

"It's the thermostat. It's been sticking partway open. Monk said he was going to fix it. Said it wouldn't take much. I hope he's feeling better today than yesterday."

"Was Monk ill?"

"Not exactly. But he had a look on his face like he wanted to kill someone."

"You know, if this keeps up, Meredith, they'll send the children home from school."

"We won't stay long, I promise. I simply want to see the dog again. To make sure he's right for us."

When they arrived at Bill Lill's, the druggist was seating himself aboard a red garden tractor, its rear wheels reinforced with chains and heavy-duty weights. Lill spotted them coming up the driveway and waved.

"I picked a great day to be off this week," he shouted at Tome. "Go on inside. There's a pot of coffee. Introduce yourself. Irene! It's great to see you!"

Engaging the tractor's gears, Lill lowered the plow and snow began to roll like surf from the driveway to its edge.

Tome watched him through the blizzard of flakes for a moment, then scuffed around to let Irene out of the van. A yellow Chevy Blazer was next to them and they tramped around it.

They entered the house through a side door under a

portico, first brushing the snow from each other's coat and hair.

"Good morning," a pleasant voice greeted them.

"Good morning," Tome answered automatically.

"Looks like the two of you are on the same wavelength," said Irene, "however wrong it is."

"Bill and I have been sitting around, doing nothing much but drink coffee. The day still has the morning feel to it. I'm Drew Pendleton."

"Meredith Tome. My wife Irene."

"Come inside where the heat's a little stronger. Would either of you like a cup of coffee? It's a fresh brew. We can put something in it, too, if you'd like."

"Nothing for me," said Tome.

"I'll have a cup. But without the something," said Irene, smiling.

"Where's the dog?" Tome asked, looking around the room.

"I believe he's outside with Bill." Pendleton poured the coffee for Irene. "If this snow sticks around through Monday and Tuesday—and they're saying it will—it'll be murder on doe. Sure I can't put something in this for you, Irene?"

Tome then remembered that there were two other visitors besides this man.

"I'm surprised you're all staying this long. Most hunters remain a week at best."

"Just me. My friends got doe permits for down home."

"And you were lucky enough to get one for here?"

Drew Pendleton shook his head. "I don't have any doe permit. Bill invited me to stay and hunt the second week of buck on my own. My school is already out on winter break, so I said, why not? It's been relaxing. I'm glad I accepted."

Irene seated herself on a sofa, Pendleton on a stiff-backed

chair. Tome continued to stand, moving a step or two from time to time around the room.

"When I get up here each year, Meredith, I read your weekly. It's a fine paper, although I wouldn't mind if it explored controversy to a greater degree. Still, I understand the caveat against doing that. It seems with everything nowadays, you have to couch your words so you don't get sued."

Tome glanced at his wife, but did not gloat.

"This murdering of hunters—"

"—Do you think that's what it's about?" said Tome.

The professor's face froze in a position that said that one of them was crazy and it wasn't himself.

"What do you think it's about?"

"Nevermind," said Tome.

"All right. But for a moment I thought maybe, as a journalist, you're holding onto something to which the rest of us don't have access."

"If you're asking if there are any breaks in the case, there aren't," said Tome, certain that was not what the man was asking.

"So what do you think the Patron Saint of Animals, Saint Francis, would think of what has been going on in your county for the past week and a half? Think he might applaud it?"

"Sounds like you might be considering the gesture."

Pendleton let go a polite smile. "Yes, I might one day trade in my Marlin for a Minolta, that's true. I've put a fair number of deer to rest myself, yet I must admit seeing a certain kind of nobility in a person who would take up the plight of animals, the most silent of underdogs, and gun down their aggressors."

"Isn't that the idea behind endangered species laws?" said Irene. "That the government will be their voice?"

"'Species' is the operative word with that, Irene. I won't say it isn't a good idea. It's obviously saved some animals from extinction. However, it doesn't deal in respect for the individual. Just think if it was people. Think if Hitler had said, 'We'll destroy all the Jews but a hundred. We don't want the world to think of us as completely uncaring heels.'"

The analogy amused Tome.

"Groups like FGC and the Flora & Fauna people are doing a better job," said Pendleton, "but they have their work cut out for them. Daily slaughter on the highways. Steady encroachment of animal habitat by land developers. Mistreatment on filming sets—I believe that continues to happen on occasion. Show dogs and cats left to dehydrate in the cargo bay of airplanes. All kinds of unnecessary medical research. Bears being killed just for their livers and elephants being destroyed just for their ivory. Now baboons and other animals are being sacrificed for the temporary transplantation of their various organs. Mind, all that only covers the portion of the planet on which we walk. Then there are the oceans with pollution and drift nets. No, I can't applaud people getting murdered for it. Nevertheless, I do see nobility."

"Man doesn't hold dominion?" said Tome.

"Really, Meredith, don't you think the word invites more than ever was intended?"

Maybe it was because they had switched to Bible talk, but Tome noticed how the room thereafter became silent. After a while, Pendleton, without explanation, rose and left..

Tome decided after all to have a cup of coffee as he waited for Lill to come in from the outside. He poured brandy into it from a decanter on a nearby shelf. The wind fluted atop the chimney with its more violent surges pushing hard against the exterior wall of the house. Once or twice in each passing minute, it bombarded the window with icy blasts of small white crystals.

Except for the obstreperous wind, the muffled tractor, and the rumble of chains, sometimes chinky when they bit into the cleared asphalt, all was quiet both inside and out. Irene selected a book from the bottom shelf of an end table and flipped through its pages. Tome moved next to the window and watched the pharmacist work the plow. It was a long, arching driveway, and more than half of the pavement still remained under snow, even though Lill was operating the plow with deftness. It seemed to Tome to be labor in vain, this clearing of snow while the storm was in progress. Perhaps it was Bill's way of having fun.

He switched his attention away from Lill and searched for the dog. He spotted the animal in the long field that led away from the house and down to the highway. The dog seemed unimpressed by the nasty weather, as its coat was piling up with unmelting snow. It was a dog of size, a mix, the most prominent characteristics being those of German Shepherd. Lill called the animal Manoovers. Two O's, he'd said, no explanation. Perhaps that was fun too. Tome didn't imagine the druggist had much fun at all since the departure of his wife, Anna. It was great that Drew Pendleton was able to visit for such a long period.

Irene became absorbed in the book on stone walls and stopped flipping pages and started reading some. Tome remained at the window, all the while smiling to himself. It was gorgeous in Bingham County, and winter days like this always underscored it. He felt quite contented just to stare out the window and watch.

At the highway where the field turned into woodland, a yellow Chevy Blazer pulled onto the berm. Momentarily, Tome thought it belonged to Pendleton, but realized that couldn't be, although he couldn't say where the man had disappeared to, unless it was the bathroom. Drinking coffee all morning would do it. Another vehicle, a Jeep station wagon, came to a stop behind the first. Three men got out of the Blazer, two from the Jeep. All but one were dressed as hunters. They immediately began to point in the direction of the field occupied by Manoovers until the driver of the Jeep, a man wearing gloves and a fine gray overcoat, turned them around to face the field on the opposite side. Although he was unable to read the magnetic sign on the door of the blue station wagon with its stylized first word and dependable Bodoni second, Tome nevertheless could recognize the overall configuration of the familiar logo to know that the man was a real estate agent representing Drake Realty. The hunters were about to be shown their future campsite. How successful a salesman this agent was he couldn't say. But the sell was not completely foreign to him. So, for some amusement on this great wintry day, he decided to play a game. He decided to extemporize with each of the man's actions.

The agent extended his left arm and the hand swept over the crest of the mountains at the rear of the field on display. *Deer, herd on herd. You only got to walk out your back door and do a little climbing. During evenings, some mornings, you won't find the need to do even that!* Now one of the hunters ought to pull up like he's holding a rifle and utter a crisp, muffled, dignifying *kur-punj* at an imaginary ten-point. *Some of that steeper terrain, it's no mystery to you, I'm sure. That's prime bear habitat. You'll find some turkey roosts, too. The state's elk herd was even once reported in the area. Yes, elk! You never heard about the elk? A lot of people haven't. We have maybe a hundred in all.*

Without transition the hand then dropped, and with the chopping motions of a cleaver, sectioned the field. *Enough space here for several camps should each of you decide at some future point that you'd like your own. You know, so you can bring your family along.* Some grins, maybe a cocky nod or laugh depending on the ages. *All right, maybe a honey from here.* Cockier nods and laughs. The agent's hand was next joined by the other and they seemed to be pointing and pressing at the same time against the mountains. Tome thought hard, momentarily stumped by this movement. *If you're not afraid to walk— you boys all appear to be in good shape—there's plenty of tremendous brookie streams back in aways. Naturals, red and pink inside, and tasty to the palate, too. Not that cardboard quality of the hatcheries' pellet-fed trout.*

The agent whirled in an about-face and pressed his hands in the same manner into the mountains behind Lill's home, and then whirled back to his original position. In the instant that he had turned in the direction of the druggist's, Tome had followed with his own eyes, and he saw the solitary whitetail barely emerge from the trees in the vicinity of the dog who, although downwind, took no notice, probably because the wind was too gusty and frivolous. The lone doe was not so close to Manoovers that it was in danger, but neither was it at a distance he would have expected. Tome put his head against the window and searched the portion of Lill's acreage visible to him, on the idea that someone had ignored the druggist's signs posting the land to intruders and was pushing through, or perhaps even putting on a drive, thus influencing the whitetail to make the strange move it had. He detected no movement, but for obvious reasons, realized that meant nothing. The drivers could be two, three hundred yards back. He gazed again at the highway. The agent once more had his back to him, but he was now standing in the center of Route 6 with his arms outstretched in opposite directions. *Not to forget, easy driving distance to either Killdeer or the county seat.*

One of the hunters, tired of the pitch, disengaged his

attention from the agent. When he transferred his gaze over his shoulder, he became studiously erect, and he glided to the yellow vehicle and withdrew a rifle. Tome switched his line of sight from the hunter to the deer. There was no set of horns that he could make out. But it failed to matter. Four shots rapidly succeeded each other, and he figured typically the deer to be a barely legal spike, observable only to the hunter because of his use of a high-powered scope—until he saw Manoovers arch fluidly upward and collapse in the snow.

Without a word to his wife, Tome rushed from the house and started across the field, breaking into heavy breathing because of the greater physical effort mandated by the deepening snow. Lill confirmed his terrible thought. The druggist had the steel plow raised, and the tractor was thundering along like a miniature tank in line with the hunter who had not fired another shot but was continuing to survey the scene through the scope. The other men were now gazing in the same direction, but they gave not the slightest indication of knowing what had taken place just seconds before. Their ignorance prevented them from understanding the intent of the angry man who was speeding toward them. Unimpeded, except by the last-second dodge of the shooter, Lill impaled the man's calf onto a corner of the steel plow, carving a rich red swath of blood and exposed muscle. The hunter fell back. The garden tractor hooked onto the yellow vehicle's rear bumper, then spun around to free itself. Lill flew from the seat. The hunter's companions caught hold of him and forced him face down over the hood.

Tome found the dog stretched on its side, blood pooling onto the pure white snow from a wound behind its heaving stomach. The animal was alive and its eyes seemed to acknowledge his presence. Nonetheless, he could not gauge the gravity of the wound, except that the amount of blood told him the dog was in need of medical attention. He yelled toward the highway for Lill, but the commotion there was too much. He stood, began running again, his chest pounding, throat burning. When he reached Lill, restrained through arm-bending by one of the hunters, he felt the frigid oxygen sucked into his hot lungs was certain to make him sick. He shoved the hunter off. Lill bolted across the road and up through the field toward his dog. The hunter attempted to substitute with Tome who, consciously fighting further discomfort, flung a fierce forearm into the side of the man's head, knocking him off his feet.

He stared down at the injured man being attended by his other companions. "You better quit fooling around... quit fooling around with rags and shirts," he advised them between massive gulps of air. "Get him to Paul Bingham."

"You bastards!" one of the helping hunters cried. "You'll pay! You bastards will pay, I swear!"

Tome ignored the enraged man who looked like a brother to the injured. The agent was in his car punching the cellular. At a reduced run, Tome began to retrace his steps to the dog. Irene had come out of the house and was heading into the field.

He called to her. "The van, Irene! Bring the van around on the highway!"

She whirled around to go back, but stopped when she saw Drew Pendleton standing on the driveway. She called the same order back to him. "The keys are in it!" she shouted.

"We have to get him to Doc Thomas," Lill said to Tome.

"Let's see if he'll let us carry him."

Tome cradled the dog in his arms and the animal didn't resist.

"I think he's going into shock," Lill said. "What can I do?"

"He's heavy. Just stay close in case I can't hold him to the highway."

The van was already leaving the driveway. Tome struggled and stumbled, but managed to keep his feet through the uneven terrain. His arms would give out if he wasn't out of the field soon.

Pendleton pulled the van off the road, and then thought to swing it around, taking care that he didn't get onto the shoulder. The Blazer and Jeep passed in front of him. Lill put his arms under Tome's and the dog, but they were close enough that Tome could hold on.

"Push that other stuff to the side."

Pendleton, who had gotten out to open the rear doors, did as Tome commanded, and they gently placed Manoovers in the center of the van's bed, closing the door after.

"I'll drive," Tome said.

"I'll get my car, and Irene and I will follow," Lill said.

"Call Thomas before you leave."

Once underway, Tome pushed the van beyond the reasonable limits of the icy roadway, but he was used to handling the vehicle whether it was empty or loaded with a thousand pounds of newsprint. The wind shook the box throughout the drive, and he found steering a straight course impossible.

"Was there even a deer?" Pendleton asked.

"Only one that I could see. But he wasn't after it."

About three-quarters of a mile from the veterinarian's offices, where some rocky hillsides pinched at the road, he slowed because of the blinding white turbulence swarming at the back of a high-stacked lumber hauler. Immediately on braking, a resounding pop shot through the spacious metal box and a sliver of glass entered the tip of Drew Pendleton's ear, causing him to cry out from the unexpected pain.

Tome swore a mixed obscenity, sparked as much by the incredulity of this new bizarre incident as by fear, and plunged the gas pedal to the floor. The van swerved around the precarious truck and was soon traveling faster than seventy miles an hour as he tried to distance himself and his passenger as quickly as possible from a second shot. Crazy were the thoughts that were passing one after another through his mind. Was the sniper changing his game plan? Or was it the men they'd just had a run-in with? Had one climbed the hillside to wait for them to come along, expecting this drive to the vet? Or was someone now attempting to deliberately kill him, the publisher of a newspaper that couldn't help but promote the county in some ways? Or was it merely an accident, the occasional stray bullet that one read about ripping through an unsuspecting motorist's window?

He darted his head at sections of the van to find which of the windows had taken a bullet. He couldn't find any. He asked Pendleton to look.

"I don't see any."

"There must be. Check again."

Pendleton looked again in all directions, but it was not until they came to a stop at the veterinarian's door that Tome finally accepted the fact that they had not been shot at. He caught the tang of something beginning to dilate his nostrils. On his left sleeve he discovered a portion of it—brown, turbid, and frozen. When he scooped it with his fingers and brought it under his nose, he chuckled softly.

Pendleton smelled it too.

"Cider," said Tome.

Chapter 19

"I mean to tell you they've got one for almost everything. They've got a 'You Can't Park Your Car in the Street at Any Time' ordinance. They've got a 'Dog on the Leash at All Times' ordinance. There's 'Garbage Picked Up Only If in Plastic Bags *and* Properly Secured.' There's the 'No Backyard Fires Excepting Barbecues' ordinance. Sure, you all laugh, think it's funny. You probably all live around here too, or someplace like this. We've also got a 'Keep Your Lawn in Good Shape' piece of legislation. Let me tell you, even the insects don't cross my grass anymore. About the only thing that does and we unfortunately *don't* have an ordinance for it, are the kids."

It was an hour before white-haired Doc Thomas, the town's veterinarian and one of its historians, completed the suturing of Manoovers. The bullet had passed through the dog, taking with it a small chunk of bowel.

"He'll be okay. I want to keep him a day to make certain. By the way," added Thomas, curiously, "I removed a tiny piece of glass from his neck. It was a fresh wound."

Tome quickly related the story of the exploding glass jug.

"Really. I didn't realize it had gotten that cold out," said the vet, who began cleaning up. "You can see him, Bill. He's still on the table. Before he stirs, I'll place him in one of the small enclosures in the back where he can't hurt himself."

Tome and Lill moved before a window framing the operating room.

"Meredith," Lill said, "I want to thank you for what you did. But I also want to take back my offer. I'm keeping the dog. I'm going to take him with me to the store. If some customers are offended, so be it. They'll get used to it or go somewhere else."

A door behind them opened and Drew Pendleton returned. He had delivered Irene home when Doc Thomas's assistant informed them that school officials were sending students home early because of the storm.

"How's Manoovers?" he asked cautiously, more to Tome than Lill.

"Doc said he'll be okay. He's going to keep him."

"Do you want to head back then, Bill?"

Before Lill could answer, Thomas was back among them, first drying his hands with a towel, then lighting a cigarette. He sported the big nose of a lifelong alcoholic and his skin was mottled by dots of red.

"Something like this occurs, I'm always reminded of what happened around here over twenty years ago," the old vet began. "I don't know offhand whether either of you were residents at the time, but cats were being killed. Shot, one after another, out in The Buckseller. It's why our Clara up and marched out of The Buckseller and deep into Devil's Den when she did. At first, AmeriCon Paper moved her and her feline friends off. That's their property, you understand, Devil's Den. More than once over the first year or two they scooted her off, but every time she moved right back and set up her tent. Then, later on, they did an about-face. Maybe some higher-up was a cat devotee, I don't know. That was my hunch, but I was never able to prove it and I tried. My phone bills from that time would back me up on that! In any case, they stopped bothering her. Just the other way around, in fact. They did a feature on her for their company magazine, pictures and all. Then, when they sent in their cutters to do some culling, they sawed up a lot of the smaller stuff for her to use throughout the winter months."

Tome had heard the old vet could just pick up and ramble, needing no invitation, no eye contact, no nothing.

"Either of you familiar with Beryl Victor?" Thomas asked after a long exhalation of smoke.

"I've heard of him," said Tome. "Owns all of Buckseller Hollow."

"Beryl never did come into town much, and nowadays he doesn't seem to come in at all. Back then, however, Beryl Victor himself was living in The Buckseller and he had a hankering for a woman and one who was more than half his age. That turned out to be our Clara, who appeared one day out of nowhere and took up housekeeping with him."

"You've lost me regarding the cats," Tome interrupted.

"Clara loved 'em!" exclaimed Thomas. "As for Beryl, he didn't object, he was so glad to have himself a woman. So that quicker than you could say armadillo, there was more than a hundred of them ranging in and around The Buckseller. Now you might think that the others living there at the time would have had a problem with so many cats stealing around. That's what a lot of people from here in town thought. But they were forgetting something, or they didn't know it in the first place. The Buckseller's a close community. Closer than most imagine. The people there have always known that nobody is going to do anything for them, and most of them probably don't want it done for them either. But they're always on the lookout that something is going to be done *to them*!"

"Some of this is beginning to sound familiar," said Lill. "I had Ferm Bacorn at the house doing some carpentry for me a couple of years back. He got to talking about this, but I only half listened."

"Bacorn would know some, that's true. But not all."

"So go on," said Tome, genuinely interested.

"Ferm said someone took to shooting the cats," said Lill.

"Yes, that did happen as I already mentioned," said Thomas, "only not at that time. At that time it was done legally."

"Somebody made a complaint?"

From behind rising blue smoke, Thomas ran his vision up and down the questioner Drew Pendleton, as if this were the first time he had noticed him.

"No names were ever mentioned that I recall. But the story went, and I checked it out, that residents in town began seeing too many strays in their own yards, and the commissioners acted. For the record, I can attest the cats were healthy, fed on a regular basis, and Beryl, he delivered a dozen or more to yours truly for shots and medicine. You understand, don't you, they couldn't just remove the cats for cruelty reasons, and the health hazard approach failed to work, too. Undaunted, as our commissioners down through the years have been in these kinds of matters, they became inventive. They passed a nuisance law, complete with quotas."

"That was legal?"

"Don't know, Meredith. Don't think they knew either. Or cared. Don't think they even asked the opinion of their own county solicitor before drafting the legislation. Thing is, you see,

Beryl might spend a few dollars getting a cat to convalesce, but they all knew that he wasn't going to initiate a legal challenge."

"So they took away the cats," said Lill.

"Rounded them up and removed them," said Thomas.

"Then where does the shooting come in?" Tome asked.

"Two years later, and if you were in town, I'd be surprised if either one of you knew what was then going on in The Buckseller."

"Obviously we didn't," said Tome, "if it's the shooting you're referring to. What happened?"

"The number of cats had again increased. This time, however, there were no complaints and no lawful attempts to remove the animals. A small band of hunters simply started driving through The Buckseller at all hours of the day and night."

"That's sick," said Pendleton.

Tome had the feeling there was a question begging, or that the garrulous veterinarian was holding something back.

"Was it authorized?" he dared ask after a moderate period of silence.

Thomas stubbed out his cigarette in an ashtray filled with butts. The dog was awakening from anesthesia and a woman gently lifted the groggy Manoovers off the table and carried him into another room.

"I can see how you got into newspaper work, Meredith. You have a nose for things just like myself."

"Who authorized it?"

"Aufderheide."

"Bacorn never mentioned a word of that, or I would have remembered," said Lill.

"I'd be surprised if Ferman knew," said Thomas.

"How did you learn of this information, Doc, if you don't mind my asking?"

"I don't think it will be sufficient for you, Meredith. But it was for me since I was there. Our Commissioner, he grinned."

Tome inclined his head at the old veterinarian as if to say "Gimme a break." Instead, he repeated Thomas's words as a question. "He grinned?"

"Hear me out. Aufderheide owns a big beautiful cabin between Slate Lick and Berks Run. It'll fully accommodate upwards of twenty hunters. For the longest time he turned it over to Creighton Halthrop, who saw that it was rented out for Karl throughout the year, every year, and often to a group from outside of Pittsburgh. It was they who were responsible."

"All right, but what about the grinning? Come on, you can't leave us hanging."

"No, I don't intend to. He was in my offices here—this was maybe ten, eleven years following the shooting of the cats—he was here with a rather strange request, as he isn't a farmer now and wasn't then. Outside in his pickup he had toted along a pig, and he wanted me to examine it. Tell him if it was okay to slaughter. Of course the animal was fine. At the time there was also a woman in my office with a wheezing Siamese, and I saw him regard the woman and the cat, but especially the cat, with a most loathsome scowl. I thought at first that it was just that the cat was a Siamese. Some people plain dislike the breed for no good reason. But it wasn't that. I asked him. It was a cat and that was enough. Then, jokingly I asked if he had had anything to do with the slaughter of the animals in The Buckseller. That's when he flashed me the grin. He didn't say anything. There was just that grin."

"That's it?"

"That's all of it. Like I said, it's not much and it's probably too little for you."

Tome really didn't know what to think. He glanced at Pendleton who was nodding at Lill. Time to exit.

"Give me a call tomorrow, Bill. I'll let you know how the dog is doing."

Tome and Lill both started for the door. But something crossed Pendleton's mind and he hesitated.

"That was a rather engrossing story you told us, Doc," he said. "But I'm thinking you had a point to telling it that was never made clear."

"You might consider hiring him, Meredith. I thought you would be the one to ask. What's been occurring these past couple of weeks? When it's all over, they're going to find that it connects directly back to the shooting of those cats. That it's all about revenge. The sniper is from The Buckseller, remember where you heard it first. Check into that hunter from Pittsburgh. See if he and his friends didn't use to stay at Aufderheide's cabin."

"So you think that old-timer was destroying people's cats?" Lill asked.

"He was twenty years younger then," said Thomas.

"What about Chandler?" Tome asked pointedly.

"A mistake. I didn't say the sniper was a hero. I read where he keeps his distance."

"And the boy?"

Pendleton stared at the vet, waiting on an answer to his question. But Thomas, though he met the black professor's eyes, ignored it.

Chapter 20

"They attempt to portray themselves as rough and tough, but as a friend of mine who moved from these parts to the Southwest likes to say, it's a watered down brand of Western rough and tough. They hunt, fish, smoke, drink beer, eat leeks, sit on their ass. That other stuff—backpacking, hiking, skiing— that's what outsiders do."

The snow finally stopped—twenty-three inches the official measurement at the Bradford Regional Airport. It was a great day to live in the Northern Tier and most everyone agreed.

Among them was Tome, who that morning told his wife Irene it was a more beautiful day to play hooky than the previous, and all across Bingham County others were sharing similar thoughts. The parking lot for the carbon factory was but half-filled. The same was true at the plastics plant. Schools remained closed, their parking slots empty of all vehicles. The old courthouse stood virtually vacant. The frightening logging trucks that pounded the roads seven days a week had disappeared.

The day after publication of the *Sentinel* activity was traditionally slow at the print shop, and although Tome made an appearance and remained past noon, he accomplished nothing. Mary Kiel also had managed to come in on time despite the weather, and she too accomplished little more than a few office-keeping chores. She told him she would stay a while longer and if there were any important calls, she knew from where she could "flush" him, her word.

The Buck 'n' Doe Lounge was where to find Tome, and many others, for it was also a day to abstain from one's usual beer or liquor, and order the bartender to break out the brandy and cream sherry. Yet the lounge was not packed with people as some might have expected. The reason for this was the approaching end of the buck season. Most buck hunters had already returned home, and the doe hunters, those from downstate who possessed Bingham County permits, would not begin to roll in until Friday evening.

Although the afternoon tones inside the Buck 'n' Doe were not the soft and muted ones outside, neither were they the raucous tones of opening day. These were pleasant, non-argumentative, overcast tones compatible to the sky enveloping the county. They were tones filled with good cheer. Whenever the door opened to the lounge, all those inside paused at what they were doing or saying to see who was entering, for on a day like today many customers were not the expected, as was the case with Tome entering at 12:45, according to the grouse.

"Meredith!" Forster greeted him heartily. "Where's Mary Kiel? You should have brought her along."

"I offered, but she declined. What are you doing here? Are you the only bartender who could make his way in?"

"That's right," said Forster. "The only one. And if they don't do a better job of plowing the roads, I might be here right on through doe season."

Tome ordered a brandy and a burger, then surveyed the room to see all who were present.

"Oh, it's getting good," said Forster. "In that booth by the jukebox there's a bevy of high school teachers. They've been having one helluva good time. Coppersmith and another councilman stopped in briefly and said they would return before long. Karl Audferheide is somewhere in the back room jawing, and Emil's there too. His mechanics called in and said no way, so he just closed the shop. Ravishing Suzanne is with him, as you'd expect. Let's see, who else?" Forster pushed the snifter containing the brandy in front of Tome, and bunching his lips together in thought, looked over his domain. "Oh yes, Popov is here, too. Check that. He *was* here. Told me he left his fatties taking care of the restaurant. His fatties. All of sudden he's getting uppity. But boy, he's looking good from all that exercise. Have you seen him lately?"

"Popov hunt, Forster?"

"Don't think so. He shoots, though, I'm sure of that. He's a member of that gun club down in Gunther. Likes to blow apart those clay pigeons. Why do you ask?"

"No reason."

"Sheriff Fennell, he was in before noon distributing posters on Perly Bechtel, who's been served a Peace Bond."

"He's still searching for Perly, is he?"

"This got nothing to do with Robin Hood's cows, Meredith. Since then, Perly's busted up a couple of bars in the county. That's why Fennell was here. If Perly walks in, we're to call his office."

"Maybe the reason he can't find him is Perly's dead in the woods."

"Let's see, Drake's agent, Jim Wilson, the one who was on hand for that action out at Lill's, he left just before you arrived."

"What about Bill? Has he been in?"

"Haven't seen him."

"Ed?"

"Him neither." Forster then raised his voice to one of two men sitting at the end of the bar, sipping beer and eating jerky, "But Clyde here doesn't want to leave. Are you at it again?"

"New recruit," the man responded amicably, waiting to draw Tome's attention. "You don't know me, Tome, but I know you. Are you familiar with the state's official hunting magazine?"

"Who isn't?"

"Exactly. But am I the only one to notice?"

"What are you noticing?" said Tome with a smile of skepticism.

"Ah, don't ask," said Forster.

"Anthropomorphism," stated the man. "I'm sure the word isn't new to you as it is to some." And the man threw an accusing glance at Forster.

"They hate it in that magazine," said Tome.

"They certainly do. But are you aware of just how hypocritical its editors are?"

"Can't say that I am. I've been a glancer, not a reader."

"Forster!" the man called. "There has got to be a copy around here somewhere. Any one will do"

"Yeah?"

"Yeah."

"And you want me to find it. What am I, your slave?"

"Go ask a few customers. Maybe there's one out in a car."

Forster reluctantly left the bar to see if he could fulfill the request. He came back sooner than any of the three men expected with two copies of the hunting magazine and dropped them on the bar in front of the man who had asked. The man beckoned Tome over. The other man offered jerky from a jar.

"It's homemade venison jerky," the second man said. "I made it myself."

"It's excellent," said the first man. Forster agreed as he took another piece.

Tome slipped a strip from the jar and pulled on it. The first man opened each of the magazines to a section wholly allotted to cute anecdotes supplied by the small army of game wardens stationed throughout the Commonwealth. Line illustrations accompanied many of the stories. In them the animals danced away from stupid hunters, conspired against unscrupulous hunters, read weather maps, ribbed each other, and shook their fists in madcap fashion at a trapper who had caught them by mistake. Those with balloons above their heads expressed a critical attitude toward human progress and were even assigned a primitive inventiveness. Most noticeable was an absence of sullen, pitiable behavior. Always, the animals were feisty, as if moxy were the capstone of their libidos.

"You see what I'm talking about? They've been working both sides of that street for longer than I can remember and no one has ever called them on it." The second man was stretching his neck to improve his view of the illustrations.

The regular feature in each of the issues was more than a spread, and Tome turned the page on one to discover a contribution from Harry Rumsey involving a raccoon. The animal had been drawn with an ambiguously crazy eye, and it was wringing its front paws as a scheming villain might his hands. A pair of hunters, at a distance behind it, were arguing. One said the coon was rabid. The other scoffed and stated the animal was simply sanitizing its next meal.

Forster brought out Tome's burger from behind swinging doors.

246 • F. E. Mazur

"Where do you want it?"

"Down where I was," said Tome. He looked back at the man with the magazine. "What about you, Clyde?"

"That isn't my name. That's just what Forster likes to call me."

"Are you a hunter?

"I certainly am," the man answered. "But I hate this sort of thing. It's what gives credibility to some of the claims made by the anti-hunting groups. That's the reason I've been pointing it out to everyone I see."

Tome wondered if Nila Ellenger was aware of the state's blatant hypocrisy. He couldn't recall any mention of it in her letters.

"Well, good luck with your effort," he said to the man. "And thanks for the jerky," he said to the second man before he moved away. "It is tasty."

At the new hour, Rusack entered the lounge.

"Guess no one will be heading off to prison today," quipped Forster upon seeing how the D.A. was dressed. Rusack wore a thick winter coat, a watchcap, and bright yellow boots reaching to his knees. He ignored Forster and marched directly to where Tome was sitting.

"Grab your drink and sandwich, Meredith. Let's take a booth."

"You want a drink?"

"Is that brandy? I'll have the same."

"Bring another brandy over, Forster," said Tome.

"Anything from the kitchen?" Forster asked.

"I'll pass," said the D.A.

"Things at a standstill over your way?" asked Tome.

"Two witnesses scheduled to testify today can't get out of

the driveway. It's just as well. A day like this, I'd rather sit and drink. Stare out the window. Don't do enough of the really simple things anymore."

"It's awfully pretty out, isn't it?"

"Magnificent! This is when I really love living here, Meredith. You can't beat it."

Forster delivered the brandy. "I hear Mr. Triggerhappy is pressing charges against Lill," he said to the D.A.

"He has, that's true."

"Are you going through with it?" Tome asked.

"You'll have to excuse us, Forster. I have some questions to ask Meredith, seeing he was there for the incident."

Forster put up a hand of understanding and returned to the other side of the bar where he started transferring clean glasses from a wash tray to a shelf.

"You were there. I'm correct in saying that, am I not?"

"I was there, yes."

"Did you see what happened?"

"I saw it all," said Tome, biting into the burger.

"Then you saw the dog chasing the deer?"

Tome forced a swallow. "The dog wasn't after deer, Ed!"

"They're all saying it was."

"There's only two people who saw what happened. The shooter and myself, and he's lying if he holds that the dog was chasing a deer. The rest were listening to a pitch from one of Drake's agents."

"Was there a deer in sight?"

"Yes, but the dog made no move in its direction. In fact, Manoovers—"

"That's the dog's name?"

"Yes, and he was facing in another direction when the

fellow fired."

"What about Lill? Where was he?

"He was outside, too, but he was unaware of what was happening until he heard the shots."

"You would testify the same if you were in court?"

"I would. I won't hedge either when I write the story for next week's edition."

Rusack lifted his snifter. "Cheers, then." They clinked each other's glass, and the D.A. settled back in the cushioned booth.

"How's the dog making out? Is it going to live?"

"Doc Thomas seemed to think so. By the way, before we left his office he laid out a rather interesting story."

Rusack shook his head. "Don't believe half of what he tells you."

"Excuse me?"

"Don't believe him."

"Isn't he recognized as the Town Historian?"

"Not by everyone he isn't."

"Cliff Addy published two books by him."

"And he didn't publish two others! Ask Mary. The reason Cliff Addy refused to publish them was on account of what he discovered about Thomas as a historian. The man makes it up."

"He indicated to us that he does a lot of checking."

"Oh, he isn't weak on labor, I'll give him that."

"So what's the problem?"

"He establishes a direction and conclusion at the outset and then attempts to make his findings corroborate them. That's why Addy wouldn't publish his stuff any longer. Too much of it was fiction. I would presume Thomas never came to you to publish because he thought Mary had apprised you. If you want the town's history as it actually happened, Meredith, consult with

Emil Carter's mother-in-law. She's the one who has it straight."

"Suzanne's mother?"

"Yes. She's in her seventies now, but anyone who wants to learn the truth of something out of the past regarding Sagerville and other parts of the county, they pay her a visit, not Thomas."

"So why haven't I ever set eyes on any of her material?" Tome asked, curious.

"Cliff Addy wouldn't publish her work either," replied Rusack, suddenly laughing at the reality of these small town facts. "However, it was for a different reason that he refused her. She wouldn't let him edit her material."

"Why? Was she afraid he'd screw up the spelling?"

Rusack laughed again. "Nothing like that. She had an attitude about her, as they say. It's pervasive in her writing. She didn't spare too many people, and never the politicians! She saw how they all wanted to develop the place and she took exception. It's hoped, however, when she passes, that her daughter might hire someone to edit the work and free it of all denunciations. I've seen some of it. It'll stand on its own, which apparently the old lady doesn't understand. It doesn't need the rough stuff."

"You know, Emil and his wife are in the back room, according to Forster. Although I have yet to see them."

"Once we get a second drink, we'll move about. It's the perfect day for socializing. But, first," said Rusack, "let's hear some of the story Thomas related to you. What's it about?"

"He thinks someone from The Buckseller is responsible for the killings. He links it to a flurry of cat shootings by hunters who were put up at a cabin owned by the Commissioner."

"That sonovabitch," said Rusack, shaking his head. "Don't look at me like that. I know for a fact he never once voted for Ed Rusack." The D.A. glanced at Forster who was funning with the cook and a waitress over the swinging doors. "This story, does it have Beryl Victor and Clara shacking up?"

"Yes, it does."

"Forget it then. Most of it is fabrication. Those two never were together. Beryl did her a good turn when she arrived in our area by letting her stay free-of-charge in one of his shacks which, truthfully, weren't all that bad at the time."

"He said the cats were the reason Clara moved into the mountains."

"Sorry. Wrong again. When you were on the search and you all stopped to question her, how many cats did you observe?"

"There was one. There may have been more inside the tent."

"Take it from me, Meredith, if there were, it wouldn't have been more than a couple. She moved to the Den because she wanted to."

"How is it you're a scholar on this?"

"Beryl Victor came to see me back then on both occasions. That is, first following the new legislation to eliminate the animals and then later after the killings. I wasn't D.A. then and my practice was new. He trusted me, plain and simple. I think he liked how I dressed down."

"Are you saying what Thomas said about the cat killings and all, that's true?"

"Yes, all that happened and more."

"Well, he thought Weatherby, if one investigated it, would turn out to be one of the hunters who used to reserve Karl's cabin."

"He's wrong. That hunter and his friends, they own a camp not far from here, and they've owned it a lifetime. How did he explain Chandler and the boy?"

"He couldn't, I must admit."

"Apparently he can't make them fit into his story. But give him time, he will."

"Why did you call him a 'sonovabitch,' Ed?"

"Because I had already heard this story and was wondering where it started. Sherman Coppersmith was passing it around at Popov's last night. Peg had me stop in and pick up a pizza on my way home. We don't need any crackpot theories and that's exactly what Thomas's theory is. It only works for one of three murders."

"Did you set the young councilman straight?"

"I didn't have to. Popov was doing it for me. Let's refill and make the rounds."

They slid from the booth, went to the bar, and placed their glasses before Forster who poured them more brandy.

"Here's four quarters," said Forster. "Plug 'em in the box. Make sure you play G9 for heartsick Betty."

A pair of big eyes rose up over the swinging doors and attached themselves to Rusack and Tome.

"What's G9, Betty?" asked Rusack, holding the quarters.

"It's a Freddie Fender," said Betty, and she wiggled her fingers at Tome. "Hi, Meredith. Where's Irene?"

"School's called, remember?"

"Oh, of course. She's home with the kids. Tell her 'Hi.'"

"Will do."

Rusack deposited the money in the jukebox and punched in the requested tune as well as five country songs to which he was partial. Afterwards, he led Tome and himself into the other room.

Aufderheide hailed them as soon as they entered. "Gawd,

look what the cat dragged in! Must be nobody's working today."

"Karl," said Rusack. Then, allowing the politician to surface in him, he quickly acknowledged others in the big room.

"You're sounding like me," the big Commissioner joked.

"Come on over and join us," shouted Emil, waving an arm. "We'll put some tables together."

Rusack and Tome accepted, and Aufderheide set himself down as well, at the same time calling to a waitress for a round on his purse.

"How you going to catch this killer, Ed," teased Emil Carter, "if you're in here?"

"I don't catch them, Emil. I prosecute them and put them behind bars. Catching them is others' jobs. It doesn't matter anyway on a day like this. If this sniper wants to pop a hunter today.... You know, I believe you could fit all the buck hunters remaining in the county on the head of a matchstick."

"He's got that right," said the Commissioner. "Who would want to drag, let alone track, a deer through snow this deep. It's worse up in the mountains, too." Three teachers peeked in from the outer room and Aufderheide, spotting them, quickly waved them over to join the party.

"Call Irene," Suzanne Carter said to Meredith.

"She's home with the kids," said Tome.

"Meredith and I were just talking about your mother in the other room," said Rusack.

"Now there's someone you can talk about," said Emil jokingly.

"You just clam up," said his wife, feigning a punch to his arm.

"No, nothing like that, Suzanne. I was telling Meredith how she is the bona fide historian for the town. That if he wants to learn the truth of things that occurred in and around Sagerville, he ought to consult with her."

"He said also that she has a bad attitude, Suzanne."

Emil laughed. "He's right about that, Meredith."

"It's just that my mother has always wanted things to stay the same," explained Suzanne. "I've lectured her many times that she should keep her feelings and opinions out of what she writes. They won't discourage change, I told her. But when did a mother ever take the advice of a daughter who was almost half her age."

Listening, Tome found himself curiously studying Suzanne Carter with respect to Forster's label that the woman was 'ravishing,' although the bartender might have been speaking sarcastically, because who really knew Forster? But in either case Suzanne Carter was certainly a good-looking woman in a plain, unassuming way. Plus, she exuded plenty of sex appeal, especially when she was sitting or standing idly in one spot. Emil was aware of it, too, it wasn't hard to tell, and folks who interacted regularly with the couple said Emil would do anything for his wife.

Over the next hour the party in the Buck 'n' Doe grew. Two of Popov's massive waitresses who had finished their shift at the diner joined the company. Coppersmith returned as promised with the other councilman and they immediately pulled up chairs. Forster came back and joined them, also, for a time. The teachers remaining out front, two men and a woman, soon surrendered to the developing fun in the larger room. Eight other men and women from the community entered the lounge at various times and they also ended up at the long table. The tone had escalated, but it remained civil, social, and full of fun. It was a great day, Tome heard more than one person say.

And then the percentage of alcohol increased in the bodies of all, and the conversations took a turn. Someone dropped a smile and asked Rusack how the investigation was going. Another ceased laughing and urged Tome to relate the details of the incident out at Lill's. Emil Carter, too, was forced to answer questions concerning the searches he and his men had recently conducted. Soon, however, the percentage of the alcohol grew again and the frivolity resumed. December days were short enough in the mountains, and when the sky was gray, they became even shorter. For a time Tome peered out the window, and when he saw the descending darkness, he thought of calling Irene, for he knew she would enjoy this camaraderie. But he knew also that she wouldn't come. The children were still too young to be left alone.

He hailed Forster, who was coming back to the table with more frequency. "A round for everyone," he said. One more, he told himself. The rest of the day in the Northern Tier he would spend at home with his wife and family. After all, there was brandy there as well.

Chapter 21

"But we have a general concept of growth around here that is greatly out of sync."

"You mean traditional, the Oklahoma stuff, I take it."

"Exactly what I mean."

"You and I and a number of others don't feel that way and we've said as much. They can all go home and leave us alone. You're shaking your head."

"Because it has nothing to do with feelings. We react the way we do because they push too hard, they grate. If they didn't shove their weight, we'd accept plans tomorrow for the biggest development imaginable."

Friday morning. The phone rang.

"Harmon Drake."

"The Buckseller," Nila Ellenger declared at once.

"Nila. Where are you?"

"I'm in New York. Where do you think I am? Did you hear what I said? I want The Buckseller."

"Are you sure? A couple of the other sites would be absolutely dynamite."

"Too remote, Harmon. I have no difficulty imagining a disgruntled hunter approaching the structures I intend to have built and torching them. And I can't believe that paper company would come through in the end and sell that acreage, even as a favor to you for solving the mystery of the missing deed. When have you ever heard of that? But regardless, the risk of arson is less with The Buckseller because of its proximity to the highway and Sagerville."

"I'm just making certain. Drake Realty doesn't want any complaints from your organization later on."

He was glad of Nila's decision. To see the Buckseller transformed, its filthy inhabitants forced to go elsewhere, was something he had been wanting to happen for a long time. He was convinced Beryl Victor would sell. In the past, others had approached the old man regarding the purchase of some of the bottomlands, but in the end their interest was always rescinded. No one desired to build something new amid the miserable shacks. Nila was the first prospect wishing to buy the entire half-mile stretch.

That afternoon he borrowed the Jeep from his agent Jim Wilson and drove out to Beryl Victor's place. The old man lived in a well-grayed, story-and-a-half log house at the end of an unpaved road that narrowed to almost nothing. Victor invited him inside the house without hesitation. The old man's face resembled that of a toughened Siberian husky, and the rest of him advertised power, too. An aging basset hound slumbered noisily next to the wood stove. A woman with her hair in a bun peeked out from a kitchen, but did not enter the room. A calico cat snoozed on the sofa. Two parakeets stared at Drake from a corner. Tropical fish flitted about in a high, octagonal aquarium, rich with plastic plants.

"You've got some nerve coming out here with snow like this, Jeep or no Jeep," said Victor. "Could you stand a drink?"

"No thanks," said Drake.

"You know, I recognize who you are, so you must be out here to see if I don't want to put this place on the market. I've had people stop by before, although never in weather like this. They usually offered a good price, too. But I wasn't interested then and I'm not today. So I'm sorry to say, you ventured out here for nothing."

Drake smiled and lowered his gaze.

"Now, you sure you don't want that drink? Make you a hot toddy? Might as well get something for your efforts."

Drake declined the drink again. "You do have a beautiful home, Mr. Victor. But that isn't why I'm here. I've a client who's expressed an interest to purchase The Buckseller."

"You don't say. How much of it are they wanting to buy?" asked Victor, skeptical.

"They want it all, from one end to the other. The offer, I assure you, is generous."

"My my. I've had some of your competition out here over the years, but they never asked about all of it. You're the first."

"Should I interpret that to mean we can talk a deal?"

"Normally you could," said Victor. "Except for one important detail. I don't own it all. And I can see right off that surprises you. You figured you knew the owner of every piece of property there is in the county, didn't you?"

"If you don't own it, sir, then who does?"

"Chandler owned his piece, one of the fellers who was shot on opening day. Who owns it now, I don't have the foggiest.

Pardon me for saying it, Mr. Drake, but you look even more surprised by that information."

"Pig Chandler had enough money at some point in his life to actually buy a parcel of land? Yes, that surprises me, Mr. Victor."

"He didn't have to buy it," Victor corrected him. "I gave it away. I gave Fogger Dann his piece, too. Do you know Fogger Dann?"

"Yes, I've recently met Mr. Dann."

"The two of them, you see, put a stop to some problems we all were having in The Buckseller a long time ago. I appreciated what they done and gave them the land. It wasn't worth near what land in the county is worth today. I'll tell you this, Mr. Drake. If Fogger Dann wants to sell and you can find out who owns Chandler's piece and they also want to sell, then come back and see me. I never heard that Seneca Chandler had family, but maybe there's someone."

"What about a will? Would he have had the foresight to draw one up?"

"One never knew about that man," said Victor, going to the door to let out his guest. "It wouldn't be registered, though, that much I can assure you. Find Dann. Speak with him. They were good friends, those two."

"Out of curiosity, Mr. Victor, have you ever regretted giving away that land?"

Victor looked down at his feet for a moment. "Many a time. The wife and I could use the money, of course. And I knew when the value of land started on the steep climb that this day would come. It's awfully beautiful earth down there in Buckseller hollow. Somebody was bound to want all of it. On the other hand, what those two done was special to all of us who lived in the 'seller at that time. So the real answer, Mr. Drake, is no, I don't regret it. I don't regret it at all."

Returning to town, Drake pulled Wilson's Jeep in front of the *Sentinel* and went inside.

"Meredith around?"

"No," said Monk, placing cardboard boxes in a corner.

Mary Kiel emerged from the back and Monk left the room.

"Can I help you, Mr. Drake?"

"Meredith's not around, I understand."

"No, he and Irene went shopping across the line. I can't help you?"

"Maybe you can, Mary. Meredith interviewed Pig Chandler before he was murdered. Was he aware that Chandler owned his piece of land in The Buckseller?"

"I doubt it," said Mary Kiel, revealing minor surprise of her own at the revelation. "I think he thought like all of us that Chandler was a tenant of Beryl Victor's. Why are you asking?"

"I'm curious who the property goes to, now that Chandler's dead."

"Talk with the people who live out there. They'd have the answer, though I'm not sure they'd be eager to give it to a man dressed in a suit and tie."

Drake looked down his nose a moment. "Why do you think I stopped in here, Mary?"

Monk returned with more boxes. "Mr. Drake, I have some business cards belonging to you."

"Good. Bring them over."

"Have you heard the news?" said Mary Kiel. "The State Police made an arrest in the murders of the Liottis brothers. They've determined that the bullet did not come from the same gun which killed Max Rayburn's son. They also located the gun."

"Anyone we know?"

"I don't recall the name right off. But he was a former employee of theirs from the other side of Killdeer."

"Which reminds me. Can I make a call?"

Mary Kiel pointed to the phone on her desk, and he punched out the number of Jim Wilson.

"Jim? This is Harmon.... Not like I was hoping, no, but it was an interesting visit nonetheless. Listen, I want to make another stop and I'm certain the road isn't cleared. All right if we exchange cars later?"

"Keep it," said the voice on the phone. "I won't be needing it until Monday morning. Then I'll need it to get me in place to blow away my next hunter.... Joke, Harmon, just a joke. Hey, really, don't worry about getting it back here tonight. We can switch tomorrow morning."

📖

The needle for the fuel tank rested all the way left. Drake steered the Jeep into the economy station and got the agency credit card ready. Studs came bounding out.

"Where the devil have you been, Studs? I stopped first thing this morning to see how Max is getting along. He told me you hadn't been in at all yesterday. Even said he got a call from your boss, wondering where you were since you didn't show up for work last night."

"I don't always hang out with him."

"Sure you do. Don't start making up lies about something like that. Is there something wrong? Max was worried. Did you stop by the Highland today?"

"No," said Studs, somewhat sheepishly. He stuck the nozzle into the filler hole and pulled on the trigger.

"What's wrong, man?"

"Ah, you don't really care, Mr. Drake. I know that. You gonna be a congressman. What do you care why I wasn't around town for a day?"

"I do care, Studs. You've been a fixture around these parts, and you work hard every day. I don't want to see anything bad happen to you. Something's wrong, I'd like to know. So would Max. He doesn't want to keep his store open, but he got to, and you could help him keep his mind off his sorrow just by being around."

Studs appreciated the reassurance.

"Okay then, I left town," he said, only glancing at Drake with obvious reluctance. "I was in some serious trouble. Naw, naw. Nothing to do with that. Don't look at me like the one 'at's been plinking unsuspecting hunters, Mr. Drake. Don't even think it. This was something else I was doing that I'm not gonna tell you about. Anyway, I wasn't going to come back, but then I realized how much my Mumma needs me."

"She does, Studs. She'd be lost without you. Max needs you, too."

"After a while I thought, I bet if I just stop doing what I was doing, it'll be all right. So I came back this morning and I swear I ain't going to do anymore what I was doing. I think I'll be all right."

"You don't want to tell me what it is?"

"No, Mr. Drake, I don't want to do that."

He let it go. Studs was a weird bird, but he did work steady.

"Anyway, where you headed this hour, Mr. Drake? Too dark now to sell houses, ain't it?"

"I got business in The Buckseller."

"Then you be careful, you make sure. There's talk around now that someone out of there is the one who killed Max, Jr. and the others."

"I heard that. Something to do with the cat killings fifteen, twenty years ago."

"Mumma and I was there when all that happened, too."

"I never knew you lived in The Buckseller."

"Just for a time. Mumma and me, we lost our trailer in a fire and Mr. Victor put us up without charge in one of his places until we could get back on our feet. He's a nice man."

Studs scratched the bottom of his nose with the credit card. The cents and gallon digits were racing.

Drake continued to watch him through the lowered window.

"You're a little older than me, Mr. Drake, and a lot of what's gone on around these parts isn't news to you. Still, I bet I know something you don't. I know something that most folks don't, unless they lived in The Buckseller back then."

"Are you going to tell me? Or are you leaving me to hang like you did with that other item?"

"This I can tell you," said the little man. "You do want this filled, don't you? ...Do you know how that all came to an end?"

"I always thought it just did. No more cats, that was the end of it."

"They never got all the cats, no way! Because Pig Chandler and another man, Fogger Dann, those two waited one night after midnight. And they waited with their guns."

"So they threatened those responsible?"

Studs shook his head slowly like a storyteller.

"They fired off a couple of rounds?"

"They fired off more than a couple, Mr. Drake. There were two cars and a truck coasted in that night. They looked more like boats than anything. I'd just quit school a little while before and I remember it all. Three vehicles. Only their parking lights on. Pig Chandler and Dann, they didn't wait for nothing. They opened up on all three and they didn't stop firing until after them cars turned around and were out of sight. I was surprised no one got killed or even injured. But then later, I thought maybe somebody did get hurt and those in the cars weren't going to let anyone know. But I never heard nothing after that."

"Interesting, Studs. I confess I was not aware of that. What's the matter? Now you're all of a sudden frowning."

"Just that maybe what I heard, Mr. Drake, maybe it's the other way around. What I heard is that the first man who died was one of those riding in the cars and that someone out of The Buckseller murdered him. But I'm thinking, maybe it's someone in those three cars that's doing the killing. They might have been waiting all this time to kill Pig Chandler, and now maybe they're looking to kill Fogger Dann, too. Doesn't that make sense?" Studs eased off on the nozzle and replaced it upright on the pump. "I'll be right back with your card and receipt."

Drake watched him go inside the station and run the credit card transaction. Studs was back quickly and he offered Drake a pen to sign the receipt.

"You keep the yellow. Give me back the white," he said.

Drake restarted the Jeep and allowed it to idle.

"But doesn't that make sense?" Studs repeated his question.

"I suppose it does," said Drake. "It makes as much sense as the other."

"What do you mean, Mr. Drake?"

"Studs, in either case you're forgetting about two additional people who were murdered. If you go with the first theory that someone out of The Buckseller is behind these recent killings, how do you explain that Chandler, a resident of The Buckseller, was murdered also?"

"See. That's another reason why I told you be careful. You going there to see someone?"

"I want to talk to this Dann fellow about Chandler. They were the best of friends, and you just explained a minute ago how that friendship was solidified."

"Now see, that may not be true. So I'll tell you again to be careful, Mr. Drake."

Drake became exasperated. "Studs, whatever are you talking about? Everything's a dark mystery with you tonight. What do you mean they may not have been the best of friends?"

Studs eyes narrowed and Drake was reminded of a weasel.

"I'm sorry, Mr. Drake. I'm not trying to mix you up or nothing. It's just that there's something else that I know, and there's only one, maybe two others that know it, too."

"You going to tell me?"

"I can't, Mr. Drake. I really can't. I can only tell you to be careful. Pig Chandler and Fogger Dann may have been good friends, but it might have come to an end a few months ago."

"And you won't tell me the reason."

Studs shook his head.

As a sign of further exasperation Drake jammed the shifter into gear, then pulled onto the highway with hardly a glance east or west for oncoming traffic.

📖

In darkness, the infamous stretch of bottomland with its

single streetlight spreading its weakened rays on the tiny hovels that hugged the earth appeared not so much a world of dregs to the real estate broker as it did a small, tight community connected through mysteries and secrets. During daylight when he had had occasion to examine it with his realty eye, the long strip of land seemed extremely vulnerable to him, a place on the planet with no strength or character revealed under the sun. He felt he could have flicked his fingers against any building and it would have fallen away like an insect on a table submitted to the same action. But in darkness he knew well enough that he was a stranger, and the light from the streetlamp, although now bolstered by the layered whiteness and the reflection thereby afforded, did nothing to dampen the fear that tautened both his breath and gut.

No state or county agency and certainly no individual ever plowed The Buckseller road, and so Drake steered the Jeep in the tracks of earlier vehicles that had packed the snow and thus delineated the road from the drainage ditches on either side. Just as it had appeared when he brought Nila here, the bottomland revealed no inhabitants. Every man, woman, and child was inside and the smoke rising from all chimneys but one attested to this fact. He turned the vehicle around in front of Chandler's home, the only building without smoke and light, and proceeded back toward the highway. He couldn't remember exactly which shack he had seen Fogger Dann beside when he and Nila were exiting last Sunday, until he saw the unusual cartage sled. It stood next to a woodpile behind a pickup truck. It had not been visible on his approach. He slowed to a stop just down from the ramshackle dwelling and extinguished motor and lights. He stared at the rundown shanty before him. The shifting white light of its television provided a choppy, phantom glow to the three small windows in the building's front.

He went over his reason for being there. It was simply an effort at efficiency, he told himself, as Nila Ellenger wasn't one to waste time in getting after her objectives. He expected the division of The Buckseller to pose no more of a problem for him than did any parcel of land. He had no doubts Dann would sell his piece. He had no doubts that whoever inherited Chandler's would likewise sell. At the moment the problem lay in determining the status of Chandler's estate so that he might get it through probate more quickly than would normally be the case. There were friends in the courthouse who would help. While, admittedly, it had been a big surprise to learn that the Buckseller man was the owner of any real property, the estate surely couldn't be large. It would be dispensed with swiftly.

After talking with Studs, and despite the little man's admonitions, Drake nonetheless expected Dann to be the most likely inheritor of Chandler's estate. *Which would really make the whole thing a lark*, he thought to himself. Despite Studs indicating that some trouble might have come between the two Buckseller men, if their split was recent, then the chances were good that the will had not been changed. If, in fact, a will existed, he reminded himself. That was the first thing he had to determine. For an instant he considered searching Chandler's hovel. But the idea was discarded after another thought came to mind. This one told him that Chandler's shack had already been ransacked by every sorry piece of protoplasm living in The Buckseller.

He got out of the vehicle, softly closing the door until the interior light went out. He tramped a careful gait to reach the shanty, pausing at each splotch of black in the snow, of which only a tire rim and a galvanized water tank, partially flattened, could be identified. The door to the small building was ajar, and several split logs from the woodpile adjacent to it had tumbled in front. He could hear two voices, neither clearly. Something told him to refrain from knocking on the door. The same thing told him he might first peek through a window.

He silently backed away and moved toward the nearest window at the front. It was dark inside the structure except for the television. *What a dump!* he thought, looking in. The building lacked even a single interior wall, and the outside walls had no finish to their inside. Strips of insulation hung about the perimeter. The ceiling was an amalgam of discarded offset printing tins from the past. What a sorry place to call one's home!

He hunched himself to avoid being seen. The television picture changed to show a solitary bird floating in the sky, and the room lit up eerily with white light. There in a corner behind the television set, he saw Dann and, to his surprise, Clara. He could see, too, that the tent woman was clothed in her familiar coat, a long and shaggy thing. She was kneeling in front of Dann, her head buried in the lap of the Buckseller man, a moment of tenderness between the two. But Drake, already grinning to himself in the cold air, saw it otherwise. What was it she was doing?... Yes, that was exactly what she was doing, wasn't it? He grinned even wider.

📖

"So the weird little feller was getting some action. I'll bet Mumma wasn't aware of that!"

Drake laughed to himself on the way back to town, all the while rethinking his quick conclusions. Bingham County's lady of the tent was putting out and Studs, obviously, had managed to get a little for himself. But Fogger Dann was also drinking at the trough, as he had just discovered, and he didn't like sharing Clara. Thus, Dann must have threatened Studs who disappeared for awhile before returning to town and swearing off any further sexual interaction. And when Studs had warned him earlier at the station that Dann and Chandler might not have been friends prior to the latter's death, wasn't he really suggesting that Chandler, too, had been screwing the woman and that Dann had murdered his best friend out of jealousy?

Drake looked in the mirror and shook his head in disbelief. "You didn't think the riffraff could surprise you, Harmon, but they did." *Someone should know of this*, he thought.

Chapter 22

"So you're back. That means you didn't get your buck, didja? Now you're gonna give a go at them doe."

"Forster. Come here."

"The coolers are filled, Sweetie. The only guy running a tab is down at the end."

"Do you really understand what he's saying, or are you just making it up."

"Who, him? You can understand him as well as I can. It just takes some getting used to. There's no scale, you see. Hey, what if I get him to lift the swatch and you put your ear right up to the hole."

"You're nuts."

"What now?"

"It's just that he doesn't look like he's too far from dying himself. Why does a man like that want to go out and kill something?"

Tome had expected the percussion pad to be similar to the one he had practiced on as a kid, an elevated block of shellacked wood with a square piece of rubber in the center. Old Uncle Rennie had shipped his son an electronic device. Dial a number to get snare, bass, tympany, cymbals. His son was dialing all the time and Tome was feeling what he thought his parents must have felt themselves when he had been a kid trying to boss the drums around: Were they the right instrument after all? Maybe the harp would have been a better choice.

He was sitting at the kitchen table, attempting to compose an editorial for next week's *Sentinel* and allowing himself to become annoyed. He decided to turn his attitude around. With his forefingers he tapped out a single paradiddle, *THUM tip TIP, THUM tip TIP,* then went into a rapid double paradiddle.

"You still do that very well," said Irene on entering the room.

"Nimble fingers. No arthritis."

"What is that you're writing?"

"How to safely kill the uncle to your son."

"No. Really."

"Did you see yesterday's editorial in the *Era?* Reamer is promising to reopen hearings on permitting business into the Killdeer Reservoir. Apparently he's polled some people and believes it will help in his bid to become a U.S. Senator. It isn't right. The people already expressed their view."

"Can I see what you've written?"

"It's nothing. I was merely putting down some thoughts." He reached out and grabbed hold of her hand. "Irene, what say you and I go out this Saturday night? Do the town."

"And which of Sagerville's seven delightful establishments would be our choice?"

Tome smiled. "It is a great state, isn't it? A little town like ours and a variety of bars to sidle up to? Let's call a sitter. Let's go to The Buckseller Inn."

"And listen to Leopold? …Oh, why not. I could stand to get out and have a drink."

"I'll give Ed a call. Maybe he and Peg will join us. I want to talk to him anyway."

"Do you think the place will be packed?"

"I'd imagine. Doe hunters have been arriving all day."

"Then let's make sure we leave early enough. I don't want to stand at the bar like a forgotten package."

Smiling at her, he did another rapid paradiddle, this one a double, *THUM thum TIP TIP, THUM thum TIP TIP,* and rose from the table. "You start getting ready now. I'll call Ed and the sitter."

Deer hunters once again filled The Buckseller Inn, but not to the elbows that characterized the opening day of buck season. A dubious fairness toward the female whitetails accounted for this fact. Had there been only a hundred buck in all of Bingham County, every hunter in the state wishing to stalk after them could have done so. Doe, on the other hand, required special permits, and these were limited in quantity. Not every hunter wanting one, got one, and so there were bound to be considerably fewer hunters. Even so, the region's drinking establishments were hardly depleted of customers, the reason for this being the family members and friends who meandered into the woods to drive the doe toward the posting permit-holders. The drivers, too, usually hit the bars.

"Myrtle, Myrtle, Myrtle," Rusack trilled, coming through the inn door.

"Peggy, you let this man o' yours dance with me tonight."

"You can have him," said Peg Rusack. "But watch your feet, Myrt."

"Where's John Meredith this evening? Or are the two of you on your own?"

"They were coming up the road as we were coming in," said Rusack. "They'll be here shortly, Myrtle."

"Irene, too, then."

"Irene, too," said Peg.

"Well, it's good John Meredith is letting her get out," said Myrtle Faner beneath a single raised eyebrow.

Rusack was under no illusion what Tome wanted to talk about. It's what the *Herald* and *Era* had wanted to talk about, and it wasn't Orleau and Drier who had called. It was their editors. It's why Dolf Meixelberger had telephoned him at home early this morning. It's what Rumsey wanted to discuss, and Fennell, too. It's why Rynes had requested they meet at his office, forget it was Saturday. Even Emil Carter had come to see him yesterday at three, inquiring if there was a plan for Monday and Tuesday.

"If someone has a strategy, Meredith, they're keeping it to themselves," said Rusack across the table. "Anyway, I don't have one! And if I'm right about what I secretly conveyed to you to be on the lookout for, then nothing is going to happen on either Monday or Tuesday."

"What secret?" asked Irene, interested.

"It's all right, Meredith. We're at the end of it. I told Peg last night."

Tome explained for his wife. "Ed isn't convinced the sniper

is only after hunters. He thinks whoever has been squeezing the trigger is after everyone who travels here to enjoy themselves."

"What was Meredith supposed to be on the lookout for, Ed?"

"I wanted him to keep his ears open, that's all, Irene. We both cover a lot of ground throughout the week. I was hoping one of us would hear my hunch on the matter from someone else. That might have indicated that the killer himself was spreading the belief."

"If you're correct, you believe there won't be any trouble come Monday?"

"Irene, if I'm right, then the killer's message hasn't gotten through. So why murder another hunter? It would be a pointless act. What's more, it could get him caught. No, I think he'll wait and go after sledders, backpackers, fishermen, campers, all the rest."

"But you could be wrong, too," said Peg Rusack to her husband.

"And if that's the case," Irene added, "then Tuesday might well be this murderer's farewell finale. Farewell until next year, that is."

"Of course she's right," said Tome.

"It's another reason I haven't any plan... Irene, you said Tuesday. I'd bank on Monday. If I'm wrong and this is about heaping revenge on hunters and nothing more, then the first day of doe could produce a mass of killing. This individual has been playing in a stadium that the rest of us continue to remain unsure is home to him or not. But the stadium empties big at the close of Monday. Tuesday the ranks of hunters in the woods will be depleted by more than half, and the sniper will be on his merry way home, wherever that is, along with everyone else. It won't be easy to ask questions, and the investigation will go dormant." He turned back in Tome's direction. "Of course, there's also the theory that all this is connected to the slaughter of cats down in The Buckseller nearly two decades ago."

"But you dismissed that out of hand when I related what Doc Thomas had to say."

"I did, and I still do. Except that Rynes has information suggesting that it might be someone out of The Buckseller who murdered these people, only for a completely different reason. The fellow who did me a turn the last time you and I were here, Meredith? It seems he's been having an affair—I'm not sure what else to call it—with our lady of the Den. Take a guess at who else might have found her entertaining as well?"

"This is about jealousy?" said Tome, astonished. "One theory makes Chandler the exception to be accounted for. This would make an exception of the boy."

"It's crazy," said Rusack. "Rynes said he asked himself the same question and so he did a little checking. So what does he discover? Just this: Rayburn used to be a wild one. Didn't seek respectability until he bought the business. So maybe he climbed the mountain and there's some connection to his son. For all we know, maybe Junior was in on the action. Like I said, it's crazy and it remains a mystery. In any case, I have no plan and I'll be surprised if there's anyone who does."

III
Doe Season

Chapter 23

"Okay, you harbor resentment toward me. I have contempt for you. What's it worth knowing that? You'll go on living here. I'll keep coming up."

As no crickets were present in December to rattle the quiet of darkness, so there were no fireflies to light it. Only a sickle of moon rushed above high gossamers of cloud and cast a ghostly hue upon the snow-covered landscape.

The killer stood outside the house in the center of the lawn, each arm hugging the other.

"You'll catch your death out there," said the second inhabitant who came up behind.

"It's melting. Listen. You can hear it."

"You remember to be careful. Keep your distance, too, for godsakes. As yet, there's no call for anything, but by morning that will change. They'll feel they must do something."

"I'll be careful."

"You know I'll do what I can."

"It's all right. It's always been all right. I understand that you can't promise more."

"Please. Come inside. You're bound to catch your death out here."

The killer pushed a slippered foot in the snow. The snow mushed, became liquid. All was quiet except for the steady, relaxing dribble-down of water through the gutters and downspouts.

The other inhabitant led the way back inside the house where it was warm and where the satisfying smells of their earlier meal remained. On the kitchen table the killer had spread out the clippings. There were dozens of them, some yellowed from age, others fairly new. Together, they read them again. First, the higher voice, then the tenor.

THOUSANDS HERE FOR BUCK OPENER

SPRING TURKEY ATTRACTS
THOUSANDS FROM CITIES

TROUT OPENER EXPECTED
TO DRAW BIGGEST CREEL YET

11TH ANNUAL CANOE RACES
TO EXCEED ATTENDANCE RECORD

FOLIAGE LOVERS A-COMING

KILLDEER PARK, RESERVOIR
TO BOOST TOURISM, ECONOMY

CANOE REGATTA TO BE BIGGEST EVER

ARCHERS GATHER FOR START
OF NEW SEASON

INTERNATIONAL SNOWMOBILE RACE PLANNED

FOR GUNTHER

**SLEDDERS BRING EXTRA REVENUE
IN DEAD OF WINTER**

**THOUSANDS ATTEND
24TH SNAKE-BAGGING FESTIVAL**

NEW SUBDIVISIONS PLANNED

**NEW SPORTS-A-RAMA FESTIVAL
DRAWS THOUSANDS**

"Let them go elsewhere," the killer said dreamily. "Let them all go where it isn't minded. But let them leave us alone."

The other inhabitant squeezed the shoulders of the killer, who all at once brightened.

"And wasn't this a stroke of luck? Almost like it was planned by a higher power. Roman could have picked it up, but instead he went for the cans and bottles. And I might have thrown it away then and there when Meredith offered the trash can."

The once crumpled page of newspaper, now smoothed out, carried a recent date. "It's almost like they'll be doing in themselves. Tomorrow, everyone will get the message." As had been done several times before, the killer read the small obscure piece in a bottom corner of the page.

"A combined force of 100 members from two anti-hunting groups are expected to disrupt the opening day activities of doe season in the state's most heavily hunted county. Members from Friends of God's Creatures will be joining their counterparts from Brothers & Sisters to the Flora & Fauna and will take their protests directly into the field on Monday."

"It'll shock them at first," said the man. "But this time they'll get the message. For sure they'll get the message! You're right. This was a stroke of luck."

The woman turned around in the arms of the man.

"Probably it's mother who should have done this a long time ago. Did I ever tell you it was she, not my father, who taught me to shoot?"

"Come to bed, won't you?"

"In a little while. Emil? ...Thanks for helping."

"Hey, I love you. You know that. I'll always love you."

The killer reached up and kissed him.

"Good night, Sweet."

"Good night, Emil."

Chapter 24

"Hear this. I've been coming here for years, since I
was a kid. There was never this friction."

"It was there. It just wasn't talked about."

Few people of the Commonwealth were aware that its
District Game Protectors held as much power as their fellow law-
enforcement officers, the State Troopers. In some ways, they
possessed more. For one, they could stop any motorist in the
Northern Tier and force the person to unlock the trunk. The
men in the brown uniforms were aware of their powers,
especially the older ones like Harry Rumsey. They were aware of
their shortcomings, too. The DGPs numbered considerably
fewer than the troopers and it was unlikely many could be
mustered for the problem facing Bingham County.

Never a man known to sit still, except when forced by a
meeting, Harry Rumsey had been frequenting the restaurants
and diners throughout the weekend, from Popov's Pantry in
Sagerville to the Old Route 6 Diner several miles the other side
of Killdeer to Kirby's outside of Gunther, eavesdropping on
what many hunters were saying: "If the powers-that-be can't put
a stop to this murdering son-of-a-bitch, then the rest of us
should!" He wished he had heard the words late at night in the
watering holes. Then he might have written them off to the

alcohol. Unfortunately, they had come to him during daylight hours in the county's most famous diners. Sunday night he had telephoned Rynes and, together, they devised the only possible plan. At 4 a.m. they marched into the fire hall to wake up the volunteer on duty for the night.

When the siren sounded, Tome had no doubt of the reason. Another terrible chimney fire was roaring out of control and was putting yet another family out of house and home. Rusack phoned and informed him otherwise.

"Get dressed and get over there now, Meredith! I'll meet you. Remember to wear your boots."

The fire hall, brightly lit, stood out like an oasis in darkness. Dozens of cars and pickups filled the streets. Others were angling into the many parking slots bordering the square. The snow continued to melt. Tome caught up with Rusack on the sidewalk. The D.A. had provided few details over the phone.

"What sort of manhunt? Are you talking about hundreds of extra police officers?"

"Rynes plans to deputize Emil's men."

"But one of them could be the sniper."

"That's partly the reason it's being done. There's a lot of talk about vigilante action coming from incensed hunters. They don't like being threatened. They don't like the fact that no one's been arrested. Some are friends of Max Rayburn, and they aren't about to let the crime go unpunished. Others are angry because they won't be able to take their kids into the woods next season."

"This is going to require a great deal of luck," said Tome.

"Then you understand why so few police. Really, Meredith, this is little more than an attempt to consolidate the anger, fear, and frustration of these people and make them responsible to someone in command. Without it, they're likely to end up shooting each other, and you know the free-for-all doe season already is."

Celebrated widely—the schools again closed for the first day—doe season was intended by the State Game Commission to trim the fawn-bearing portion of the whitetail herd in each county so that available food was under less demand. Heralded by its inventors as a humanitarian attempt to prevent starvation and as a means to sustain good health in the herd, it often went before firing squads of anti-hunting groups who challenged such inherent sovereignty. Others argued on occasion, when the matter was brought up at all, that doe season provided a more legitimate hunt than did the longer buck season. By this, they meant there were seldom bragging rights to a doe. Men and women went out because it was their last-ditch effort at putting some venison in for the winter. Yet still others countered by stating that this same legitimacy cut out much of the sportsmanship of the hunt as many hunters banded together to assault the doe in a somewhat primitive fashion. Compiling a roster as the law required of them, the group moved out to favored terrain. Those with permits and guns then fortified a fairly straight line with a hundred yards between shooters. The remainder of the team then started a half-mile away to tramp noisily in the shooters' direction. Deer bolted out ahead of the drivers and when in sight of those posted, they instantly became targets. And unlike their male counterparts with the coveted rack of antlers, doe instilled less of the pride to be taken down one animal to one man. Teams often agreed beforehand that any member could bring down as many doe as there were hunters in the party willing to apply their tag. Some people—and Tome counted himself as one of them—believed it to be the real reason that a small faction of hunters went out after doe at all. A man couldn't just sit and pick off Indians or buffalo as was once done in the past. But it was okay today— not legally, but among friends—to slaughter a half-dozen of the whitetails in a matter of seconds. Concerning the females, this action afforded about the only bragging right there was.

"I don't know about this," Tome said after a time. "How's Emil feel about it? They're volunteers, but he's their chief."

"Rynes was the first to sound the whistle. Then he phoned Emil. Don't forget, Meredith, Carter's a volunteer himself."

Men had already packed the fire hall when they arrived, and others continued to enter. Rynes ordered two vehicles moved outside so that everyone could assemble into a mass. The detective stood at the back of the hall on a concrete dais with the men in front. Rumsey stood off several feet at his right. Emil Carter postured at the other side.

The detective peered beyond the men into the darkness behind the open doors and seemed satisfied that all who were coming were on hand. He nodded to the man on his left.

Carter spoke, "Let me have your attention." The men quieted. Some were smoking, while others sipped coffee they had brought from home. "In a couple of hours it'll be first light and the doe season will begin. I needn't tell any of you what that means, as we've all been thinking the same thing. The only question has been whether it will happen today or tomorrow. We're betting on today."

There was an echoing ring to his words inside the hall's concrete walls.

A volunteer spoke next, addressing the detective. "Someone said that you might be deputizing those of us here. Any truth to that?"

"We need your help," Rynes said. "We can catch this sicko if we work together."

"Maybe so," shouted Robin Hood standing at the rear. "But what about our guns? I don't want to hear you say we can't take our guns along. No way I'm going to be stumping in the woods without a gun!"

"Take your guns," said Rynes. "Look. If you're a lucky one who holds a doe permit and you see a doe, by all means shoot it. I didn't ask you here to ruin your day. I gathered you here so that we might put an end to this matter."

The detective waited. The man who had once informed him that the corpses of teenager Max Rayburn, Jr., and a whitetail deer weren't quite ready for the dining fare of a bear appeared satisfied with the detective's answers. Everyone, in fact, seemed okay with what the law officer had said, and so he ordered everyone to raise their right arms.

"Where are we going?" someone asked following the en masse deputization. "Devil's Den?"

"I can't think of a better place," said Carter.

"I can," countered the man. "We should ride the roads. Go where there's plenty of vehicles. Why would he dare climb up to Devil's Den again?"

"Because he's comfortable there," replied Carter. "Obviously, he's familiar with the terrain. He thinks he can get in and out undiscovered."

The large assemblage started to break off into smaller ones.

"There are several things I need to inform you of," Rynes said, raising his voice. Everyone quieted and faced the dais. "First of all, we're looking for a man—"

"Fogger Dann!" someone interrupted. "We've heard the latest, Detective. It's no secret."

"Then I'll forgo the details. We've been unable to locate this man from The Buckseller. However, you need to remember there are no charges against him. At the moment he's wanted only for questioning. Make sure you bear that in mind if you run up against him. At present there are no suspects. That's a special detail each of you shouldn't take too lightly when you're in the field today. Don't let your suspicions override your good sense. But don't let them underride it either. If you come across a hunter, do an examination. Check to see if he's wearing a license. If he hates the sport, it's unlikely he'll be supporting it. Look, also, to determine if there's a knife or rope attached to his belt. The absence of either is only circumstantial, but it should cause you to up your alertness."

From the rear of the hall, Robin Hood spoke out again: "What if we do find him, Detective? That is to say, if I run across a hunter who has another hunter in his crosshairs... You see what I'm gettin' at."

"That's a good question Jimbo's asking. Some guys like to scope out other hunters. See what they're up to. But it doesn't mean they intend to blow them away.

"Understand I realize this isn't an easy assignment. Each of you will have to use your judgment," said Rynes. "That's all I can tell you."

"Now, anything else?" Carter broke in. "If not, we best get ready. If you're not dressed for the weather, then return to your homes and collect what you'll need. We'll leave this station for the Den at 5:45. Some of us will enter from the backside, others from The Buckseller."

📖

Sitting in his pickup and clearing the window of fog, Fogger Dann stared at the fire hall, idly thinking it resembled a faraway space ship that had set down in the middle of nowhere. Some men, he could see, were leaving the hall, climbing into their vehicles, and driving away. Many others remained inside and milled around. He watched Tome and the shorter district attorney as they advanced toward him on the sidewalk. They crossed the street in the direction of the courthouse that was dark, except for the soft globe of light to the right of the main door, and shuffled up the courthouse steps.

He got out of the truck and moved toward the steps himself, making sure to stay out of the light until the D.A. unlocked the door. When that was done, he raced up the steps and followed the two men inside.

In the dim light Rusack did not recognize the intruder. Tome did.

"Mr. Dann."

"I want to talk."

"It's the fellow from the Inn," Tome said.

"The police are looking for you," said Rusack. "Would you like me to summon the detective across the way?"

"I want to talk. For starters, only with you. I haven't killed anyone."

"No one's said you have."

"Don't play me for a fool. I've heard what's making the rounds."

"Meredith and I were heading up to my office. Why not come along. We can talk there."

The three men mounted the steps to the second-floor office of the Bingham County District Attorney. Rusack opened the door and switched on the lights.

"Find a seat."

Tome pointed out one for Dann in front of the D.A.'s desk and took another for himself off to one side.

"Before you begin, Mr. Dann, I believe I need to express my gratitude. I want to thank you for diverting a punch that might well have found my face."

"That's why I feel comfortable talking with you," said Dann. "I'm not saying you owe me, but maybe you'll listen with a more open ear than the others. Buckseller folk don't engender much of the fair shake in outsiders."

Use of the word "engender" caused Rusack to eye the man more attentively.

"All right. What's on your mind?"

"Like I said, I didn't kill nobody. I didn't kill my friend, and I didn't kill Max Rayburn's young'un either."

"But you know why the police want to question you in regard to those killings?"

"There's nothing to the cat killing stuff. That was settled a long time ago."

"It was never settled, Mr. Dann. It was only stopped. What about the other reason that's making the rounds? That you killed Chandler over a woman."

Dann looked to the window and back. This was something he preferred not to talk about. It was really nobody's business.

"Well?"

"We shared her. Seneca was fine with it, she was fine with it, and so was I. Despite what some people think, she's a good woman. You got something wrong with you, she overlooks it. Something missing, she fills it in like it's not missing at all. Because my ass might be on the line, let me tell you, also, that we weren't the only ones. We shared her with others, and some might surprise you."

He glanced at Tome, thinking he might mention Monk's name, but then let it go. Monk didn't need anymore bullshit in this life either. Tome could find out about Monk and Studs and a couple of others on his own.

"So are you wanting something more of me than just my ear?" asked Rusack.

Dann shook his head. "I wanted you to get the first impression, that's all. I'll talk with the police, I've got nothing to hide. But I'd prefer it be done later, if that's all right with you. I'm one that didn't get a buck either, and this year I got a doe permit all legal and such. I can use the meat. I haven't been working steady, you understand."

"You're giving me your word, then, you'll be around."

"My word. That's right."

Rusack thought it over, never taking his eyes off The Buckseller man.

"All right. Rynes probably won't want to talk to you this instant anyway. He's up to his neck in coordinating this morning's affair."

This caused a faint smile to form in the face of Dann.

"I say something funny?"

"If the detective isn't eager to question me, then maybe he thinks it's a crock, this idea that Fogger Dann is the sniper."

"Ask him yourself when this day is over."

Rusack strode over to the window at the rear of the office. He could see the firehall. The amount of activity appeared to be about the same as when he and Tome had left. A few vehicles were returning volunteers from their homes, now clothed for a day of hunting, not fighting fires.

He stepped back to the front of the office.

"When you're out there," he cautioned Dann matter-of-factly, "remember to stay away from Devil's Den!"

"You think it'll go the same way? Come on, that's crazy. Why would he chance another stab at the Den when he's got the entire county to pick from. I figure it's the Den that'll be safest."

"He's not referring to the killer," Tome explained. "He's referring to those gathering at the fire hall. That's where the detective and Emil will be taking them, to the Den. He—" Tome nodded at the D.A.— "he doesn't believe there will be any more murders committed in the woods today."

Puzzled, Dann glanced from Tome to Rusack.

"Why's that?"

"Mr. Rusack doesn't believe this is just about hunters."

"Then who is it about?"

"It's about everyone who travels here to play in the great outdoors," said Rusack. "Deer hunters just happened to be first on his agenda. He's killed three hunters, inspired a copycat murder of the Liottis brothers, and yet his message hasn't gotten through. It'll be counterproductive to his goal to murder more hunters at this time. It's my opinion anyone in the woods today will be perfectly safe."

Dann's eyes slowly hardened. "You know, if what you're saying is true...." He broke off in thought and stayed there a while.

"What is it?" Rusack finally had to ask.

"What if you extend your theory?"

"How's that?"

"What if it's more than just people who come here for sport? What if it includes anyone who shouldn't be here?" He shifted his attention to Tome. "You remember the woman in your office the night that house went up in smoke?"

"Nila Ellenger?"

"I received a letter from her a few days after. She wanted to know if myself and others would be upset if she purchased all of The Buckseller, since she thinks everyone of us living there would be forced to leave. Apparently she's unaware that I own a piece of it. But none of that's any matter. At the end of the letter, she wrote that members of her group and another would be in the area during doe season and that if they showed up in The Buckseller, I was not to be shy about introducing myself."

"Are these people intending to harass hunters in the field?" asked Tome.

"That's what I figured when I read the letter. They've done it elsewhere. Usually they have someone around capturing the whole thing on videotape, which they deliver to the TV stations."

"He may be onto something," Tome remarked.

"Do you have any idea where they're going?" Rusack asked.

"Not with certainty. But they all were staying at several camps off 6, just a mile east of the turnoff to the 'Seller. This morning when I was heading here, I recognized a couple of their cars ready to leave the highway. They were turning north onto the gravel road that leads to Berks Run."

Tome and Rusack exchanged looks.

"But how would the killer know this?" Tome asked. The question was for anyone to answer.

"What's it matter?" Rusack said. "These past couple of weeks he seems to have known everything, the rest of us nothing. Maybe this is where things shift around."

The D.A. picked up the phone on his desk.

"Rynes?"

"He won't change his plans at this hour, but if I request that he send a couple of cars out to Berks Run, he'll do it."

"I'll be going," said Dann.

"One moment," said Rusack, holding the phone. "I told you to stay out of the Den, but wherever you go, keep looking over your shoulder. There's yet another theory in the breeze that whoever killed your friend is out of one of those cars and that they'll be looking to put a bullet in you. You know the cars I'm talking about, don't you?"

"I do," said Dann hesitantly, "but I didn't think too many others did."

"Too many others don't. Your benefactor informed me of it all when it happened some twenty years ago."

"What are you two talking about?" asked Tome, nonplused.

"These other theories don't account for everybody who's been murdered, and so they don't hold water for me, Mr. Dann. All the same, if I were you, I'd be careful."

📖

Moving effortlessly through the melting snow, Suzanne Carter thought of her aging mother who had been a strong woman in earlier days. Not only had she instructed her daughter how to shoot, but she had taught her also never to be afraid, especially in the wild and in the dark.

"Make whatever's out there fearful of you," Suzanne remembered her saying. "That includes other people, dear."

The sickle moon continued to race through thin banks of cloud as if it were at war. The temperature was warming to almost balmy under the front rushing in. Suzanne Carter had wedged her husband's rusty four-wheel-drive vehicle into a section of snowbank on Allison Run. Although she had been walking now for over a mile to get to Berks Run, her breathing barely labored. Pink light spread outward and around her from the east.

The Berks Run finding, like the crumpled out-of-town newspaper, had been another stroke of luck. Of course, if it had not occurred, she would have been forced to risk her identity by approaching the woman who, with her short hair and square shoulders, looked so much like a lesbian, as did some of her companions. She would have sidled up and asked her directly, pretending to be in admiration of the anti-hunting group. But the woman had made it easy for Suzanne. The woman had inquired of the store clerk if topographical maps of the Berks Run quadrangle were available. The clerk answered "yes," and the woman, trying to be cool or something, held up six fingers. Suzanne wasn't so familiar with Berks Run as she was with Devil's Den. Nevertheless, she had been in the woodlands often enough, and she had her own compass and topographical map, both of which she understood how to use.

Berks Run resembled a flatiron in its lower center where the water ran. It was a beautiful stream at every point, paralleled by walkable rock and populated with brookies. Studying the area earlier on the map, she had been uncertain how the doe hunters would approach it, but Emil told her how he would hunt it and that's what she was banking on. She headed for the base. That's where the shooters would be, at the base of the iron. It's also where she expected to find the others, and her first sign of them was not long in coming.

Pausing to listen, Suzanne soon became aware that she was laughing to herself. These people were absurd, these harassers of hunters. The sound most offensive was instantly recognizable to her. A party noisemaker, the rattle, the kind she and Emil themselves had twirled at several New Year's Eve festivities when they were younger.

At the very least, they should be shooting off guns. Preferably, of a caliber that can be heard in the next county. But rattles and tiny paper horns?

Her laughter escaped her momentarily and she slapped a hand to her mouth.

Moving on, she soon spotted the first posted hunters, forcing her to realize that she had made a mistake. Emil and she had forgotten for an instant in their planning that this time her target wasn't hunters. These anti-hunters she was after would not be found where she was now standing. Such ridiculous people, blowing their horns and spinning their raucously grating rattles, would be moving in between the posters and drivers, attempting to encourage the deer into the mountains on either side.

She changed course without hesitation and made her way around the side of the iron, onto the slope. And there she saw the first of them: two women— one with horn, one with rattle. Both were laughing, guffawing actually, shaking their heads, delighted at themselves and the turmoil they and their friends were producing. No sign of laughter now anywhere on her face, Suzanne peered about like a cunning fox. When she saw no other human being in the surrounding vicinity, she raised the rifle to her shoulder and placed the gossamer on the rattler, then fired. The woman dropped like a stone, her blood spraying onto her friend like cleaner onto a carpet stain. Suzanne placed the crosshairs on the second woman, now a statue, and coldly squeezed the trigger a second time, producing the same results. No more horn. No more rattle.

Still, the matter was hardly finished, as Suzanne wanted a

man from among their kind. She wanted no one saying at the end of the day that some hunter had gunned down these crazy interfering women. The message must be clear. It was not about men. It was not about women. It was not even about hunters, like so many thought. It was about everyone who came and by their presence alone, threatened to change her life and the lives of others who wanted things on the Tier to remain as they were.

She kept to the slope, stealing along the outside curvature of the iron for several hundred yards. Eight deer rushed by, breaking off brittle tree limbs in their way. She peered beyond the spot where she had first seen the deer. In the distance, amid a tiny opening of trees growing near the water, she saw four of them and one was a man, a short, roly-poly of a man. She could see that this little man was holding a pair of noisemaking rattlers and she watched him spin one, then the other, in a processional rhythm that was religious and faintly familiar to her.

As Suzanne watched, the woman who had purchased the topo maps in town approached the man and curled each of her hands around a rattle, silencing them both. The man moved his head sheepishly. He was sorry. Then all four huddled together to make a plan. Fingers pointed in several directions, and there was more laughter. Shortly, the man and another woman started in the direction of those Suzanne had shot. She followed them from above and at a distance. The woman eventually broke off on her own and started to blow a noisemaker as she forded the water in the other direction. Roly-poly was headed just were Suzanne hoped.

📖

Rusack pulled the Landrover to a stop beside several other

vehicles parked helter-skelter at the head of Berks Run.

"Let's go. There's no use waiting in here."

"What about the troopers?" Tome asked.

"We'll wait, but not long. The sky's lit. That means the hunt is on."

The D.A. got out and reached back into the vehicle for a rifle. He pulled back the bolt and inserted a handful of shells into the magazine underneath.

"Are you sure you want to do this?" Tome asked.

Rusack turned himself around to invite inspection of his back. There pinned in the center of his hunting coat was a deer license inside a holder and the white slip of a doe permit pushed in front.

"I don't believe you," Tome said with a shake of his head.

"I've been so busy with cases, I haven't been out this year. You should have worn yours. I noticed all you brought was a camera…. Meredith, you don't have to go along on this if you don't want to. But if there's any truth to what Dann said, I'd appreciate having someone watch my back."

"I'll accompany you, don't worry about that. Peg would never forgive me if I let this sniper put a hole in you. Can I presume you'll return the favor and keep my butt from getting blown off as well?"

Rusack smiled. "Do you want a gun? I've got an old .243 along that belonged to my father."

Tome extended an arm and Rusack reached back into the vehicle to extract the second rifle.

They tramped to the edge of the woods just as two hunters were walking out.

"Anything happening?" Rusack inquired of the men.

"Sounded like somebody got something."

"Heard two shots, not too far apart. I saw deer running myself, but couldn't lay a bead."

"Any of the anti-hunters in the area?" Tome asked.

"Fuckin' A, they're here, and they're making a mess of things. That's the reason we're leaving, going elsewhere. You know, it's a wonder someone doesn't put a bullet in one of them. Sounds like you knew they were coming."

"Good luck to you both," said Rusack.

"Yeah. You too."

"Shoot straight," said the second hunter.

Two pairs of headlights were winding up the road in their direction, one close behind the other.

"That must be Rynes' men."

The troopers pulled to a stop, staying on the road. One lowered a window and shined a flashlight on Tome and the D.A., whom he recognized and to whom he jokingly remarked about being up so early.

"The detective tell you anything?" Rusack asked, going over to the window.

"Not much. Why don't you fill us in?"

The trooper got out and signaled to the other one to join him. Rusack told them what he had recently learned.

"And the two of you are going in there to do what?" asked the first trooper, looking more to Tome to get the answer. "What I was afraid of. Hang on a second. We've got some gear in the trunks we can change into."

A short time later, Tome and Rusack advanced into the woods, maintaining about seventy-five yards between them. They followed the ridge that gradually sloped down to the base of the iron. There was a trooper to their left and right.

Fogger Dann's mind underwent a change. He forgot about the hunting of doe. With the anties in the area, his intuition was telling him that Berks Run could be the end of it. He owed it to his good friend Seneca to make certain the killer did not escape.

The pickup pushed hard through the slush. The roads were becoming treacherous. At Berks Run he saw the police cars and Rusack's vehicle. They had gone in at the bottom of the run. He would go another hundred yards, enter near its tip.

Daylight fully established itself, and Tome was the first to see the ominous triangle begin to form. No mistaking the slighter frame, Tome realized that one of its points belonged to a woman, but he failed to recognize Suzanne Carter who, garbed in her hunting get-up, was raising her rifle at the same time that she gracefully twirled her body to the right. Tome searched hard for the doe, what had to be the object of the female hunter's attention, but all he could see was a chubby little man many yards below them both. The chubby man was experiencing difficulty navigating the uneven, slick terrain beneath the melting snow. Slipping and sliding, both arms flailing about, he tried his best to keep his body from getting pitched into the cold slush. The balloonish head bobbed like a fighter's to avoid the jabs from low-hanging branches.

The second point, some two hundred yards to the left and away, was Fogger Dann, and his rifle was aimed unmistakably at the woman, confusing Tome further. Had the Buckseller man lied to Ed and himself? Had he fooled his own friend and led poor Pig Chandler to believe that the pair were lifelong companions before killing him with a bullet to the head? No, that seemed absurd!

The trooper on his left identified point number three. Tome drew a line parallel to the barrel of his weapon. It appeared to zoom straight at Fogger Dann.

Glancing over his shoulder, he next saw Rusack rumbling toward him like a shaken woodchuck, staying low to the ground. The D.A. busily switched his vision from one point of the triangular shape to the next while he moved. Tome himself now revisited the changing shape that was thinning, becoming more oblique. The woman's rifle had swung ninety degrees, now pointing away from Tome, and he determined, still not so readily, that there wasn't a doe for quarry. The quarry appeared to be the chubby little man. *No, the quarry is the man.* Why was he having a hard time accepting what his eyes were seeing?

He further amazed himself as he remembered that he was hauling about a rifle on his shoulder. Awkwardly he brought the .243 up and positioned the crosshairs of its scope on the woman. Who was he fooling? He still had doubts. Or maybe he didn't want to believe. Or maybe he refused to believe because his mind and body knew he could not kill another human being, certainly not a woman.

A shivering stone, that's what he had become; and as he looked toward his friend, it appeared that Rusack was undergoing an identical transformation. Thank God, the triangle's shape was continuing to change.

Roly-poly soon stumbled onto the scene that contained the lifeless, bloodsoaked forms of his two friends, but he made no close inspection of either as Suzanne Carter was expecting. Instead, the little man whirled immediately in the direction of the wooded slope, meticulously scouring the upper terrain with his vision. He spotted her just as she squeezed off a shot. Flinging himself to the earth like an infantryman. the roly-poly man rolled like a perfect log, over and over. When he ceased rolling, he whipped out a large pistol from underneath his coat, and with no indecision he began to shoot at Suzanne Carter on the slope. She managed to fire off two additional rounds before the little man took her down while she was vigorously sliding back the bolt to chamber a third. The slug from the .356 Magnum hit her first in the front base of the neck, then caromed upward into the back of her brain. Her long body snapped for a moment to beautiful attention and then collapsed.

Tome, Rusack, Dann, the troopers, the little man, they all rushed to where Suzanne Carter lay in a pool of crimson slush. The roly-poly man, breathing heavily, offered no apologies. Neither did he brag about his lucky shot.

"Who is she?" is all he asked

"Her name is Suzanne Carter," said Tome, sadly.

Surprisingly, the face of Suzanne Carter remained intact. An odd, almost revolting thought passed through Tome: Forster was right. The woman all of a sudden did look ravishing.

Chapter 25

Tuesday morning before noon, a lone hunter, exiting the woods about three hundred yards north of where he had left his vehicle beside a narrow blacktop road, came upon Emil Carter's car. It rested upright, crushed against a large sycamore. Emil, inside, was dead. Others concluded the accident must have occurred around 10 or 11 the previous a.m. Firemen from a neighboring community used the Jaws of Life to remove his body. They abstained from making a comment of irony. A wad of deer hair stuck out from the aluminum framing the driver's headlamp. Troopers concluded Emil had been moving at high speed when a deer leaped out in front of his vehicle. He'd swerved to miss the animal but lost control on the slushy pavement, careening off the road over a steep embankment where he then hit the big sycamore which finished him off. Had the doe hunter not navigated himself so poorly out of the woods, Emil Carter might not have been discovered for days, even weeks.

"Emil never was a dummie," said Robin Hood. "Forster, give everyone another round and take it out of mine.... The search on the Den broke for awhile and a bunch of us gathered together for a cigarette and a splash of java. That's when it came over the squawkbox about Suzanne. But I doubt he heard it, as he was maybe a coupla hundred feet away. But this is why I say he was no dummie. We all knew where he was and we stared at him. He read our faces, was what he did. Read what was on our faces instantly, and then he moved off. Not in a hurry either, but more like he was regrouping some of the others so that we all could begin a walk in the other direction. But all the time he knew. He disappeared off the Den and left without a second thought. I don't know where he thought he was going or how far he thought he'd get. But he knew Suzanne had been found out and that he would be next."

"Do you think he realized then that she was dead?" asked Pollard from one end of the bar.

"That I'm not sure," said Robin Hood. "But it's hard to think he would have just up and left her if he didn't. They were awfully close, those two. Birds of a feather. That's never been disputed."

"Our little town," said Roman. "You say that Tome and Rusack are claiming it was more than hunters this all had to do with?"

"That's the word. They claim Suzanne would have been trying to kill just about everyone who visits here."

"Even those who drive in during the fall just to admire the leaves?"

"Yep. Them, too."

After this, all the men became silent and sipped from their drinks as Forster set the new round before each. Pollard assumed a look that was close to stupid and elbowed the man beside him. It was time for ribbing.

"Hey Jimbo," he said, raising his voice and grinning. "Someone told me when you first heard about it, you asked if they were certain it was Emil and not your buddy Perly. Is that right?"

"I hadn't realized that Emil was driving Suzanne's car,"

explained Robin Hood. "That's all. I'd thought it was the Bronco. Look, I always liked Emil. Suzanne too. Perly Bechtel, however, is another story."

"We understand," Forster said, arms across his body, his head nodding a straight face while winking at the others. "Wondering if Perly might bust in at any time and butcher you instead of a cow, it can't be much fun sitting on the toilet."

"Hey Jimbo, tell the others here how you missed that twelve-point during the snowstorm. Or was it a fourteen-point? Or twenty-point?"

"Forster, Clyde can pay for his own drink."

Everyone began laughing, even Clyde.

📖

"Ravishing? That sounds a little sick, Meredith."

"I don't mean it like that, Irene. Forster was the first to call her that and I plainly couldn't see it. But he must have spotted something in her the rest of us didn't. He didn't call her beautiful, lovely, gorgeous. He said she was 'ravishing.'"

Irene Tome continued to stare, wondering why her husband was obsessing over a simple word as he sat at the kitchen table. She was not sure what to think or say, so she said nothing.

From an upstairs bedroom came the sound of paradiddles, one after another being laid down in a slow, rhythmic, hypnotic manner. Finally, becoming louder, they captured the father's attention. Tome waited a moment, his ear cocked to the second floor, and listened. The paradiddles continued to gain speed and emphasis. Finally, he started to echo them with his own, softly at first, then with a greater demand.

Irene watched and listened. Her husband wasn't missing a beat, and for the first time in a long time she had a hunch he wouldn't.

Note

This book is not available for purchase by libraries through their usual channels. If you enjoyed the story and believe it is a volume that should be easily available for others to read, ask your librarian to order a copy either from your local bookstore or from any of the online bookstores, such as Amazon.